KEEPERS

BOOK 1 - THE EDEN EAST NOVELS

SACHA DE BLACK

COPYRIGHT

CONTENTS

GLOSSARY

Balance - *The fundamental rightness of fate; the result of a met destiny; the correctness that comes from following the right path. Peace, unity, clarity and light must be strived for in order to achieve Balance.*

Balancer – *The Keeper or Fallon Bound to another; the one true soulmate.*

Balance Scriptures - *The Balance Scriptures are a powerful fate reading device capable of being read only by the First Fallon.*

Barrier – *The fabric of the universe that separates each world and realm.*

Binding - *The moment two perfectly Balanced souls are joined for eternity.*

Binding Scar – *The physical mark of a Binding. Usually* in the form of string-like scars in the state colour of both Balancers in the Binding. The scar resides on the right forearm stretching from wrist to elbow.

Bound – When a Keeper or Fallon has been through their Binding Ceremony and has a Balancer.

CogTracker – A handheld cog-like computer device that has multiple functions: a communications mechanism for CogMail and CogCalls and it's also a Balance scanner.

Double Binding - Double Binding – Myth, a Binding that occurs between three Keepers. Dryad - A form of Keeper closely related to the trees in the Ancient Forest. They have particular abilities to heal others, to aid in the keeping of fate.

Dust – A magical particle used in funerals that can Bind to the essence of a Fallon and subsequently forms a protective barrier over their city for a short period of time.

Dusting - The funeral ceremony of a Fallon.

Dustoria - The momentary euphoria a Keeper feels when a particle of Dust makes contact with their skin.

Elemental – A form of Keeper with particular abilities to control one element – their essence trace, to aid in the keeping of fate.

Essence – The core of a person; the sum of the soul. The essence is the manifestation of the heart and spirit of who and what a person is.

Essence heads – *Physical and immortal representations of a pair of Keepers or Fallons that manifest during a Binding. The essence heads are the record of a Binding's life and a physical representation of the Binding and the unbreakable bond it forms.*

Fallon – *A royal Keeper who is able to control all of the powers of their state.*

First and Last Fallon - *During the creation of Trutinor, the First and Last Fallons were born. Sisters of Balance, they were created to bring peace to the worlds they preside over.*

Imbalance - *A fundamental wrongness that must be eradicated. A darkness that infects the soul, leaving damage, destruction and chaos in its wake. It must always be eradicated.*

Inheritance - *A mythical occurrence when two Fallons (parents) die simultaneously; part of their essence is transferred to their eldest heir. There are no official recorded instances of this happening.*

Jugo - *Unlike a Binding, which seals souls and magic, a Jugo connects two lives. If one lives, so does the other. If one perishes, they both do.*

Keeper – *A being from Trutinor, whose purpose in life is to keep the Balance of fate.*

Obex – *The world between all worlds. Nestled inside the fabric of the universe where time no longer exists.*

Potential - *the most likely candidate fated to be Bound to a Keeper or Fallon, as decreed by the First Fallon.*

Shifter – *A form of Keeper with particular abilities to shift into one animal – their essence trace, to aid in the keeping of fate.*

Simulator – *An augmented reality machine used to recreate Earth-like situations in order to examine Keeper students.*

Siren – *A form of Keeper with particular abilities to control one emotion – their essence trace, to aid in the keeping of fate.*

Sorcerer - *A form of Keeper with particular abilities to control one form of sorcery magic – their essence trace, to aid in the keeping of fate.*

Steampunk Transporter - *A Steampunk Transporter has the duty to protect, serve and ensure the safe passage of their state's Fallons, using whatever magical means necessary.*

The Six – *Trutinor's six highest ranking generals.*

Trace – *The physical mark of magic left on a body.*

Unbound Baby - *The birth of a highly Imbalanced baby caused by the lack of Bound parents.*

MAP OF TRUTINOR

TRUTINOR

NORTH STATE

KEEPERS SCHOOL

EAST STATE

WEST STATE

ANCIENT FOREST

AURORA'S COVE

SOUTH STATE

DRYAD CITY
& HOSPITAL

EDEN'S TOWER

TREY'S BAR

THE DARK'S
CASTLE (1ST
HOUSE OF
THE NORTH)

LUNAR CASTLE
(ARDEN'S)

HOUSES OF
THE NORTH

STRATERA
ACADEMY

TRUTINOR
COUNCIL

TREY'S
MANSION

DATCH
PRISON

For Atlas and Chloe: my life, my world, and my oxygen.

ONE

'*Where there is Balance, there is Imbalance.*'

First Law - The Book of Balance

Father always said not to trust a Fallon that can't keep the Balance. I should have listened.

MY MOTHER and father are fidgeting. Perched, along with everyone else's parents, on the front row of the lecture hall's steep tiered seating. Someone must have opened a door because a ripple of air drifts through the auditorium and makes the stage's velvety green curtains wrinkle. I close my eyes, letting it wash over my skin and take a deep breath. It doesn't help. The wind is carrying everyone's anxiety, and my Elemental power can't help but seek out the anomaly and feed it into my system like a virus.

I snatch a glance at the Earth simulator door. It's in the middle of the stage, entrance dark, exterior plain and cube-like; a solitary shape; a grim reaper ready to make me fail my exams. Behind me, the last couple of classmates are waiting their turn, chewing their nails and watching the current exam play out on the screen above the stage.

They're useless, of course. A virtual sim is nothing like being on Earth. But the Council won't allow anyone in the field until they've been Bound and passed their finals. Especially not if they're me.

"You're too precious," Arden, the Council deputy said every time I begged him to let me go on the school field trips. "Your Fallon blood is too royal to risk injury or death before you're properly qualified. You know that, Eden."

I do know; I just wish I could change it. Frustrated, I scan the sea of parents in the theatre seats. But their faces are as strained as my classmates. I focus on Father instead. He sits up a little higher, and for a brief moment, we share a knowing look. Then it's gone. Replaced with a poised expression and a smile befitting any Fallon. He broke the rules and smuggled me through the barrier into Earth to practice. Under normal circumstances, as a Fallon, I'd have an unfair advantage because I'm stronger than most Keepers. But today, Victor is on my team, and he's more useless than the sims. Worse, his score impacts mine. And *that* is exactly why Father smuggled me out to practice.

Victor's lanky figure slides into place next to mine. His white-blond hair is muted with grease that's turned it a mousy shade of beige. The sloppy top knot is, I imagine, an attempt to hide the oil. I swear I can see the strands twitching and moving like bugs crawling over his scalp. I turn away to stop my nose wrinkling.

Victor might be my Potential, but it's still a mystery to me why the Council of Trutinor think Victor is the most probable candidate to become my Balancer. How is *he* supposed to Balance my soul?

"Victor," I say, struggling to hide the distaste in my voice.

His clawed index finger extends until it pokes me in my ribs.

"You better not mess this up for us, East," he says.

You can't practice with magic for long without it leaving a trace. I like to think of it as a magical signature. I'm lucky. My eyes, like Mother's, are turning violet, like the bright glow of a lightning flash. Victor isn't so lucky. As a Fallon and a Shifter, with the ability to shift into any animal he wants, he could have had any animal trace. But our traces reflect our truest selves, our magical essence, and his is a wolf. One of his hands is gnarling up and forming a mangled wolf paw. A paw that I'll have to hold.

I knock his dog nail off my side and glare at him. Fire elements flicker in my belly, daring me to retaliate. But my parents are watching so I stay composed, stand a little straighter and under my breath say, "We both know I'll carry your whimpering ass across the finish line, Dark. So why don't you play nice and I'll let you thank me after. Hmm?"

He bares his canines, and for a second, I think I hear a growl emanate from his chest. Before I can call him out, Professor Kemble signals the auditorium's silence. Two students exit the sim door, they're pale, eyes darting over the crowd as they weave their way stage right and down into the waiting room.

"Fallon Victor Dark? Fallon Eden East?" Kemble says and gestures for us to approach the Balance simulators.

Victor's face pinches like he's sniffing something sour. It takes all my willpower not to slap the expression off his face. Even though he's never said it, I know he can't stand the thought of being Bound to me any more than I can to him.

The stage stairs creak underfoot as we climb. I flash a final glance at the front row. Mother's violet eyes are bright as she nods and urges me on. I look at Father and smile to myself. Physically, I am like him with the same stocky stature and dark, curly bird's nest on top of my head. But behind Mother's sparkling eyes I see the grit and determination that's burning in my gut too. Her palms cross in her lap, an attempt to hide her tension. But even from the stage, I can sense the electricity sparking like hot static between her palms.

Victor doesn't bother to look at his parents and it's that ego that'll catch us out in the sim if I'm not focused.

Professor Kemble moves center stage, his floor-length green Keeper robes a stark reminder of what's at stake. If we mess up, we won't secure a place at Stratera Academy, and we won't keep the Balance or get a place on the Council.

Kemble opens the sim door. I take a deep breath. Then Victor and I step into the darkness.

TWO

'It is the duty of a Keeper to keep the Balance of fate.'
Second Law - The Book of Balance

THE DOOR CLICKS plunging us into a darkness that clings tight to my skin like a wetsuit. The only sound is the fast rattle of Victor's nervous breath against the blackness.

Somewhere in the room, the sim's cameras whir to life and cogs grind under the strain of a full day of testing. Any second now, our image will be projected onto the auditorium screen and our every move will be scrutinized. This is my last chance to set things straight with Victor; both our grades depend on it.

"Listen," I breathe, fumbling for his hand.

As I slip my fingers through his, he flinches.

"Whatever we've done to each other in the past, let's just forget it, okay? This is about both our futures now. Bound to each other or not, if we want to go to Stratera Academy, we need to work together."

"You broke both my arms, Eden," he says, his grip tightening around mine.

"I did. But that was a really long time ago and I only did it because you killed my dog and strung him up on the classroom door frame."

"That's because your father..."

"Victor," I snap. Pausing, I take a deep breath, "We don't have time to go over this. Can we just forget our family's history and the Council and whatever we've done to each other at school? You know as well as I do we're going to be Bound tomorrow... Probably."

He fidgets under my grip as if he's deciding whether that's a good thing.

"Look, the point is, we might as well get used to working with each other before it counts."

My stomach churns like the belly of a maelstrom; I know I don't have a choice, that I can't out run fate. But that doesn't make the prospect of being tied to his family for the rest of eternity any easier. At least if I pass our final sim, I'll get to keep studying. If that means telling Victor a few white lies now, then I'll say whatever I have to.

"Fine," he says, and drops my hand as a speck of bright white light appears a few feet in front of us.

The light hovers at eye level and explodes into a frenzy of swirling sounds and colors. Then it quietens and places us in the entrance hall of a small cottage.

"I have a feeling this one's for me," I say, examining the contents of the hall.

The walls are the same faded mint green you find in an

old people's home. The paper peels at random intervals. Photos hang crooked along the wall, covered in so much dust I can barely see the people underneath them. There's an eerie quiet in the house that makes my chest tight. The kind of quiet that appears after something dies.

Victor stays behind me as I approach an open door. I inch my head around it and pull away slamming my back into the wall. I count to three and peer around the door again. But the same set of creepy, empty eyes are still staring at me.

This is just a sim, get a grip, I think, slowing my breathing.

Ten years ago, some professor or other, and a student, died in a training accident on Earth. Since then, we've had to use the sims. But how can you practice if you don't have real risks?

I place my index finger across my lips, playing along with the simulation. Victor rolls his eyes, takes a look, then recoils faster than I did.

"There's a dead cat in there. It's rotting," he says scrunching up his face.

"Yeah and there's also an old lady knitting in the corner, oblivious to it."

"How can she not smell that?"

"I have no idea. Dementia?" I observe her through the crack in the door again. The perm shaping her head is faded like the paint in the hallway. Instead of chocolate brown, her curls look like sepia photographs. Her skin is leathery, and her eyes hollow sockets in her shriveled head.

"She's dying," I say, "go see if you can find something. A pattern, a clue. Anything. There must be something wrong." He disappears into a room at the end of the corridor leaving me alone.

There's always a pattern. Humans, Keepers, and Fallons, while separated by power and dimensions, are all the same. We think, feel and behave predictably because we're fallible, Imbalanced and that's why there's a pattern; just like the scarf the old woman is knitting. She repeats loop after loop, after loop. Keeping the Balance is as simple as looking at the pattern and correcting the miss-stitch.

Her living room is filthy and cluttered with soiled food trays, newspapers, and medicine bottles. The fetid, musty stench is overpowering. The entire house is rotting around her while she dies, and yet no one is looking after her. That's the miss-stitch. I take one of the photos off the wall and wipe the dust away. Two young boys are paddling in the sea next to her.

Victor appears empty handed and shrugs.

"She has two sons," I say, pointing at the photos. But as I move down the hall and the photos get more recent, I see that one of the boys is missing.

"No. She *had* two." I take down a couple more photos. One of the boys is middle aged in these. He has a rabble of his own children at the same beach, but there's no sign of his brother.

"What happened to the other one?" Victor asks.

"I think he died. My guess is something happened for the living one to stop talking to her. That's why she's all alone. We need to reconnect them."

"Okay," he nods.

"Can you shift into the cat? If she's senile enough not to have noticed it's dead, maybe she won't realize it's alive again."

"Why do I get all the good jobs? It stinks in there."

Victor's body plummets to the floor forming a fat, ginger

cat, identical to the one decomposing on her living room floor. I put a couple of photos in his mouth and he trots in.

"Eddie," the old woman says, smiling, and puts down her knitting needles. "What have you got there?" She leans down, groaning with every movement, and takes the photos out of his mouth. Victor rubs his body against her legs as her eyes glass over with tears. Her bony finger strokes the image of her son and she lets out a soft whimper.

I put my hand up to the crack in the door, summon the wind element and push a gust of air at the telephone next to her. The receiver rattles and slips off the handset. The old lady frowns but replaces the handset.

Come on. Come on. Just call him. The seconds roll into a minute and still, she strokes the photo but doesn't call him and I realize, maybe she can't ring him even if she wants to.

I run down the corridor till I find the kitchen. Scanning the worktops, I lift papers and packets, and rifle through stained documents searching for anything with a number on it. It's all covered in a film of dirt and crumbs that stick to my fingers. A phone book falls to the ground, but I don't pick it up because I don't know her son's name. Then I notice a faded notelet clinging to the fridge, its edges crinkly and worn. On it is a phone number with the letter 'A' and three kisses underneath. It's all I have, but it's worth a shot.

In the corridor, I find the wire for her house phone. It leads to a power box near the front door. Committing the number to memory, I close my eyes and put my hand on the box. Electricity pops and buzzes as it flows through the line. I form the numbers in my mind and funnel as much power as I can through the box. But the wires are old and the connection fights against me. Static and bolts flicker around the box zapping my fingers making the pads tingle.

I pull my hand away, unsure if this is even going to

work; I've never forced a call both ways before. But I have to try, so I replace my hand and channel the numbers through the power lines again. In the living room, the phone rings and the old lady calls out in surprise.

"Albie," she says, "Oh, Albie, I'm so sorry."

Then the hall melts into darkness.

The next sim is Victor's. We're in a field. A large, white building sits nestled at the bottom of the grass. Colored chalk dapples a sea of gray tarmac circling the building.

"It's a school," he says, "this is mine for sure."

Victor's body shudders then dissolves into the shape of a Labrador.

"Good choice."

For the first time, I'm grateful he is on my team. Victor's sim record is substandard for a Fallon, but at least he *is* a Fallon, which gives us an advantage over our Keeper class-mates who can only control part of their State's power. But as Fallons, we wield all the power of our people: Victor can shift into anything he likes while I can control all of the elements.

This sim is fast. Victor is slow. The school bell shrieks; children flood the playground and scatter, darting like ants. Victor hides in a shrub, with a poor line of sight to the children. The last child to exit the school is a young girl wearing a pretty, pink dress; she's limping, and she has a black eye that someone's attempted to hide with makeup that's far too orange for her skin. A big girl dressed in red walks in front of her blocking my view.

Move Victor. Be both our eyes. But he stays put. I raise my hand and pump a huge gust of wind, parting the bush and shoving him out. He looks over at me and bares his teeth. The big girl in red scruffs the little girl and drags her to the side of the building. *School bully case.* I put my hand up, this time drawing on water. A patch of ice appears in front of the girl in red. She slips and lands on her knee; blood erupts from the cut and dribbles down her shin. But she's back on her feet without so much as a moan. *Impressive*, I think, and search for Victor. He's still lagging back. What is he doing? I pump another gust of wind with one hand and point at the girl being bullied. He gets up but not before grunting at me first, then trots over to the girls, taking a position in front of the girl in pink. *Don't worry, Victor, take your freaking time.* He sits there like a limp rag as the bully rounds on her victim. *Do I have to do everything?*

This time, I fire a shot of electricity right at his throat, forcing a growl out as the bully approaches. She falters and steps back. The sim is over. Victor realizes what he has to do and stands up, finally guarding the victim, snarling and bearing his teeth at the injured bully. But it's already over: Victor's response, and the bully's hesitation, were enough to give the girl in pink the confidence to stand up for herself.

As the vision fades the girl in pink says, "Touch me again, Lara, and I'll set Bruno on you."

Sim after sim plays out; we resolve arguments, prevent accidents and connect soulmates. We save lives and make things right. Our job is to read the Balance of fate, to remove Imbalance, and realign everyone to their intended path. We influence, bend and push, until people find their way back to their destiny. We are the silent memories that tiptoe through your dreams giving you comfort from lost ones. The magic hand that prevents you crossing the road into a moving car, and the thunderstorm that makes your soulmate share his umbrella.

There is a pattern. There is *always* a pattern. Which is why, when the last sim appears, I know something is very wrong.

THREE

---

*'And with the creation of Trutinor, so shall
the First and Last Fallons be born unto it.
Sisters of Balance, destined to bring peace
to the worlds they preside over.'*

Excerpt - The Book of Balance

IT'S PITCH BLACK, again. But this time I'm shouting,
calling out for Victor. My voice sounds disjointed, hollow,
and it echoes, making Victor's name ring in my ears. I
freeze. Sims don't echo.

I shake my head, "This is just a test. A bloody good test
but a test nonetheless." A nervous laugh bubbles out. I'll
congratulate Arden after this is over. I was wrong. The

Council's investment has worked; these sims are *really* convincing.

My scalp prickles like someone's watching me, only it doesn't feel like cameras or the auditorium full of parents. This feels like something else. Like I'm somewhere else. But that's impossible.

The air is suffocating. This darkness is almost tangible, like wherever I am is full of Imbalance. *This isn't funny anymore. Where are you, Victor?*

My heart races, beads of sweat form on my brow. Holding my hands out, I fumble forward reaching for a sim wall to orient myself, but instead of a wall, I hit something hard and lumpy. Lights flash. A white face, smeared in blood and half chewed scraps of flesh, is glaring at me.

I scream, stumbling back, and hit a cold wall. Instinctively, I ball my fists, igniting them with electricity, and take a defensive stance: hands out; feet split; violet electricity pulsating around my hands.

Panic grips my chest like a vice, but I manage to bark, "Stay back," with as much authority as I can.

The creature twists its head at a strange angle, like its spine isn't quite connected and its deep red eyes narrow as it scans me up and down.

"It's definitely her," it says, as a grin peels so far across its face I swear its lips aren't attached. "Now we need to find him."

Everything goes black. I blink, and I'm standing in the sim next to Victor, the next simulation rippling into focus.

"What the hell just happened?" I say.

"What do you mean? The sim switched. I think this is the last one."

"Did you not...? Were you...?" I don't finish my sentence

because he is staring at me with a blank expression. Whatever happened to me, did not happen to him.

"Forget it," I say, and turn to the scene in front of us. The air is cold and crisp and makes it sharp to breathe. I'm grateful for the chill as it dries my sweat and slows my breathing.

"I don't understand it," Victor says. He rubs his palm over his top knot, and then shoves both hands into his black trousers.

We're in a cemetery. Row upon row of neatly arranged tombstones dot the plush field. The sweet scent of flowers laid in respect of loved ones fills my nose and beneath us, is an empty grave. Placed on top of the grave's blank tombstone is a hypodermic syringe with the word 'cure' written on it.

"Something's not right," I say frowning and pick up the needle.

As soon as it's in my hand, the scene dissolves, and we reappear in the middle of a hospital ward. There are only two beds in here, and the body-shaped mounds under the covers look too small to be adults.

"I hate hospitals," I say. The stench of rubbery plastic and chemicals clings to your clothes for hours after you leave.

I glance at the single syringe and back to the beds. Stepping closer, my stomach sinks; I was right. The beds contain identical twins: children.

"It's a choice," I say. "One lives, one dies."

"Well, makes sense, I guess," Victor says shrugging as if he couldn't care less.

"Maybe. I mean everything else has been about what we can do; this must be about how we reason."

He nods in agreement. But even as I say it there's a gnawing in my gut; an itch I can't quite reach.

"Something's not right. This is too easy."

"Maybe not," he says, passing me the two medical charts from the ends of their beds. "Nothing between them. Their stats are the same."

"What about the CogTracker? What are the Balance readings?"

Victor pulls out three black cogs joined by a pivot and flips them open. The first cog is a screen, which lights up as lines of text scroll down the page. The second cog is a Balance scanner, and the third is a keyboard.

He hits a button, the screen goes dead, and the scanner flares to life. He waves it over both bodies and then holds the screen up to me.

"Why am I not surprised?" Both twins are equally matched for Balance and Imbalance. There's nothing between them to help us choose.

"This is ridiculous," Victor says, "obviously, it doesn't matter. We just have to choose. Give me the needle; I'll do it." He reaches out to grab the needle, but I step back. My boots clunk against the lino floor, making the distance I put between us awkward and stilted. Victor's jaw clenches.

"Give me the syringe, Eden."

"Just wait a minute. Let's think about this. What sim is ever that simple? Especially the last sim of our finals."

His lip quivers like a snarl is simmering.

I tilt my head at him, "Come on. Be reasonable. Remember what we promised each other?"

His black eyes harden, a steely look washing over him.

"The twins are matched perfectly. There's no differ-ence in Balance levels, nothing. This isn't a real choice because it obviously doesn't matter. We just need to save a life and get out of here."

Something he says clicks. I replay his words, 'This isn't a choice because it doesn't matter.' My eyes widen. He's right; this isn't a choice. There's nothing between them on the tracker, nothing to differentiate in their medical stats and they're identical twins. Every sim so far has tested our ability to realign or remove Imbalances. Somewhere in the patterns, there's been a clue for us to find; enough Imbalance to weight fate in one person's favor or not. But there's nothing between these two. It's unheard of, but maybe we're not meant to make a choice. Our whole lives we've trained to keep fate, but what if this time, we can't?

"I know wh..." I say, but Victor lunges at me, and I'm so lost in the realization of what we have to do, I don't see him coming. He knocks my shoulder sending me tumbling to the floor. The syringe flies out of my hand and straight into his.

"Wait," I say, scrambling to my feet. "Victor, just wait...."

He pulls the cap off the syringe and hovers over the twin nearest us.

"When are you going to learn, just because you're part of the First Family, doesn't mean you're always right."

I put my hand out as if that will stop him, "This isn't about us...We're not meant to..."

But he doesn't wait for me to finish. He plunges the needle into the closest twin's neck.

"...Choose," I shout, but it's already over: the sim dissolves, and the door opens.

FOUR

'The First Family of the East shall rule Trutinor.'

Fifth Law, The Book of Balance

THE HOLDING AREA, despite being full of my class-mates, is gray and silent like the air has been sucked out and we're walking into the vacuum that's left. Maybe it's not the room at all but me. Worry over the consequences of Victor's mess up is making me breathless. Father's right, I should never trust Victor. I can't believe I thought he would work with me. Now, because of him, both of us will fail our finals. How are we meant to be Bound if he can't even keep a simple promise to work with me?

Several eyes glance at us as we walk, four feet apart, into the seating area. Victor doesn't speak to me, or look at me, or even acknowledge me. He knows he screwed up, but instead of just admitting it, and apologizing, he stalks over to his friend, Trat Riplock - a wolf Keeper.

Trat's father, Obert is the head of 'The Second' of six Houses in the North. Which makes Obert a member of The Six - an elite fighting group responsible for policing Trutinor – it also gives Trat a chip on his shoulder that rivals Victor's.

Chairs line the walls and fill the room in neat little rows like dominoes ready to be knocked over. Two ominous screens hang on the back wall, one projecting the final couple in testing, Rita Runskall and Tiron Galsworthy, Keepers from the East and South. The other screen contains only a heading 'FINAL SIM RESULTS' and a blinking caption beneath it, 'COMING SOON.' I watch Rita and Tiron's sim noting that it looks nothing like the horror show we just experienced.

Tearing my eyes away, I scan the room, eventually spotting my best friend, Bo.

"He's an ass, Eden," she whispers, as I reach her. She gives Victor a pointed glare. "Sometimes I don't understand how I'm even related to him. Look, you nailed all the other sims," she says, waving a dismissive hand in his direction, "and it was obvious you knew the answer in the hospital even though my idiot brother didn't. And if I could see that, the professors will have seen it too. It's going to be fine. Trust me."

She forces her bright red lips into a smile. But I'm too deflated to be positive, so I slump in the seat next to her. She twirls her white ponytail around her fingers and blinks at me. I know what she's thinking because it's what I'd be thinking in her position. Will this be one of those times when our families' history gets in the way of our friendship? It won't. Like always, she's already taken my side. Even when I broke Victor's arms, she said he deserved it because Mustard was an innocent dog. If we do fail our finals, it's on Victor's head, not hers.

She reaches in her bag and pulls out a cog shaped mirror and her signature red lipstick. I bet she applies five more layers before Rita and Tiron are even out of their sim.

I smile as she plasters makeup on. Despite looking like a doll with porcelain skin and pin-straight hair, if you messed with Bo, she'd cut you and leave you for dead without so much as a backward glance. That's what I love about her most. She cares more about keeping the Balance than being a Fallon. Both of us would give up our royalty in a second if it meant we could be Keepers on the frontline. I fire Victor a glance, he's pulling and pushing at his paw-knuckles. His trace must hurt. I get eye ache sometimes from the change in my irises too, I guess it's the consequence of magic binding to our essence.

"Well, at least if you and Kato come top of the class, our head boy and girl at Stratera Academy will be hot badasses instead of a scruff bag and scrawny wolf."

She peers over the mirror and raises a perfectly penciled eyebrow. "Would you stop. It's going to be fine. Besides, you're like twenty points clear at the top of the class score-board anyway. It would take a miracle for me and Kato to beat you now."

The screens on the wall go blank. Rita and Tiron walk in, and all eighty-seven Keepers in my year group take a collective breath.

I sit up, and this time the air really has disappeared from my lungs. All eyes are on the screens. No one moves. No one even blinks. The 'COMING SOON' caption is still flashing. Only now the motion has slowed as if it's teasing us. It flickers, once. Twice. Three more times, then it disappears. Bo grabs my arm, her nails digging into my flesh as hard as mine cut into the seat.

I glance at Victor; he looks how I feel. His usually white skin is a sickly shade of yellow and a sheen of sweat covers his forehead. He has to pass, he just *has* to. Because if he fails, so do I.

Under the squeeze of Bo's fingers a rapid heartbeat thuds. I'm not sure if it's hers or mine. Victor must know I'm looking at him because he squirms and looks everywhere except at me. I refuse to turn away and make this easy on him. My whole future is on that board, resting in his actions. What if I've failed? What if I can't fulfil my duty as a Fallon because he screwed up? I can't look. I can't even breathe for fear of throwing up. And then the results appear.

Bo draws a sharp breath. Victor's mouth falls slack, and eighty-seven students turn to look at me. Victor stands. My eyes are glued to him as his chair scrapes along the floor, screeching. I know, with all certainty, we've failed. He made us fail. At last, he looks at me; it's a hard stare that penetrates my skin. Then, he spins on his heel and storms out of the room, slamming the holding room door so hard, the pane of glass shudders.

Arsehole.

I turn to the screen and my mouth gapes open.

"I don't understand," I whisper to Bo, "that's impossible."

Something must be wrong. My name is at the top of the pass list with the highest score. Victor should be right next to me. But he isn't. He isn't anywhere on my list. I look at the second screen and there, at the top of the fail list, is his name.

FIVE

'Only the worthiest students shall be trained.'

By-Law 12 – The Book of Balance

I CAN'T DANCE. Like, really can't dance. This isn't one of those left feet, bad dad-dancing things either. There is something wrong with my DNA. Put me in a training ring, and I'll fight like a tornado. But put me on a dance floor, and my body ceases to function, let alone obey ballroom commands.

Every day for the last six weeks Professor Nyra's drilled our class on the formal 'acceptance to Stratera Academy' dance. But at the end of every session Nyra's had a red face and been muttering things at me in an old Trutinor language. And I'm pretty sure whatever she's said isn't becoming of an etiquette tutor.

Nyra's pressed, green sorcery robes swish behind her as she strides up and down the corridor outside the West's Great Hall inspecting my class. Because I somehow came top of the class, I am last in line and last to enter the hall. Nyra pauses in front of me, looks me up and down, purses her lips and walks on.

I give Bo a sideways glance, and she smirks. We both went for the unconventional choice. Something Nyra and our parents disagreed with. Instead of wearing ball gowns smothered in diamonds and jewelry, as a Fallon should, we're wearing the same formal uniform as the rest of our Keeper classmates. When we walked in, Nyra's face went white, then a rich shade of plum as she mumbled something about outrage and bloody Fallons. Bo and I prefer to think of it as a protest against not being allowed to serve on the front line with our classmates. Once we're Bound tomorrow, even though we're attending Stratera Academy, Fallon duties will begin which means we'll only get the boring, difficult cases that last forever and where nothing ever happens - typical Council work.

Bo's wearing the Shifter Keeper's uniform: black trousers and smart shirt with a full-length cape lined in fur and embossed with the Northern State's wolf symbol, and of course, she's wearing her signature red lipstick. I'm in fatigue trousers and a high collared violet shirt with no sleeves. It's the same color as my eyes and the circular symbol of the East with the four elements we control: earth, air, fire, and water, emblazoned in gold over the right breast.

"Where is Victor?" I mouth at Bo.

She shrugs, "Sorry."

Neither of us has seen him since he walked out of the

results room. Despite failing, he's still my Potential; he should be my dance partner this evening.

Bo grins at Kato, our mutual friend, and a Siren Fallon from the South.

"Get a room," I breathe, and she feigns innocence at me.

Failing an exam is bad enough, but not turning up to our dance just because he failed and I didn't is a low blow. I scan the line to my left and see two glum looking students who also failed. If they can suck it up, why can't he? Is his ego that big? Or is he punishing me?

I still don't know why I passed and Victor didn't. But there's no time to think about it because the music from the Great Hall flares to life and the huge oak doors open. I can just imagine Father's face when I walk through the doors and Victor isn't opposite me. If I'm Bound to him in the morning, the last thing we need is another dispute between our families.

The procession moves, like soldiers marching onto a parade square. Everyone's stood tall, eyes twinkling, uniforms sparkling, shiny and neat. As we enter the hall, the music reaches a crescendo. We are in an enormous square with intricate tiles under our feet. To our left and right are dining tables stretching the length of the room and deco-rated with either maroon, blue, lilac, black, or royal green tablecloths. Each color represents one of the Fallon families: violet for the East and the Elementals, black for the North and the Shifters, maroon for the South and the Sirens, green for the West and the Sorcerers, and blue for the Ancient Forest and the Dryads. The tables are smothered in cande-labras, highly polished cutlery and enough food to feed my entire class for a year. The smell from succulent cuts of meat and roast potatoes makes me salivate, and I'm not alone. A few of my classmates' parents are already eyeing up the vegetables.

At the top of the room, is a raised stage and the head table. Our professors and Council members, including mine and Victor's parents, are sitting alert and straight faced. Mother and Father spot me, and give me a quick nod before they clock my outfit. Father's jaw hardens, and he glares at Mother whose mouth twitches. She tilts her face down for a moment and then looks up again, a blank expression pinned in place. She doesn't know it, but she gave us the idea. There's an old rumor that her and Nyx - her oldest friend - pulled a similar stunt at their acceptance ball.

The procession comes to a halt. Those with the lowest grades are nearest my parents' table. I am near the door with Bo to my right and Kato opposite us with the boys. I try to ignore the space in front of me and remind myself that at least it means I can slip out and avoid embarrassing myself in the dance. The music stops, and Arden Winkworth, Father's deputy and the Head Professor of Keepers school makes his way around the table to a lectern in the middle of the stage. As a Sorcerer Fallon, his robes are green, but his belly sticks out too far for them to look neat. He sports a full head of thick, cropped hair, although, with age, the salt and pepper speckle has spread to his trimmed beard too. I've known Arden my entire life, and I don't think I've ever seen him with another style of beard. His mustache drops into angular points and a goatee making him look like a motorbike riding anarchist who sets fire to schools rather than being the head of one.

"Keepers, Fallons, Council members... Welcome to this evening's celebration," Arden says, smiling. "Tonight is the end of an era. I appreciate that many of you are eager to get on with proceedings and be accepted into Stratera Academy, but I urge you to be present this evening. Take stock of this celebration because Stratera Academy will not be easy. It will test you in ways you never imagined. Enjoy this evening, take advantage of the rest period over the summer break and prepare yourself for rigorous study in a few weeks' time."

He pauses and takes a sip of a blueish liquid that I know for a fact isn't legal on campus. After Arden's wife died ten years ago, Father spent a lot of nights in a lot of different bars consoling Arden as well as making sure he didn't go off the rails and jeopardize his position on the Council. When your Balancer dies, it takes a while to readjust. We have Balancers for a reason: to ward off Imbalance. They're entwined in our lives and our destiny. Mother once told me that our souls are like puzzles with a piece missing. When you're Bound it's like finding the missing piece; it makes you whole and complete. When your Balancer dies, that piece of you dies with them. Not everyone can survive that kind of loss. But Arden was young when Tilly passed and he has a daughter to look after: Ren. Father was too stubborn to lose his friend or let Ren suffer another loss. No one else seems to have noticed the drink, so I keep my mouth shut and scan the room.

One of the floor length curtains behind the stage catches my eye as it moves. Frowning, I squint at the figure hiding in the darkness. A flash of white skin and dark eyes tells me it's Victor. So, he is here after all. I stare at Bo's cheek hoping she'll turn around. She does, so I flick my eyes in Victor's direction. When she sees him, she stiffens. If I don't kill him first, she might kick his ass for me.

"Usually, I would be the accepting professor," Arden says, interrupting my thoughts. "But today, I have an announcement. As you're aware, we have a head girl for Stratera Academy."

Everyone's eyes shift to me and murmurs trickle all through the room bar the top table. My cheeks burn, and I stare straight at Arden. *Thanks for that.*

"However, we need to appoint a head boy. There's a Fallon, who, as yet, has not attended Stratera Academy. But with special dispensation from the Council, it is my honor to present your new head boy. At just nineteen years old he is one of the most powerful Fallons in Trutinor. Ladies and gentleman, it is a pleasure to welcome back, Trey Luchelli, Siren Fallon of the South, and Stratera Academy head boy."

Trey? I can't help myself; I break rank and grab Bo's arm. Both of us frown at each other and then fire simultaneous glares at Kato. Trey used to be my best friend and happens to be Kato's older brother. Before we can be annoyed at Kato for keeping this a secret, his mouth falls open.

"He didn't know either?" I breathe to Bo.

"Can't have done," she says through the corner of her lips.

We've both known Trey and Kato since we were young. Their parents, Lani and Kale Luchelli were on the Council with ours. But Lani and Kale died mysteriously when Trey was twelve and Bo, Kato and I were all ten. Supposedly Trey Inherited some extra powers in a weird by-product of their death, but it was all hushed up, and no one talks about it. Because of what happened, Trey was taken out of school and tutored privately. I haven't seen him since. He just disappeared one day and that was it. Although Kato lost his parents too, he got to continue life as normal at school with us. I lost my closest friend, and couldn't even support him through his parents' death.

Arden steps out of the way and waves Trey forward. There's a stilted clap which eventually breaks into cheering as a tall, toned guy steps onto the stage.

"Holy sh..."

"Eden," Bo snaps, digging me in the ribs.

"Sorry but, damn. I barely recognize him."

Apart from his piercing blue eyes, Trey was a plain kid. Now, he is anything but. His skin is bronzed, making his blue eyes pop. I can tell, even under a light layer of beard, that his jaw is chiseled. Brown hair scoops over his shoulder in thick waves, and he's wearing skin tight black jeans and a maroon string vest. He's showing off way more skin than necessary, and I'm not sure where to look.

"Good evening," Trey says, his voice silky with a hint of grit.

Bo's eyebrows pinch at me. "You feeling alright?" she says.

"I... Umm...Yes, sorry. Just a bit taken aback by how much he's changed."

"Well, don't get too attached. That there..." She nods in the direction of a tall woman sat on stage who has waist-length golden hair that flows down her back and bright green eyes, "is Evelyn de Lest, his Balancer, and she's a total bitch. I should know. I've met her."

"I'm honored to hold this position as head boy," Trey starts, "because of the unusual circumstances, and the fact I've not studied with you in school, I've been asked to accept each one of you into Stratera Academy with Fallon Winkworth. So, without further ado, shall we begin?" He nods to the Sinfonietta of musicians on stage, and they strike up a ceremonial accompaniment as he makes his way down the line with Arden shaking each Keeper's hand and giving them a bronze cog – a key to their new locker on the Stratera campus.

It takes forever for Trey to make his way down the boys' line followed by the girls' line. By the time they reach Bo, Arden taps Trey's shoulder and leaves. The back of my knees ache, and I am desperate to take my cog and get out of sight before the dance starts.

I focus ahead, but whatever perfume he's wearing is intoxicating, and I can't help but sneak a peek at him. He smells like hot summer, the ocean and frankincense all mixed together.

"Eden East, Fallon of the East," he says, taking my hand and placing a cog key in it, "congratulations."

"Thanks," I say trying to ignore the heat between our palms.

The music cranks up a notch, and several Keepers further down the line move into place for the dance. I twitch, eager to get off the floor. But Trey grips my hand. I look up at him and get caught in those blue eyes I remember.

"So, you're the head girl. Nice to meet you, I'm head boy," he grins at me.

"Uh," I mumble, "yeah. Nice to meet you too."

"We can discuss the specifics of how we should work with each other, given we aren't Bound at a later date."

I nod. For some reason, this feels awkward. I try to recall memories of him and of us from childhood, but my brain is foggy, clouded like I can't quite reach them. How can one person change so much in seven years? I swear I look the same as I did back then, except maybe with a few extra scars and a curvier figure.

"I see you are 'Potential-less' this evening," he says, breaking the silence and glancing at Victor's empty spot.

The music crescendos and the beat changes flowing into the acceptance dance.

"In which case, may I have the honor?" he says, dropping my hand and bowing.

"Sure. I mean no," I stutter and freeze. The brain-fog vanishes leaving me focused on what he just said.

"I'm escaping," I say, "I can't dance, and Victor isn't here. Therefore, I'm using my get out of jail card."

Then in my head, I add, *I couldn't get the dance right with Victor, let alone an estranged friend, who also happens to have become extremely attractive.*

He laughs and takes my hand anyway kissing goodbye my chance of escape.

"What are you doing," I growl under my breath as he pulls my body so close to his, our cheeks brush.

"Ensuring my childhood friend can enjoy her night," he whispers, "let's start again... Hello, Eden, it's been a while..." He swings me around before I can answer, twirling me under his arm and guiding me back in like I'm a feather instead of a fully-grown woman. I'm stiff, uncomfortable like I've slept on the floor all night, but despite that, moving with him is easier than it was with Victor. For the first time in weeks, my feet find the beat and tap out the right steps.

"How are you head boy? And why did I pass and Victor fail? Was that something to do with you too?" I say, narrowing my eyes at him.

He smiles at me, displaying crooked but perfectly white teeth.

"Why?" I ask. "Why did they pass me and not Victor?"

His eyes flash to my father, who nods back at Trey as he swings me out in a loop, his feet gliding over the tiled floor like he's trodden this route a thousand times before. Couples move around us like we're starlings dipping and swooping over the dance floor. Then we're close again, body to body, skin and breath melting together as his face draws close to mine and his hand slips to the small of my back.

"I owe your father. He's been good to me since…" His voice fades. "Well, anyway, I figured the least I could do was to pay him back for everything he's done over the years and a couple of the scoring professors used to know my father and owed me a favor. Besides, they couldn't fail you because of Victor when your scores were so exceptional. Which left them a head boy problem I easily solved. Evelyn's already been to Stratera Academy and I haven't. The Council figured it was a spot of good timing to slot me in as head boy."

"So, the Council only thinks I deserve the place because you convinced them?" I ask, my body becoming rigid. I don't want a place out of sympathy. I'm about to tell him where to go when his palm touches my bare arm. A rush of calm washes over me like the cool kiss of a spring breeze and my body involuntarily relaxes.

"Don't do that," I snap, my feet now stomping out the dance steps.

"Do what?"

"Don't use your Siren magic to calm me down."

"Interesting," he says, "most people can't feel it when I do it. I'm not like the other Sirens, one of the many consequences of my parents…"

"Yeah, well, I still don't want you to do it, and you can tell the Council and professors they can keep their head girl position. I don't need a pity place. I'll go back and take the exam with Victor again just like everyone else has to."

"Is that what you think? You think you got a place out of pity."

"Isn't that what you just said?"

"Not at all. You deserve your place. You scored top in everything, and you didn't drop a single mark in the final sim. It was Victor's error. The professors knew that. Your father and I just needed to point it out. Besides, I thought it would be fun catching up with my old friend."

"Friend? I haven't seen you in nearly a decade, Trey. I barely remember you."

"Ouch," he says, halting, and taking a step back to bow with the other boys as the music ends. "Well, it's impossible to forget you, Eden."

He shows me his crooked smile again and disappears off the dance floor leaving me bewildered. What was that supposed to mean? It almost sounded flirtatious. It wasn't. Obviously. But my insides twist like it was anyway. I stare at him as he greets Evelyn and kisses her on the cheek. Her face pinches as our eyes meet and she forces a quick smile in my direction. I tip my head at her and walk off the dance floor unsure whether I'm annoyed with how I got a place, or grateful to have it.

What I am certain of, is that I don't understand Trey. He's confusing and intense and nothing like the Trey I remember.

"Mom," I say, as she almost crashes into me.

Her expression is wide, startled. Her hair, pinned in a tidy bun, is misshapen, and a few stray hairs fall loose as she straightens herself out.

"Everything okay?"

"No..." she says, her eyes skirting the area around us. She reaches out and pulls me into a hug and whispers, "There's so much I want to tell you. So much I should have told you, but there's no time now. We can't talk here. There's an Imbalance. It's serious and it runs far deeper than any of us understand. Your father needs me to go with him."

She lets me go and fidgets with her dress, tugging at a thread. When she finally looks at me, her eyes are warm and round, full of the love I'm used to seeing, but the corners of her eyes are creased, like her brow, and she's twitching.

"What kind of..."

She cuts me off with one curt shake of her head.

"Mom, you're scaring me. When are you coming back?"

She hesitates.

"Mom? When are you coming back? You're going to make it for the ceremony tomorrow, aren't you?"

Her mouth smiles, her eyes don't. "Of course, honey. If I could change this, I would, but I've run out of time." She takes my hand and squeezes. "We'll make it back," she clears her throat and adds, "I promise."

Her words hang in the air like a veil I can't see through. She's never broken a promise, and yet this time, I don't believe her. Mom doesn't go on work trips. She's the face of the East, meeting with our Keepers, attending ceremonies, dealing with the Council stuff I dread.

She pulls me into another hug, grasping so tight it hurts, then she kisses me on the forehead. When I see her face, tears spill over her lids.

"I'm so proud of you," she says, "you've grown into the most beautiful woman. You were fantastic in the sim, and even if Lionel isn't, I'm rather fond of your outfit." She laughs through the tears. I try to smile back, but inside panic grips my chest.

"No matter what happens tomorrow, even if you are Bound to Victor, we will find a way to make it work. But will you promise one thing?"

"What?" I say stepping back, probing her face for clues. *Be logical, Eden. The Binding Ceremony is in less than twenty-four hours, they can't be going far, or they'll miss it.* But the way she hugged me, the way she's speaking tells me not to let her go.

I open my mouth to ask a dozen questions, but she cuts in.

"Promise me you'll always follow your heart." Father's voice fills the air, and I lose my chance.

"Eleanor?" he says softly.

Her shoulders tighten. "Here, take this," she says and hands me a set of three silver cogs, her Balance tracker.

"But I have one, and this is yours."

"I know. Just take it. Check the C-drive as soon as you can." Her lips tremble like she wants to say more but can't. Instead the words are lost, and she is silent.

Father's eyes are as wild as Mother's. What the hell is wrong with them?

He touches my shoulder, "You were amazing today, darling," he says, and I can tell he's forcing calm into his voice.

"Thanks, Dad."

"Eleanor, if we don't go, we won't make it in time."

Our conversation is over. Father grips me as hard as Mother did. He gazes at me taking in every part of my face as if it's the first time he's seen me.

"I love you, darling," he says and presses a kiss into my forehead.

Before Mom leaves, she points at the cogs, "C-drive, you must look at it, Eden." Her eyes skirt around my face, scanning every inch of my expression.

I nod, "I will."

Her mouth sags just enough for me to know she wants

to say more. I shuffle on the spot, desperate to have a guarantee they'll make it back in time.

"Dad, Mom? You're not going to miss it, are you?" I say, my voice cracking.

"We promise," Father says; his hand squeezes the door frame so hard his knuckles are white.

I try to say, "I love you, Mom." But the words get swallowed amongst the music, cheering and dancers twirling past the door. I crane my head around the gaggle of Keepers and catch Mom whispering, "I love you, Eden East." Then she's gone.

SIX

'Potential – the most likely candidate fated to be Bound to a Keeper or Fallon, as decreed by the First Fallon.'

Seventh Law – The Book of Balance

THAT NIGHT, I dream of Trey. We're alone, in the Ancient Forest. A break in the canopy reveals a cloudless, starry sky, broken only by the occasional fleeting meteor. I am fourteen; Trey is sixteen. He Inherited two years ago and finally, the Council will Bind him in the morning.

"Who is she?" I ask, as we lie back on the mossy forest floor and watch the night sky.

"Don't be like that," he says reaching across the ground for my hand.

"Like what, Trey? Gutted that my best friend is going to disappear with his new soulmate to play happy families and never come back?"

He takes a deep breath and hitches closer to me, "Her name is Evelyn de Lest, she's a Sorcerer. A distant cousin of Arden's from another realm, so I'm told."

"Oh," I say, my hands pumping fist motions as if that will somehow squeeze the knot out of my chest.

"Don't," he says, gripping my arm to make me stop. "You know if I could stop this, I would."

"That doesn't make it any easier," I say, and roll away from him.

"You think I want this?"

I'm silent because it doesn't matter whether he wants it or not. It's going to happen, and there's nothing either of us can do about it. Tomorrow he will be Bound to another girl, and, when he is, my heart will break in two. And the one person I want to stitch me back together will be gone.

"I'm sorry," I say, and turn to face him.

"I always thought we would be..." he says.

"I know. Me too," I say, attempting a smile. "They're saying I'll be Bound to Victor. It's all but official."

"Victor?"

"Yeah. Even the thought makes me sick. You know he killed my dog?" I fall silent. He's staring at me. His blue eyes change with his mood. Tonight, they are almost navy, and it makes me wonder what he's thinking.

"This isn't goodbye," he says, and then he reaches for my hand. We've held hands before, playing stupid games as kids, or dancing in school. But this time it's different. There's a craving in his grip, like he's asking for more. Heat pours from his palms into mine betraying his Siren ability. He never could hide what he felt from me.

"Then why does it feel like goodbye?"

"I promise you, no matter what happens, no matter who we're with, or where we are, we will always be together."

He squeezes my hand, and the dream fades.

———

WHEN I WAKE on the morning of the ceremony, I go over and over the dream. It felt so real, so full. More like a memory. I shake my head and dismiss it. My brain is making up nonsense because he reappeared after years last night, and now he happens to be hot. I stick my head into the halls wondering why the school dormitories are so quiet. Today is the biggest event of the year; there should be chaos with parents and family everywhere while my classmates rush to get dressed and do their makeup. But instead, the halls rest ominous and silent.

I wash, dress in slacks and eat by myself then wander to Bo's room. She's missing. *That's odd,* I think but decide she's probably already gone to the Fallon dressing room, which is where I head next. But she isn't there, and three hours later, neither she nor my parents have returned.

"There's two hours to the ceremony. Now is not the ideal time to disappear," I say to Kato as I slouch into a dark green armchair. The Fallon's private dressing room behind the Great Hall hasn't been redecorated in forever. The chairs and curtains are made of lavish but ancient, green and gold fabrics that are spotted with threadbare patches and smell of must. One wall is full of mirrors, opposite are several wardrobes with our gowns. I pull my hands over my face and groan; my parents still aren't here.

"When I find Bo, I'll scold her for both of us," Kato says nudging my foot with his brogue shoe before turning back to his cog screens. Kato is a tech genius. He should study something Siren related at Stratera Academy, but I suspect he will do cog programming or something else technical I don't understand.

"This is serious; I haven't seen her all day."

He frowns, "Neither have I, but you know what she's like. Probably gawping at herself in a mirror making sure every strand of hair is perfect." He sits on the arm of my chair, and continues, "Besides, she's about to get me for all eternity, it's not like she's going to miss out on that. Is she?"

I look up at him, about to give him an earful, but through the arrogance, there's fear buried in the lines of his face and I know he's as worried as I am, so I try a different tactic.

"Don't speak too soon, you could end up with me."

"Don't be gross, Eden," he says, and shoves me back in my seat. "And get dressed, it's going to take you ages to look respectable."

"You're such a dick. Why are we friends?"

"We're friends?" he says grinning, the worry dispelled. He gets off the armchair and straightens his fitted deep red suit, "I'm going to look for my betrothed; I'll see if I can track your parents down at the same time."

As he strolls out the dressing room door, Nyx walks in. She sees me and her eyes widen like glowing green orbs.

"Why aren't you dressed?" The orange birthmark on her cheek darts across her face. I smile. My eyes might be changing color the more I use Elemental power, but they're nothing compared to Nyx's. She's a Cat Shifter, but even in her normal form, her big eyes are bright green with black vertical pupils just like a cat's; it makes her look like she's always surprised. When she shifts, the only way to distinguish her from any other black alley cat is a small blemish of ginger fur on her face: her birthmark.

"Where are my parents, Nyx?" I ask, pulling out my mom's CogTracker. I flip open the silver cogs and ring Dad for the eighteenth time. When it goes to answerphone, I switch on the tracker screen and search for their essences. But again, I find nothing, which means they're still out of range, and the chance of them making it back to the school in time for the ceremony, is zero.

"They'll be here, Eden. Don't worry." But the way her eyes skirt away from me, tells me she doesn't think they'll make it either.

"Do you know where they went?" I ask, the first bite of tears brimming under my eyes. I swallow them away.

"I don't. But Titus might."

Titus is Nyx's husband and the East's Steampunk Transporter, responsible for taking my family everywhere. He's been with us since I was born.

"What do you mean he might know? Is he not with them?"

Nyx blinks several times before shaking her head once, "Lionel asked Titus to put the personal train on autopilot so he could stay behind and fix the larger one. We need to get some parts for it."

"So, no one knows where they are? I can't find their essence on the tracker because they're out of range, and they're not picking up my calls."

Nyx's face softens, "They'll be here. When have they ever missed anything you've done? I'll find Titus. Just get dressed, and make sure you're ready."

Her body quivers then disappears, dropping to the floor and reappearing in her cat form. I've never got my head around shifting. The light around their body blurs like you're staring through glass and it's raining too hard. Then the edges of their skin ripple, faster and faster until they're all contorted and fuzzy. For an instant they vanish, and I swear they cease to exist. Then they reappear a millisecond later as an animal. Nyx says it's not like that. For her it feels like ages, time slows while her body crunches its bones up to shrink into her cat form. What seems like a second to me, is much, much longer to her.

Her tail flicks around the door as she trots away and I am left alone with my violet dress covered in sparkling gems, a pair of heels I can't walk in and a growing unease in my stomach.

SEVEN

'No baby shall be born to Unbound Keepers.'

Third Law – The Book of Balance

I'M STANDING outside the Great Hall doors in Keepers School, with no memory of how I got here. When I try to think about the last couple of hours, they are a haze of obsessive repeat dialing, pacing, and a growing panic that's fogged my brain like a cataract.

"They're not coming," I say to Kato. "And neither is Bo. Don't try and tell me you're not worried. Look at the state of you."

Sirens are always tanned. Kato is translucent. A line of sweat forms on his forehead against his dark blond hair. He wipes it off, but it reappears just as quickly.

"Speak for yourself, Eden, I always look gorgeous. Runs in the family, don't you know," he says smirking.

Normally I'd put him in his place, but after seeing Trey last night, he might have a point. The image of his brother's body close to mine as we danced across the ballroom floats through my mind. My stomach knots in response. I shift in my gown, grateful Kato can't read my thoughts.

There's a jostle as the doors in front of us are pulled open and slammed shut again as a couple of professors slip through. His smile fades, a tightness grips his eyes. He's afraid. I would be too.

I want my parents here because it's important to me, not because it's a necessity. Even though I can't stand the thought of being Bound to Victor, if he was missing, I'd be terrified. I'm not sure a Potential has ever failed to turn up to a Binding. In fact, I don't even know what will happen to Kato if she doesn't turn up. But I don't have time to consider the consequences because the oak doors yawn open, and my classmates at the front are swallowed into the hall.

I grab Kato's hand and whisper that it's going to be fine, even though we both know it's not.

"Fallon East," Professor Nyra growls at me as I walk past into the hall. "Eden, do you mind? He isn't even your Potential for goodness sake."

I roll my eyes but drop his hand. She's such a stickler. The Book of Balance doesn't say Unbound Keepers can't show kindness or affection. Only ancient Council members interpret it that way.

The hall is as enormous as the sim testing room with tiered seats that rise dozens of feet in the air, but in here they're sectioned off into each State's area.

In the far-left corner is the North State, filled with chairs shaped into mini snow-tipped mountains. The seat bases are carved into the mountain rocks, and furs line the cove of each one making them look like mountainous thrones.

Next to the North, curving around the room, is the West State and the Sorcerers. Their chairs are sandstone cobbled structures, their backs comprised of thatch straw like the bungalows in the villages surrounding Keepers School. Multicolored flowers and vibrant green shrubbery adorn the front of the seats and spill over peppering the floor like flowery paint splats.

On my far right is the Siren-filled South State with maroon and black Chesterfield chairs. Their chair backs are carved with intricate sculptures like mini gargoyles.

My section, in the East, is a bit different. Instead of one style of seating, there are four distinct sections. Each section represents one of the four elements. For those with the power of fire, there are several rows of seats, each one ablaze. In front of them is the illusion of a small lake, with dozens of watery seats appearing almost translucent as they shimmer and wobble. Hovering above the water chairs are white, puffy clouds shaped like floating benches for those that control air. Some of the clouds have flecks of gray, others the occasional flicker of electricity. The seats closest to the front are sand and dirt, for those that control earth. The last area in the hall is for the Dryads from the Ancient Forest, our healers. Their woven, wooden seating runs along the front of all ours, bending around the stage and all the way to the walls.

I choose a cloudy seat but poke it first, to make sure it will take my weight. It's spongier than it looks, almost like a foam mattress, so I figure I'm safe.

Scanning the crowd, part of me hopes my parents will walk in, but it's too late for that. I pull out my CogTracker anyway and check it for the millionth time to see if their essences are in range. They aren't. They haven't returned my calls either. I notice the file mother mentioned on my screen desktop. I tap C-drive, but it's locked.

The doors click shut behind me signaling for the audience's silence. I don't have time to try and unlock the drive, so I shut it down. The curtains at the rear of the stage draw back, and the final murmurs subside. Knowing the doors are shut, I sweep the room one last time just in case they did make it. But all that stares back are the unrecognizable expressions of Keepers, my classmates, and their families. I catch Kato; he shakes his head, I shake mine back. Bo didn't make it either. His eyes are wild, harried, and he's chewing his nails. I want to do something, anything to help him. But as I stand to move over to him, the First Fallon steps out of the darkness and into the center of the stage. Now, the silence is absolute, concentrated and intense like the quiet anticipation of dawn before first light.

The First Fallon is a recluse; I've only seen her a few times, and that was because of Father and the Council. She's strange, the epitome of Balance and everything good, and yet she strikes me as cold. Shimmery white robes hang off her tiny frame. Her knee length white hair swishes as she moves, and her ivory skin is so still and devoid of emotion you'd think her face was a mannequin.

Magic is power, and power is never free, it always leaves a mark, even on someone as powerful as her. She bears the physical traces of all our magic. Before her sister - The Last Fallon - died they were the only two of their kind: Boundless and able to yield all the powers in Trutinor. Her body bears the evidence, magical scars and signatures from eons of use. Her eyes are violet like mine but cooler, icy almost. She's beautiful like a Siren, but the rest of her is worn and tired like a soldier returning from battle. She has strange bark-like markings down one side of her neck which I assume are traces of her healing Dryad powers. The inside of her palm has a deep scar, from holding a wand, carving up her hand like a canyon; Arden has the same markings on his palm. As she moves center stage, she limps on her right leg; it's barely noticeable, but I wonder if, like Victor's hand, her foot is changing as a result of shifting.

Three Sorcerers in robes place a stand with a large, white leather book onstage: the Book of Balance. The First Fallon opens it, skims a few pages and lets it rest open. The Sorcerers return, wands extended, guiding a set of five levitating cogs that once connected; form the Balance Scriptures which she reads our fate from. Each colored cog represents a different State, and they hover in front of the First Fallon until she twists her hands over them and they lock into place.

I catch sight of Victor. His face is tense.

Bo and Kato are desperate to be Bound. They think I don't know they've been having a secret relationship and sneak around like it's a huge secret; even an idiot can tell they've been in love for years. I just wish I felt the same about Victor. I want to be needed the way Kato needs Bo. It's beautiful, and intense, and a little bit disgusting all at the same time. When they're together nothing else exists.

The First Fallon looks at Trey, sat on the Council table at the front, and smiles. Rumor has it that after his parents died, she took it upon herself to care for him. I wonder if that's why he disappeared.

She opens her pale arms, "Welcome, Keepers, Fallons, parents, and Potentials. It is always a privilege to read the scriptures and enact the true fate of so many of our young Keepers. It is both a great responsibility and a deep burden to keep the Balance of fate and to ensure that we, and our distant human cousins, meet our destinies and live in light and Balance. But that is a burden we must carry with pride and honor, and one we can only fulfill if we are Bound to our fated Balancer and soulmate."

She pauses, and waves her hands over the cogs making them shift and spin. Five wisps of smoke: black, lilac, blue, green and maroon, appear from the cogs and dance together until the colors aren't discernible, and there's just a haze of smoke that sinks into the center of the cogs and disappears.

"Today is a momentous occasion," the First Fallon starts, "you're taking your first step into adulthood. While there are still many years of hard work and intensive study to come, you should treasure today. It is your day. May your Bindings be Balanced." She plunges her hands into the center of the cogs.

Her first hand comes out and between her fingers is a tiny bubble of maroon smoke. A Siren. The smoke convulses in the air until it forms the shape of a boy's face I recognize: Tiron Galsworthy. That means Rita's next. Tiron's face shudders into sharper focus, and the tail that will be Bound to Rita's protrudes from his smoky-essence face's neck. As Tiron approaches the stage, the First Fallon yanks the next piece of smoke out, but instead of violet for Rita and the East, it's green.

Rita's scream cuts the air like poison. No one moves, or speaks or even blinks. Her solitary figure stands, like a lonely lighthouse, marooned in the seats. Her shoulders rock as the sobs start to flow, but no one goes to her. No one helps her as her whole life crumbles before her. Tiron glances from Rita to the First Fallon and back again. The shock is written into his slack face. He has to move; there's nothing he can do. I shift in my seat and inch my way down the cloudy seats until I can put my arm around Rita and force her into her seat.

"It's okay, Rita. It's going to be okay," I say. But it's not. She's spent most of her life thinking she will be Bound to Tiron. Much as we're told not to, once the Potentials are announced, you can't help but plan your life together. Spending hours talking about your lives, the things you'll do and see and build together. But it's made clear to us that we're only ever Potentials, nothing more; an almost promise. Errors like this are why the Council advises against families meeting. But they can't help themselves. It's an excuse for parties, meals, outings and happy gatherings. A Binding creates a profound and lasting connection, uniting families the way roots of forest trees matt together. This won't just ruin her life but the lives of both their families.

Victor's gaze skirts between Tiron and Rita. It would be better if we suffered the same fate as Rita and Tiron. The rifts between our states are so deep, hatred between Shifters and Elementals has fueled civil wars for centuries. When our Potential status was announced, our parents held a polite and brief drinks evening, and have not met other than for Council business since. Mistakes like this are rare. The chance of it happening to Victor and me as well are nil.

The essence face of a Sorcerer, Eloise Serina is hanging over the stage. She's stumbling, ashen faced onto the stage. If I remember right, her Potential was Trat Riplock, so this will be even more of a controversy given his father's high-ranking Shifter status.

"Tiron Galsworthy and Eloise Serina," the First Fallon says, "draw your power essences."

They both fumble, still reeling from shock. A small

marble appears on Eloise's hand where she points her wand. It twirls growing into a mesh of twisted vines and flowers. She has the power of plant magic. Floating above Tiron's hand is a tiny version of his face. Its lips are trembling, and lines gouge into its forehead as it shakes; he controls fear.

"Let the East Bind with the South," the First Fallon says and passes her hands over their essences. Tiron's small face and Eloise's vines fly into the air losing their structure and forming threads that knit to the neck of their essence heads. Four tendrils: two maroon, two green, protrude from the bottom of their necks and knot themselves together into a plait. Then they grow thin like oscillating worms and lunge for Tiron and Eloise's arms.

"Join hands," the First Fallon commands.

As they do, one maroon and one green tendril suckers on to each of their right forearms. Eloise whimpers as spines from the plait puncture her skin. Tiron, able to control his fear, stays silent, but the color drains from his face.

The spines splinter off and crawl like spiders' legs over their arms burning their souls together. Finally, the tendrils snap off and shrink back to the necks of the essence faces re-forming into an indestructible plait. Once sealed not even death can break their Binding.

All that's left on their forearms are identical maroon and green scars, an imprint of the plait that now hangs beneath their essence heads: the fingerprint of their Binding, and like a fingerprint, it's unique.

They leave the stage holding hands, which makes Rita cry again. I squeeze her shoulder wishing I could say something to make her feel better.

Eloise and Tiron wear the same vacant expression like they've just woken up from a lengthy sleep. Two Sorcerers coax the Bound faces off stage. They'll take them to the

Binding Chamber, a cavernous room located here in the West. All our Bindings are stored there. No one other than high ranking Council members are allowed in, but I hear it's spectacular.

"Eden East?" the First Fallon calls. Dozens of eyes turn to look at me. She must have called me once already because my smoky-essence face is hanging in focus on stage.

I stand up, and take one final glance around the room, not that I expect my parents to appear. My chest is tight. I'm not sure if it's nerves about Victor or disappointment in my parents. I consider looking for Victor in the crowd, but if I'm going to have a life time of staring at him, I'd rather keep this last moment of freedom to myself. My face and shoulders are stiff from trying to hide my emotion as I weave toward the stage. I don't want this. Everything in my body is telling me to run. Victor doesn't even want this.

I pass the Council table and avoid looking at my parents' empty seats at the top. I reach the stage stairs, climb a couple and pause. The First Fallon's eyes are wide, and her mouth has fallen open like she was about to sing but someone pressed pause. I freeze. She tumbles forward, her arm lunging towards me as if to grab me. Her movement startles me, and I misstep. My knee slams into the stairs at the same time something punches into my back.

I yelp as heat erupts across my skin; the cloying smell of burning hair and fabric pervade the air. Screams explode through the audience. But I'm locked by panic, which makes them muffled and distant. Figures run, hands grab for children as parents tear them out of the stands.

I wrench my head around to see what's attached to me. But whatever it is, hit me in the center of my spine and is covered by the brightest violet light I've ever seen.

Behind me, a man jumps to his feet. I think it's Kato, but

maybe it's Trey. His eyes flick from me to the First Fallon.

Another punch. This time to my thigh. It knocks me the rest of the way up the stairs, and I collapse on to the stage. This time I see my attacker. It's torn straight through my dress and punctured into my leg. Like a bolt of lightning, dozens of spindles split off and crawl over my skin. I scream, but now even my voice is disjointed. I'm shrieking, high pitched and loud as hundreds of needles pierce my flesh. I smack at the lightning bolt trying to dislodge it, but instead of pushing it off, it sticks to my hand like a tentacle and wraps itself tighter around my thigh.

"Get it off," I bellow, reaching for the First Fallon.

But she steps back, "I can't." Her expression is muddled, and I can't tell if she's furious or horrified. Maybe both.

"How is this happening?" a voice roars behind me. Trey appears, his teeth bared, shoulders rising and falling with angry breaths. "You assured me this wouldn't happen again. Did you not foresee this?" he barks. His fists ball. But I'm too desperate to pull the bolts off to stop and understand. Chaos fills the stands, as Keepers and parents shriek and panic surging for the exit doors.

"Do not touch her, Trey," the First Fallon says, her voice sharp, threatening. "This is impossible," she says, this time more to herself than Trey. "I made sure it would not come to pass."

I fall to my knees as another bolt hits my other calf.

The heat scorches my skin until I am certain I'll be left burnt like a roasted animal. Another punch. This time to my abdomen. I let out a guttural cry, as the tendrils crawl over my skin leaving tiny heat blisters in their wake.

Three more blows smash into my torso, making me woozy. Most of my body is encased by the violet bolts. Trey grabs my free hand, and yanks me into the middle of the stage.

"Stop. Do not..." the First Fallon barks. But he holds his hand up to silence her.

"No, Cecilia. Not this time."

Who is Cecilia? I think before another shriller voice yells to my left. "What do you think you're doing, Trey?" the woman asks, her tone harsh and full of spite.

"Stay back, Eve. Just stay back," Trey says, and waves her off too.

I'm lying on my front, splayed like a star fish, dying. Trey lies next to me, his body flat on the stage too. He hesitates, then cups his hand to my face. "You're going to be okay."

A tentacle shears off latching onto his wrist. He flinches but doesn't take his hand away.

I shake my head. I'm not okay; I'm dying. These bolts are going to burn me to death. I'm Unbound, so I'll drift through the other side, Obex, for all eternity. The thought of being a lost soul gives me a burst of energy, and I kick and lash against the restraints, trying to free myself. But the harder I fight the tighter the rope-like bolts squeeze.

"What's happening?" I scream.

Trey mouths the air like he knows but can't bring himself to tell me.

My mind races, until it settles on a memory. Kato only spoke of what happened to Trey once: maroon essence bolts had encased Trey's body and the sound of his brother's screams, mixed with the stench of burning flesh, haunted him for years.

Despite the heat from the lightning, my blood runs cold, goosebumps slithering down my back. They aren't bolts of lightning. It's essence. Someone's essence.

"No," I breathe and kick out flailing even harder. "NO." This time I'm screaming it, over and over and over like an echo from a nightmare; the words are piercing.

"Eden, listen to me," Trey says, both hands on my face, and he's pulling me close, so we're eye to eye. His hands are engulfed by the essence, and I don't understand how he's coping.

"You have to stop fighting; it will ease the pain."

Stop fighting? How can I stop fighting?

"But this. Is this...? Are my par..." I choke on the words. I can't say it.

I have to be wrong. These have to be bolts, a lightning attack of some sort. They can't be essence.

Trey's forehead wrinkles, his piercing blue eyes concentrating on me, "You have to stop fighting because there's nothing you can do to stop this. You have to ride it out."

Finally, I relax and whisper, "Are they dead?"

He blinks, but he doesn't deny it. Why is silence so much worse than an answer?

I shake my head. The essence reaches my neck. More spines splinter off and onto Trey's hands as they pierce my cheeks. Heavy tears spill onto the spines making sparks fly like fireworks around us. If it weren't so horrifying, it would be spectacular. My vision splinters. I hear a scream somewhere in the distance, but as the shriek echoes around us, I realize it's mine. Then my body gives out, and I fall limp.

The last thing I hear before the crackles obstruct my ears, is Trey saying, "I'm right here, Eden. I've always been here. I'll never leave you."

Violet light blocks my vision until there is only the deafening roar of essence filling my body. Finally the blackness comes, and I sink into the relief of nothingness.

EIGHT

'Inheritance - *A mythical occurrence when two Fallons (parents) die simultaneously, and part of their essence is transferred to their eldest heir. There are no official recorded instances of this happening.'*

'Amendment: There is one recorded case of a Siren Fallon Inheriting essence. Sorcerers suggest the act of Inheriting essence causes a massive Imbalance, the consequences of which are still being studied.'

Excerpt – Myths and Legends of Trutinor

'Compulsion, or 'to compel' - The use of

***Siren   powers   to   control   another's
emotion.'***

From the Dictionary of Balance

While I'm unconscious, my mind dreams of a life I haven't
lived. In each snippet, there is one constant: Trey. First, I'm
in the Ceremony Hall, his hand clasping my face, then
we're pulled to The Pink Lake, his hand still on my cheek,
only this time he's kissing me, his hands roaming my body,
making me hot, electric, gasping.

OPENING MY EYES, I glimpse a wooden hospital room. I
squeeze my eyes shut again. The images of Trey fade away,
replaced by the truth of why I'm here. For just a minute, I
pretend everything is okay. No one's dead. I'm Bound to
someone other than Victor. Life is good. Everyone is alive.
But as soon as I dare to breathe, the choking reality hits me,
and I know it's all a lie.

The scent of the Ancient Forest's eternal summer fills
my nose: sweet blossom and honey aromas so potent I can
taste them like a thick golden nectar. Although I've always
sensed the air, I've never been able to taste it. Everything is
different. More intense. My powers are in overdrive, and I
don't understand why. It's like the air itself is alive only now
it's a part of me. I reach out to it again; this time a softness
that feels like silk slips over my skin carrying the murmur of

birds and a coolness that tells me it's dawn. I wonder for a moment if that means Mother is the one that's dead. Her essence is... was, air. Father's is water.

A flash of my last memory screams into focus. The stage. The burning. Trey. I gasp for breath and haul my body upright pushing the images away. Everything aches, my muscles shake in protest, and I wobble before finding a comfortable position.

Does Trey feel more? Are his powers in overdrive too? Is that what he meant at the dance when he said it was weird I could feel his Siren compulsion? A quiet cough interrupts my thoughts.

"Eden?" a smooth male husk drifts through the room. It's familiar. "Are you hot?" he asks.

Odd question. Don't people normally ask if you're ok? Or in pain? But I am hot, and then I realize who the voice belongs to.

"Trey?" My throat is dry and crackles like it's the first time I've spoken in weeks.

I spot him in the corner of the room. Like all hospital rooms in Dryad City Hospital, it looks more like a tree house or a wicker basket than a hospital because large forest branches weave together to form walls.

"I'm boiling," I rasp.

He stands, opens the door and windows, and lets the breeze in. Then he moves to my bed. I groan, even the movement of him settling next to me makes my muscles hurt.

"It aches."

He nods, "That's because you've been out cold for three days straight."

"Oh," I say and pull my knees under my chin. "Where is everyone?"

"Bo, Kato, Nyx and Titus all took shifts with me; they've gone back to the central hospital building to sleep and eat."

I frown, as I replay his words, 'with me.' Has he been here the whole time? He fidgets in his seat as if he knows what I'm thinking; his cheeks flush pink, but I blink, and the color is gone.

"I know what you've been through, Eden," he says, "I know how much it hurts, and how everything you're seeing and feeling right now is heightened. It's intense, and it will be for a few weeks, until your body and your mind get used to it. You need to be Bound as soon as possible. It will help bring your Balance back to normal. That's the mistake the Council made with me."

He reaches for my shoulder making me flinch. His face drops, as though I've offended him.

"Sorry," I say.

"No, I'm sorry, I should know better."

"I need to know... Are they okay? I mean, which one...?" I falter. If I don't say it, maybe it won't be true.

"Israel is coming to speak to you on behalf of the Council."

Israel? Why Israel? Why would the Council send Victor's father? Anyone would be better than him. Heat trickles into my rib cage, and the first embers of fire smolder between my palm and my knees.

"Are you okay?"

I'm not. I turn my palm up - the whole thing is alight. I scramble back as if I can get away from myself. But I can't. I stare open mouthed at my hand. When I use the fire element it's separate to me. Something I control and manipulate that floats above my hand. This is different. Fire burns from the center of my palm, like the fuel is coming from inside me. As if to confirm I'm right, a rush of heat pumps through my arm like my veins are flamethrowers. The fire around my palm burns harder, like my panic is making it brighter. Or maybe the fire's sentient. Either way, my heart is pounding, and my breath short. With each beat, the flames pulse stronger until they consume my whole hand and a white-hot heat circles my chest.

Trey takes my other wrist, and where his palm touches my skin, cool vibrations flow into my body like waves lapping on shore. My heart slows, and the flames drop to embers before extinguishing. He stares at me, his chest rising and falling as fast as mine.

"You're not in control of your powers yet. There's a lot you need to know and understand, and until then, you need to be careful with your emotions, especially while you're not Bound."

He reaches for me like he's done it a thousand times before, and pulls me under his bare arm. I stiffen. Why is he so comfortable with contact? What if someone, Evelyn, came in?

He's wearing a thin white string vest, and as the curve of his bicep molds around my shoulder, my stomach knots a fraction. I tell myself this is just Trey, I used to know him, and he is already Bound. It's been a long time since he was in my life, but as I lean into him, for some reason, it feels like yesterday. I relax and sink into his embrace. Where his arm meets my body, gusts of arctic-like wind continue to flow through my system. I'm grateful for his Siren powers, and I decide that maybe having your emotions compelled once in a while isn't so bad.

"After I Inherited," he starts, and strokes my hair, tracing cool lines over my scalp. "I wasn't Bound for four years. Everything was messed up and Imbalanced. No one had ever Inherited before, so they didn't know what to do with me. There were so many tests, and questions and studies. That's why I disappeared. They made out it was to train me to be a Fallon leader, but that was a lie. The First F..." he stops, takes a breath and continues. "The Council wanted to understand me. It won't be like that this time. I won't let anyone do that to you."

"Is that why you came on stage? Because you knew what was happening to me?"

"One of many complicated reasons that don't matter right now," he says.

My head swims; he's only giving me half a story, something is missing, but I can't work out what. He continues, cutting off my train of thought.

"I've been surrounded by more people than ever over the last eight years. First with Sorcerers and the tests, then being Bound to Evelyn and the constant Council work..." His voice is quiet, distant as if he's reliving a hundred memories at once and they're jumbled and confused. He turns to me.

"But I was so alone. They didn't understand. None of them had ever seen this before, let alone experienced it."

I sit up, untangling myself from his arms. "Until now?" I say, "you were alone, until now?"

He nods, "Until you." His eyes are so blue, and yet they burn like flames dancing with an intensity that makes me shuffle in my seat.

I take in his words, absorb them, trying to understand their meaning. As if reading my mind, he says, "Now, no matter what happens, who we are with, or where we are, we will always be together."

I rest my head on my knees, a feeling of déjà vu making me tired and confused. My eyes close for just an instant, yet

I'm yanked back to the Great Hall. Violet bolts snake around my limbs. Keepers shriek, hollow, piercing, like shattered glass. The memory of burning flesh makes pain whittle into my muscles, so I open my eyes. If I have to relive the Inheritance every time I shut them, I'll never sleep again.

"Flash backs?" Trey asks.

I nod, too exhausted to talk.

He reaches for my forearm. This time, as he touches me, a wave of warmth spreads from under his hand and radiates into my torso. Everything I feel, anger; terror; confusion, dissolves into an expanse of sparkles like the twinkling of a starlit sky.

The sensation rushes around my body, stretching into my fingertips, up to my scalp and into my eyes, blinding me with a bright, intoxicating euphoria. The sparkles spread to my legs, and my breath catches as the sensation reaches my groin. The edges of the room fade as I lose myself to some desire I've never felt before. I want more. I need more. Then I come to my senses.

"Stop," I gasp.

He lets go instantly, but his eyes are as glazed as my brain feels.

"I'm so sorry. That shouldn't have happened," he says, leaning back with a deep pink on his cheeks.

"What *did* happen?"

"I don't know. I was trying to take your pain away, so you don't go through what I did, and it just... I guess I got caught up in our connection."

He stands, turning his back to me, and moves a couple of paces away.

"Don't take my pain away, okay?" I say as tenderly as I can.

"I was just trying to help."

"I know. But calming me down is one thing. Taking my pain away. That's... that's not right. That's like taking away a scar. Scars are memories. They're real. Moments we shouldn't forget." *That pain might be the only thing I have left of my parents,* I think, but I don't say that aloud.

He shrugs, "Do you feel better?"

"I do," I smile. "Thank you." But this is a false calm. While I still have my pain, any emotion he controls is like sticking a plaster over a gaping wound: the compulsion will fade, the blood will ooze out the sides, and eventually, so will my pain.

He helps me into a rocking chair made of the same woven branches as the walls. The scent of wood sap wafts up from the seat, and I can feel the connection to the earth running from the wood frame, through the floorboards, down the tree trunk, and into the earth. It's overwhelming, but in an odd way, it's comforting.

"Where does it go?" I ask him. "The emotion, I mean. When you take it out of me."

He smiles, "You're consistent, I'll give you that."

Before I can ask what that means, he flips his hand over. A speck of dust appears in his hand, with a tail that connects to his palm. Like the fire in my hand, his power must be connected to him too. The ball spins until it forms a dark violet ball flecked with black barb-like wisps. I lean into his hand.

"Is that...?"

"Yes. Just a small piece of your pain."

"Big ball for a small piece of pain."

His eyes skirt away, so I change the subject.

"What will you do with it?"

"I'd discard it normally, but I can keep it if you want. Give it back to you when the time's right?"

I look up at him and search his face. I do want him to keep it so I can take it back when I'm ready, but it feels weird knowing he's keeping a piece of me.

"Okay...," I say hesitantly

"I can get rid of it if you prefer? Just release it back into Trutinor?"

"No. No. I want it back. Just not yet," I say, and reach out to poke it.

His left hand grabs my wrist, making me jump.

"Don't," he says, "don't ever touch them, okay?"

"Why?"

"Just don't."

"Okay," I say, and lean back in my seat wondering what his problem is. "So, does this mean I can't feel until you give it back?"

"Nothing's that simple." He tilts his hand to stroke the air around the ball. It spins faster as if it isn't a piece of my pain but a basketball on the tip of his finger, then a wisp protrudes. "This is just a moment in time, it's the hurt you felt in the instant I touched you. It's like a memory, I guess but for your feelings."

"If you keep it, and I look back on this in a year's time, will I feel nothing?"

"In a way. You'd know what you felt, just like you'd know what you were wearing. But that's it. It would be like looking at a photo of someone else. You'd recognize the memory and the emotions you felt, but you wouldn't feel anything other than indifference, I guess."

I recoil. I have so many happy memories, with my family, what if someone took them away? What if those feelings disappeared and I couldn't get them back?

"That's awful," I blurt before I can stop myself, "I'd rather be full of pain, than indifferent. Indifference is empty; it's nothingness. Why would anyone let their memories be taken?"

He shrugs and shuts his fingers over the purple ball making it puff into the air. His blue eyes, usually warm and bright, are cold and pale like my words extinguished them. "Sometimes it's a necessity. Or the pain is too much. Or it's for someone's safety, to protect them."

I stare at him taking in his words, and realize he doesn't mean 'the pain,' he means, *his* pain. Warmth touches the top of my neck; I didn't mean to hurt him.

"You took your own pain away?" I ask.

He stays silent, but his shoulders harden like the secrets he's harboring are an impenetrable fortress; he's on the inside, and I am stuck, like a child looking through the glass at him.

Before I can push him for an answer, heavy boots clunk on the wooden balcony outside my room. Trey stands straighter running a hand through his wavy hair. His nose wrinkles, and I too, catch the faint whiff of stale blood.

"Israel," Trey says, and glances at me, all signs of the barrier he put up gone.

Don't let me cry in front of Israel, I plead silently. Trey, having sat on the Council for years, understands the politics between our families.

He walks over to me, so familiar, so knowing as if he's still my childhood friend and no time has passed. Or more likely, he's just reading my emotions. He stands behind my chair. I take a deep breath, and Israel steps into the room.

NINE

'The soul does not die but passes through the barrier to Obex. When fate determines, our souls move on to the next life, and our Bindings move with us, permeating Obex and all the realms between. They are eternal.'

Excerpt from The Book of Balance, modern translation vol. 3

ISRAEL STANDS IN THE DOORWAY, hovering like he's waiting for permission to enter. I frown; Israel is egotistical and domineering, and he hates my family. I don't understand his hesitance; I figured he'd revel in my pain.

But he just stands in the doorway shaking and looking haggard.

"Are you coming in?" I ask.

He ducks his head under the door frame and enters the room. He has the same greasy blond hair, tied in a topknot, as Victor. He rearranges the thick furs draped down his back and sits in an armchair across from me. His movements are slow, labored, and I'm not sure if he's in pain or exhausted. He leans forward, puts his elbows on his knees and his head in hands, as his cape falls across one shoulder. It occurs to me that he probably caught and skinned the poor animals that make up his furs himself. Even if it is always winter in the North, the idea of skinning an animal with my bare hands to wear it makes me queasy.

"Eden, I..."

The gravel of his voice jars me out of my thoughts. He's looking at me with those endless black pupils. Heavy purple bags hang like fruit under his eyes. His white skin, usually taut like Bo's, is wrinkled as though he's aged a decade since I last saw him.

"Just tell me which one died."

The room is silent except for the thud, thud, thud of my heart colliding against my ribcage. The beats ring so loud in my ears I fear I won't hear Israel's words. Trey must sense my rising anxiety because he leans a little closer and just out of Israel's eye line, rests the pad of his finger against the skin on my shoulder.

My chest rattles in defiance but obeys, and the beating slows. Trey's subtle, I'll give him that.

"A case has been opened. It's headed by Fallon Winkworth and the Guild of Investigations."

I nod, satisfied. If anyone can find out what happened and bring whoever did this to justice, it's Arden.

"They don't know what happened, yet..." Israel says quietly. He sounds concerned, regretful almost. I'm not used to his kindness; it's unsettling like a sudden snowstorm mid-summer.

Although I have lots of memories of school holidays spent with Bo in their house, the majority of my recollections of Israel are watching him snarl at my father across the Council Chamber. Either he's faking the sincerity, or this is a side to Israel I've never seen.

He shifts in the armchair, and rubs his forehead so hard I think he might wipe the furrowed lines away.

"Israel?" I nudge. "Which one of my parents is dead?"

He winces at the word dead, and his hands move to his sharp-trimmed beard.

"I am so sorry, Eden. I know I didn't always see eye to eye with your parents, but there's a lot you didn't see, a lot you don't know. I have so much respect for them. But... There's something you should know..."

Israel's eyes meet Trey's. *Does Trey already know which one died? Did he lie to me when I asked?*

"I was the one who found them," Israel says, his face scarlet, and I think I see tears welling in his eyes. I'm not sure if he's angry or gutted, or maybe both. His words replay in my head and it makes me icy cold. *Them? He said he found 'them.'*

The air is motionless, and the sound of birds and insects outside mutes. A fog of gray fills my vision, and everything except the roar of my breathing goes quiet.

"What do you mean, *them*?"

A pit opens in my mind; darkness spills into my body numbing everything except my hearing. At first, I was afraid to miss his words, now I plead for deafness. I will him not to speak. But his shoulders rise and fall as he prepares to tell me. Everything moves in slow, juddering motions and color fades to black and white.

Israel takes a breath. His eyes focus on me and his mouth opens, but no words come.

"Israel...? What do you mean 'them'?" I press, my voice barely audible.

A swell of frustrated heat floods my system. Trey said he was Imbalanced. Is this what it feels like? When Israel doesn't speak, it makes the first fire embers inside me ignite. Trey places two more fingers against my back. He can feel my irritation and panic; he's taking no chances.

Israel's face crumples. He puffs out a deep breath, and when he looks at me again, the hard facade I'm used to is back.

"Eden, as deputy chair of the Royal Council of Trutinor, and as the person who was first at the scene of the crime, it is my duty to inform you..." he blinks a few times. I close my eyes, electricity sparking around my insides like my body is a prison and it's trying to claw its way out. Somewhere behind me, I hear Trey catch his breath, and then the pressure of his entire hand is on my back.

There is a feverish heat between his grip and my skin. War is raging, his power versus my emotions. Sweat runs down his arm, falls onto my spine, and rolls down my back like a wayward raindrop. He's struggling. I open my eyes, hoping he can win and keep me strong.

When my gaze meets Israel's, he says the words that, deep down, I've known were coming since Trey stepped onto the stage.

"Eden, I'm sorry. Lionel and Eleanor were found earlier today. Both of your parents are dead."

TEN

'Binding – *The moment two perfectly Balanced souls are joined for eternity.'*

From the Dictionary of Balance

THICK, warm arms carry me. I press against them, eyes shut, hoping it's Father. It isn't. Father smells like autumn rain: fresh and warm from the last of summer's dying breath. This is different. But the last time I smelt it, I was just as close to him as I am now. And like last time, the cloy of frankincense and the closeness of his body makes my stomach knot. Trey is carrying me. The fleshy curve of his bicep and the strange void of emotion confirms it. I open my eyes. Is it weird I'm so comfortable in his arms?

He pushes through a set of rooftop doors. "You're

home," he says and places me down on one of the sofas overlooking Element City's maze of skyscrapers.

Dirty pink clouds coat the sky in long thin stains like someone painted their fingers and smeared them over the horizon. In the distance, the desert curls around the city block like a sandy hug. I shiver and rub my arms; the night breeze is already cutting through the warren-like city streets.

Pulling myself up, I walk to the edge of the roof and lean over the parapet. Elemental Keepers scurry like bugs below. This is meant to be my home, but everything that was once familiar, ordinary, and a comfort, is now sharp and shaded with grief.

Rickety bridges and walkways link between tower windows hundreds of feet in the air. That connection used to feel like a lifeline to my people, now it's intrusive, and I wish I could cut it off. Lights flicker to life in the windows, and I remember how, as a child, I thought they made the buildings look like giant Christmas trees.

"I don't think I can be here," I say, gripping the wall until my knuckles turn white. "Everywhere I look I see my parents." I pause, gulping air to stop myself from crying.

"What Israel said... Are they? Are both of them...?"

Trey doesn't respond. He never seems to answer when I need it most. But at least he's still here. As he steps toward me, the goosebumps tracking down my arms soak up his body heat and disappear.

I squeeze my eyes shut, turn around, and slide to the ground. I can't look at the city anymore. It's suffocating. I wrap my arms around my chest as if that will somehow make the pain disappear.

Above me thunder cracks like a drum, and Trey glances

up as rain splatters his face and the rooftop floor. Then he looks down at me.

"Yes, the rain is my fault. No, I'm not going stop it. Too tired."

He could use compulsion to stop me if he wanted, but he doesn't. So, drop by drop, the rain drenches us, and even though I'm soaked, I'm smiling because I like that he hasn't stopped me.

"You should go, you'll get cold," I say, looking at his string vest.

Instead of leaving, as he should, he sits down beside me, his warm, wet shoulder touching mine. He picks up my hand like it's an automatic movement and says, "Back in the hospital, I tried to control your anger. But when Israel started to explain what the investigation team knew, you screamed for him to leave. When he didn't, you erupted in flames. We were in the middle of the forest. If you'd flamed up for any length of time we, and all the Dryads, would be dead. The only thing I could do was make you black out. I figured it was safer for you here." His tone is soft, like cotton.

I narrow my eyes, "You can stop controlling me now."

"I don't know what you're talking about," he says, and turns away.

"Liar. Your eyes are like blue flames when you use your Siren powers. Honestly, I'm fine. Back at the hospital, it was strange..."

"Go on."

I hesitate. How well do I know Trey? Yes, we were friends in childhood, but that was forever ago, and he's a Council member as much as Israel is. Can I trust him?

"You're not alone, Eden. You'll never be alone. Not while I'm here. I know your parents are gone, and that feels like your heart's been cut out. But don't shut down..."

"You mean don't shut *you* out." I tilt my head, trying to work out who he's consoling, him or me.

I take a breath and decide to risk telling him.

"It was like I was surrounded by darkness." I eye him, trying to gauge his reaction. His face remains blank, so I continue. "Everything was muted, gray. Darkness was, or maybe is, inside me. It shouldn't be there; I need to get it out because once it unleashed itself, I had no control over my body. I couldn't control anything: not my powers, the fire, nothing. It just..."

"Exploded," he interjects.

"Exactly."

"It lurks somewhere inside me."

"You have it too?"

He nods, "It happened after the Inheritance."

Footsteps echo in the stairwell we came up. His eyes dart to the door. He raises his fingers to his lips and then mouths the words 'It's Imbalance.' Then he stands and pulls his hand through his hair, "Your city is beautiful, but I don't want to get locked in here during the Dusting."

"Of course, go," I say, standing. But I don't want him to go. I want to know more. To understand what this thing inside me is and how to get rid of it.

"I'm here if you need me...Whenever you need me," he says, hesitating before leaving.

"Where can I find you?"

"My bar, in the South."

I nod, and he goes. For the first time since my parents died, I am all alone. No matter what he says, they're gone. I can't bring them to life again so I'll always be alone. The gulf of tears I've been holding back streaks my cheeks, big, hot and round as they fall. Huge sobs rock my shoulders until I can't take the pain in my chest anymore. I launch balls of fire and lightning into the air trying to get rid of the ache. The darkness, or Imbalance, or whatever it is, must sense my anger because, like the creeping of a shadow, it appears in my mind. Black needles prick my senses making me angrier, and each bolt, ball and blaze I throw, gets bigger, louder, more dangerous. Clouds burst apart, singed gray at the edges, and shower ash over the rooftops. I scream, over and over and over, until my voice runs dry, and my throat is hoarse. Finally, I lean on the parapet, my breathing heavy. The Imbalance mists over my vision. Confusing me, controlling me, whispering wordless encouragement like a conscience. Only the whispers aren't good ones. Instead of bursting clouds apart, I have the urge to blow up buildings. I clench my fists, "No... No one else dies today."

Something fluffy rubs against my legs making me jump, and the darkness dissolves. Cat-Nyx hops between my shins. The sight of her drains the remaining fight out of me. I trudge back to the sofas and collapse, exhausted and aching worse than ever. I wonder how long she's been watching me.

"How could they, Nyx? How could they just die like that?"

She pads across the rooftop, climbs onto my lap, and nudges at my torso.

"Don't think I don't know what you're doing."

The corner of her furry mouth curls showing the point of a single tooth. She prods her head into my jaw and kneads her paws into my chest. I sigh, but I relent and stroke her under her chin until she purrs. We sit for a time, me stroking, her purring. After a while, the weight where she's sitting on my lap lifts and she reappears in the seat next to me. She slips her hand into mine, "Do you remember when you fell over and cut your leg down to the bone?"

I touch my shin where the scar still taints my skin, and smile. "Three hours you let me stroke you, till Mom and Dad got back from Earth and took me to the Dryads to get treated."

Her eyes well up, and I wonder if it's the memory or because she knows this time, they aren't coming home.

"Titus pushed that train so hard to get back for you." I think she laughs, but it sounds more like a sob, "I threatened to break our Binding if he didn't get back fast."

I attempt a smile for her, but it's half-hearted and doesn't stop her tears from running anyway. I slip my hands in my pocket searching for a tissue to offer her, but instead, I find a hard, round coin which takes the breath out of my lungs.

I pull it out and hold it up, "Dad gave me this because I'd been brave. He got it on that trip and said I should keep it as a good luck charm, then laughed to himself because humans tell each other to break a leg when they wish someone luck."

Nyx wipes her face and pulls me into a hug.

"I miss them too," she says.

But I don't miss them. Not yet. I'm too angry they're gone. I touch her cheek and say, "We're going to be okay, you know."

"I'm meant to look after you, Eden," she says, "not the other way around."

"I know. But, this time, we need to look after each other."

She shakes her head at me, her short spiky hair twitching like fur, "When did you get so grown up?"

I shrug and change the subject. "Trey mentioned the Dusting; I didn't realize it was so soon. Aren't they normally a week or two after a Fallon…" I can't say the words; I'm not sure I'll ever be able to. "I mean, don't they have investigations to do?"

"Arden's had the entire Guild of Investigations working around the clock for the last four days. They're just finishing up now. They had to speed up the process because they want to get you Bound."

"Oh," I say, thinking it all seems strange and rushed. "When am I being Bound?"

"A couple of days. As soon as the Dusting is over. They won't let you stay like this…" She doesn't say Imbalanced, but that's what she means.

"I know," I say. There's a smog of darkness thickening in my head. I can't tell if the whispers of revenge are the Imbalance, or me. I understand now why Trey silenced me when he heard Nyx coming. This isn't something that can be explained to anyone else. My brain fuzzes with thought after thought until I have a headache, but one question surfaces. Like me, Trey's been exposed to a level of Imbalance a Keeper should never experience. Whatever's inside me is carving marks into my soul, permanent changes engraining themselves in my essence. I don't need to be told I'll never get rid of this completely. Scars like that, the ones that change you forever, don't just disappear when you're healed or Bound. Which makes me wonder - how will my Binding even work?

ELEVEN

'Dustoria - *The momentary euphoria a Keeper feels when a particle of Dust makes contact with their skin.'*

'Dusting – *The funeral ceremony of a Fallon.'*

From the Dictionary of Balance

AT SOME POINT during the night Kato arrives at my home tower because when I wake in the morning, he's passed out on the sofa on the other side of my bedroom. His arm dangles off the side, and he's still dressed in skinny maroon jeans and a white top. Except for the mass of blond hair, he looks just like Trey. I throw a pillow at his head to wake him.

"Trey told me what happened in the hospital," he says, yawning and pushing his sleep-styled blond hair away from his face. "I was worried about you."

I smile, get out of bed and hug him, "Careful, Kato. I might start believing you have a heart."

"Don't be ridiculous, I'm a Siren," he grins at me and then adds, "now go get showered, you stink of smoke and ashy Elemental."

A couple of hours later, I've washed and dressed in my comfiest fatigues, boots and black t-shirt. But I fail to eat much at breakfast and leave Nyx and Kato in the doorway of my building. Kato had to get back to the South, but it still took ten whole minutes to convince them I would be fine, and even though they agreed to let me go alone, as I walk away, I can still feel their worried stares.

I haven't seen Bo since before the ceremony, and Kato didn't mention her this morning. Trey said she helped him watch over me in the hospital, but that's not the same as seeing her. I miss her. I need her, now more than ever. I open the silver CogTracker Mom gave me and scan for Bo's name to type out a message:

Where are you?

Three dots appear as she starts to respond. But the dots stop just as fast as they appeared, so I write:

I need you

But the dots don't reappear. I snap the tracker shut, frustrated.

Meandering through the narrow streets, I distract myself from Bo by stopping to talk to various Keepers. As the capital of the East, Element City is home to all kinds of Elemental Keepers. The other cities tend to have Keepers of one type of Elemental power like Ignis, which is home to a large proportion of fire Elementals, or Caelum City where all the air Elementals live.

Traders take advantage of the diverse and dense population in Element City filling the streets with stalls, and markets making the already narrow paths stifling. Awnings jut out from the buildings with trinkets dangling down like rainforest canopies. There's a heady mix of burning herbs, wet earth and cooking food permeating the air. What light reaches the ground, refracts through the scented smoke making it almost dream-like.

I leave the market area and a few minutes later, reach the entrance to Element Square - the largest open space in the city. It's covered by grass and large enough to fit several thousand people inside. As I step into the square, I falter. There's a stage in the top corner and four drapes hanging down the back. One's ablaze with an orange fire that doesn't spread further than the edge of the fabric, another drape has a disappearing and reappearing waterfall flowing down it. The third looks like it's constructed from the same clouds I sat on before the ceremony and the last drape is grainy, and ripples as the sandy fabric shifts and moves in the breeze.

In front of the drapes, are my parents. I'm afraid to breathe in case I erupt into flames again. Even from the other side of the square, I can distinguish their dulled skin. Their still figures lie on a plinth side by side, as if they're just taking a nap.

My legs wobble, suddenly weak. Arden's arm catches me before I fall to the ground.

"It's okay," he says, pulling me tight, "it's going to be okay."

Why do people say that? It's never okay, but people say it anyway like it's some sticky band-aid that will patch me up like magic. My parents are dead, and I have to turn their bodies into Dust live on stage in front of thousands of people. What part of that is okay?

Arden guides me backstage. The area is fenced off but not under cover. I slump on top of a large, black speaker discarded near the stage stairs, take a deep breath and let the sun stream across my face. As the warmth soaks in, the feeling returns to my legs and the image of their lifeless figures fades.

"I really have to do this," I say, my throat clogging.

"You really have to do this," Arden nods, and nudges me across the speaker so he can perch next to me.

"The Dust does most of the work, all you need to do is release it and blow it over your parents. Okay?"

I look up at him, unsure if I can, so I change the subject.

"What did your investigation find?"

He sits up straight. "Are you sure now is a wise time to ask? You need to be in control for the Dusting. When Trey..." He stops. "I mean... Well, we don't want a repeat."

He squeezes my hand and smiles.

"I'm fine, really," I lie. "It was just the shock of seeing them. I want to know."

"Okay," he nods, "they were found in Israel's house."

My body tightens. Maybe Arden was right: I shouldn't have asked.

"That's why he wanted to tell you himself. He was distraught, Eden, I've never seen him so upset."

I nod. Everything from the hospital room is muddled, but flashes of memory are slotting into order. When Israel told me he'd found them in his house, the Imbalance took over, clouding my head with a frenzy of emotion. I remember screaming accusations before burning up and blacking out. I drop my eyes to the floor and fidget.

"I shouldn't have got so cross in the hospital, I should have let Israel explain."

"I heard about that," Arden says, eyeing me. "Listen, we know the cause of death now. I heard from the Guild of Investigations this morning. They were poisoned."

"Poisoned? I say, sitting up. "Where would someone get a poison powerful enough to kill a Fallon?"

"The Guild are running tests on the poison found in their blood. We'll find out what happened. I promise you."

I pick his hand up and squeeze. His hands are dry, covered in callouses, the result of spray-back from wand magic no doubt. I look at him: bags paint the skin under his eyes brown and purple; his eyes are puffy like he's been crying, and even his ever-neat beard looks untidy around the edges.

"Thank you, Arden."

He shrugs, "Lionel was my best friend; he saved my life when Tilly died. He was my family; *you're* my family."

Lance Rockford, Arden's Steampunk Transporter, appears from behind the stage curtains. Lance is a giant, towering over Arden and me. He's wearing the standard issue double-breasted navy transporter's jacket and trouser uniform. Dark dreadlocks hang to his waist, silver beads adorning the dreads in random places. He holds himself proud as he walks towards us. He should too because he started out with Arden as an apprentice, and now he's the youngest brigadier on record and in charge of the whole of Trutinor's transport, which makes him Titus' boss. Something I like to poke fun at Titus over.

"It's almost time, Arden," Lance says, and touches my shoulder giving me a nod.

The sun is high in the sky; we must have been talking longer than I realize because an electric rumble oscillates through the air telling me the square is full.

Drums flare to life, kicking a heavy base note out making the crowd launch into a cacophony of cheers, and the stage rise and fall with the music.

Arden pulls out a purple velvet bag small enough to fit in my hand. I reach to take it, but the surprising weight yanks my arm to the ground.

"Bloody hell, why is it so heavy?" I ask, picking myself, and the bag, off the floor.

"There's enough Dust in there to cover the entire city."

"But the pouch is so small."

Arden smiles, "Magic is efficient."

"No kidding. So I just blow this stuff into the air?"

"Yes. Each particle in the bag will fuse with a particle of your parents as they disintegrate. Their essence will combine with the Dust and cover the city in a dome. Put the bag in the center of the stage, open it, and use wind to summon the Dust out. It will do the rest for you."

"Okay."

Arden examines me, and then pulls the arms of my t-shirt down to my wrists and drapes a thin violet cloak around me, pulling the hood up.

"Don't let the Dust touch you." It's not a question but a command.

"Why?"

"When a speck of Dust touches a Keeper, it channels a tiny bit of your parents' essence through the Keeper's powers. It's fleeting, but to them, it's like being connected to element power rocket fuel. You have too much power as it is. We don't need a repeat of what happened at Trey's parents' Dusting.

"What did happen?"

"That doesn't matter. Just don't let the Dust touch you and when you're done, come straight back to the tower to prepare for the Council dinner tomorrow. I'll be waiting for you there."

He pulls me into a hug before I can ask any more questions.

"Fine," I mumble into his green robes, "no Dust touching fun."

The scent of the West's spring is hidden in the threads of his robes: pine and wild garlic, reminders of school, and running in the fields with Bo. I still haven't heard from her; I don't know if she made it here before the roads were closed.

Arden pulls me in front of him, his face serious, "Focus on the square. Not your parents. If you keep your eyes on the crowd, you won't panic."

"Okay," I say, making a mental note.

"Your parents were so proud of you, Eden. I can't take their place, but no matter what happens, I'll always be here for you."

I smile because the kindness in his words makes my throat clamp down, and I need to save my voice for the stage.

The music stops, but my ears continue to ring with the

crowd's cheers. As the shouts and claps reach a crescendo, I climb the metal stage stairs and pause behind the curtains. I take one last breath and push through the drapes.

The entire square is packed full of bodies. Keepers from every corner of Trutinor stand side by side, united in celebration of my parents. Even the sky is full of flying creatures and Shifter dragons.

Despite Arden's words, my eyes fall on my parents' bodies. Someone has dressed them in our royal Fallon robes. Even though there's makeup on their faces, their skin has a faint mottled discoloration: a network of black strands; poison woven into their veins like spiders' webs.

My heart pounds, and my face scrunches with concentration. A trickle of sweat falls down my back. *I won't let them down. I can't.*

I place the purple bag between their bodies and open the draw string.

Thousands of eyes fall on me; even though the faces are full of sympathy it feels more like an army of rifles aiming at their enemy, focused, sharp and waiting to ambush. The silence makes my neck bristle like chicken skin. A handful of black clouds pop into existence and billow across the sky. I cannot lose control. Not now.

Breathe, Eden, just breathe. Think sun, think sun.

Yellow shards pierce through the clouds, and heat dapples my skin. I tilt my head towards it and drink in the last rays I'll see for a couple of days. For a moment, I pretend it's my parents making the sun shine and not me. The thought gives me strength and makes the warmth in the air wrap around me like armor.

To my left is a spherical microphone. I pick it up, twisting a cog around until it clicks and buzzes to life.

"To each and every one of you, I thank you for coming

to pay your respects for the loss of two great leaders and two even better parents. I'd hoped they would be here to witness me formally call an end to their reign." I swallow, tears stinging my eyes. "But instead, I ask that each of you stand with me... Stand and rejoice in their achievements. In the glory of the East, the elements and the knowledge that your Fallons died with honor, keeping the Balance."

The crowd erupts, cheering, waving and bellowing: Lionel. Eleanor. Lionel. Eleanor. The mantra of names is bittersweet; my chest swells with pride, and aches with loss.

"I hope each one of you is touched by a piece of their Dust so that you too can remember their spectacular lives and their ultimate sacrifice."

I take a breath and add, "To the Elemental Keepers of the East, I swear to serve you with my life, use my power to keep your fate and my heart to honor our State. Together, we will never forget Lionel and Eleanor. May you all be Balanced."

The music roars to life, bodies jump and dance, fueled by electric excitement.

I raise my hand over the top of the small pouch and glance at each of my parents. The knot in my throat has swollen so large it hurts, and I can't swallow. Tears prick the back of my eyes, sharp like needles, but I refuse to cry on stage.

Once the Dust is out, my parents will disappear, forever. I stare at each of them in turn, terrified I'll forget their faces. I try to burn the curves of their cheeks, and the dips of their lips and chins, into my mind, but my eyes are clogged with tears, and I can't see them.

"Goodbye, Mom. Dad. I'll always love you," I whisper, and then I pump a little breeze into the bag. It rushes out shuddering and swirling above their bodies until it forms a ball. It spins faster and faster until the sparkling black and purple atoms are indistinguishable. Two ribbons splinter off; one glides towards my mother, the other to Father. They float above their heads, and then it starts.

At first, like sand falling through a timer, their hair disintegrates and trickles into the air. Then particle by particle, their faces and bodies float up, mixing with the Dust. When the last grain of their essence flutters into the air and joins the distended Dust ball, it takes everything I have not to reach out and grab it, so that I can keep a piece of them with me. But I don't. Because, although the plinth is empty like they never existed, there is a deep aching in my chest that tells me their memories are locked in my heart. And when the Dust is all gone, melted into the sky and blurred with the stars, all I'll have to do is look up and remember.

The music beats harder, drums thunder out a rhythm. Like lightning, the huge Dust ball shoots hundreds of feet skyward and bursts in an explosion of violet light, sparkles and particles. It spreads a dome of purple and black Dust over the square. As it flies higher, it multiplies, swarming like locusts until it engulfs the sun and pours a midnight glow over the square. Within a couple of hours, Element City will be sealed inside a dome of Dust. Then, atom by atom, the Dust will fall until the last particle drops to the ground, and my parents' reign will officially end.

Figures convulse with the music; arms stretch towards the sky hoping to catch a piece of Dust. A wayward particle that didn't make it to the sky, falls and touches the skin of a short, brown haired Keeper in front of the stage. Her head kicks back. Her brown eyes flash, and her skin throbs violet with the power imbued from the Dust. Her expression glazes over, as her body moves in time to the beat and she loses herself in an essence-paradise.

I take one last look at the crowd: thousands of Keepers connected in a smoldering euphoria, each one joined to my parents in a way I'll never be. Only one body in the writhing mass of people remains immobile. Their motionlessness stands out, stark and jarring like blood splatter on snow. I narrow my eyes at the figure and freeze. It's Victor.

TWELVE

'**Imbalance** – *A fundamental wrongness that must be eradicated. A darkness that infects the soul, leaving damage, destruction and chaos in its wake. It must always be destroyed.*'

Teachings of the First Fallon

I SLIP off stage and head towards the edge of the square. If Victor wants to talk to me, he can find me in my tower; I need to get inside away from the Dust anyway. As I squeeze between gyrating bodies, the music beats so loud my heart pounds in time with it. I realize that for one perfect moment, swallowed in amongst the throngs of people, I am anonymous. I am free. A Keeper not a Fallon, my parents are alive, Victor and I both passed our exams, and I am just another Keeper lost in the Dusting. But perfection doesn't exist, and I should know better than to hope for things that can never be.

A tall figure slides behind my shoulder, leans into my neck, and drinks in the smell of my skin. I freeze.

"Victor," I say, "now you decide to show your face?"

"What's wrong with you? Anyone would think someone died. Oh, wait. Oops," he says, covering his mouth with his paw-hand.

Waves of hot needles sting inside my chest. I want to crush him, or hurt him, or better, electrocute him. But I don't. I take a deep breath and say, "It's not my fault everyone, including the professors, can see your incompetence. I guess someone's got to be the runt of the Fallons'."

His skin flickers. Ripples of scales or claws or something else unnatural peel across his cheeks. His jaw is as hard as his eyes. And I see the truth in them. The truth that our Binding will never be a happy one. There's no pretending. There is only hate.

"At least I'm loyal," he hisses, "didn't take you long to replace me with a new head boy, did it?"

I laugh, "You're intimidated by Trey?" I say, raising an eyebrow. His face stays blank. *I guess not.*

"Or are you jealous?"

A vein in his neck pulses, just once, but it's enough to know I hit a nerve.

Something floating through the air catches my eye, but by the time I realize what it is, it's too late. A single particle of Dust drops onto my cheek.

I'm sucked through an invisible tunnel, eyes first, vision narrowing. Violet essence smatters across my view like static. My chest fills with a dark gloop of resentment.

Then the heat starts, deep, angry, and burning hotter than white fire. The same gray from the Dryad hospital ward blinds me. I'm a puppet, and the darkness is my master. It sends a cold calm permeating through me, like the quiet stillness of nature under a blanket of snow. My lips pull into a strange, twisted smile. I want to hurt him. I need to hurt him.

He cocks his head at me and takes a step back as if he can sense the change in the air.

"What do you want, Victor?" I spit.

He straightens up, eyes narrowing to slits. I laugh to myself; if his mother hadn't passed on her scrawny stature, he might be intimidating.

The music beats louder. It's hard to hear conversations even a couple of feet apart. He leans close, his rabid dog breath pouring over my face.

"Seen Bo yet?"

I stiffen. I don't know who's angry – me, the Dust or whatever Imbalance is lurking inside me. But it's the Imbalance that's turned me into a predator, and predators aren't impulsive. They wait. Choosing the perfect moment for maximum impact.

"I haven't."

"Maybe you should." His words are cold, cutting and delivered with a smile.

"Is that so?"

"You mean, you haven't heard? Oh, well, in that case, Eden," he says, exaggerating my name. "As my Potential, I feel it's my duty to tell you: Bo's been given The Six."

I recoil, confused.

"How? The Six are controlled by the head of your family."

He nods. "I know. Convenient timing, don't you think?"

"What's that supposed to mean?" I say, my eyes growing darker.

"Oh, nothing. Just that it's awfully convenient for Bo to disappear right before your parents' mysterious death, given they turned up in our house and the only person that's gained anything is Bo."

In some distant part of my mind, I am screaming. Tearing chunks of skin from his face and burning what's left of him to the ground. How can he insinuate Bo has something to do with my parents' death? He must really hate me because using Bo to hurt me is a low blow, even for him. But then I see my chance.

"Thank you for telling me. Victor, I know it can't be easy to make an accusation against your sister like that. It's testament to how much you want our Binding to work."

His eyebrows knit in the middle. He wanted me to react. But I won't. Not yet.

"It means a lot to me. And I guess seeing as we're going to be Bound any day now, this doesn't matter."

I reach up, pull his face down to mine. His breath makes my stomach heave, but the thirst for revenge, is more powerful. I press my lips to his. He tenses. I doubt a first kiss was the response he expected. But prey like him, shouldn't play with predators like me. Like all good victims resigned to their fate, he relaxes into my grip. I let his filthy paws roam over my shoulders just long enough to make him vulnerable. Then I grip his neck. Hard. He stiffens, but he can't escape. I push his mouth open, close my eyes, and suck all his air molecules into my body.

I drop him, and he falls to his knees clutching his throat with his good hand. Wild panic thunders across his eyes. I've stolen his air, and I won't let him get any more. He grabs at my fatigues, but I kick him off, and he flips over, jerking. His face flushes red, then white as his eyes start to roll.

My chest spasms against the added pressure of his air. But I refuse to let go. My vision is completely gray; I know I'm not in control, but I don't care. Maybe that makes me as much a prey to the Imbalance as Victor is to me. Deep down I don't want this, but I'm doing it anyway, because it feels good, and he deserves it.

"Eden. Release him at once," Maddison's shrill voice cuts through the music, but I don't move, and I don't let Victor go. His skin is turning blue. I want to watch him pass out. Maddison slaps me hard across the cheek, making me stumble backward, and the air bursts from my lungs. I gasp. The gray, the violet essence, the Dust, all of it disappears, and I am standing watching Victor, my Potential take huge, shuddering gulps of air.

"What is wrong with you?" Maddison barks, her tomato red hair dancing with every head shake.

And I have no idea. How could I almost suffocate my Potential?

"What were you thinking? You could have killed him."

And she's right, except there is no 'could' about it. If she hadn't turned up, I *would* have killed him.

Maddison's thin lips pinch together. Her magic trace, dotted scales on her skin - marks from constant dragon-shifting –quiver with her words.

Victor struggles to his feet. I consider helping but think better of it. Maddison, as tall as Victor, leans down into my face.

"Do you have any idea what you could've done? Outbursts like that, could ruin everything we've worked for."

"What is that supposed to mean? Who's we?"

She shakes her head and glances at Victor, who's still trying to gather himself. She doesn't help him up, and for a second, I feel sorry for him. She rubs her temples.

"Once the Dusting is over, go back to the West, immediately. You must be Bound, it's imperative to everything. I knew we should have told you."

She turns to leave, then stops. Her face softens, a smile reaching her eyes; it's sad, glistening with tears.

"May your reign be Balanced."

THIRTEEN

'It is the Steampunk Transporter's duty to protect, serve, and ensure the safe passage of their State's Fallons, using whatever magical means necessary.'

Eighth Law – The Book of Balance

MY MOTHER USED to say dinners are a civilized affair. She would zip up my violet dinner dress and add, "We're Fallons, Eden." Then she'd kiss me on the forehead, and push me into the dining suite.

"I know, Mom. We're privileged to be Fallons so we must rule with the heart of our people, and the power of our ancestors."

My parroting of that phrase would always make her

smile. It's her smile I miss most because it was more than radiant. Like she commanded the sun and the moon and all the stars with it. And I suppose in a way, until the Dust falls, she is.

I am outside the Long Hall in my home tower the following day after the Dusting. The Council is inside, or some of them are at least; those not on duty, patrolling the Dusting or working.

My fingers reach up and skim an ornate, gold frame hanging on the hall wall. I can't bring myself to look at the portrait of my parents' happy faces. My fingers brush the frame; memories like that reminds me they did exist.

I enter the formal dining suite that takes up an entire floor of the tower. Three of the walls are glass windows floor to ceiling which makes for spectacular views. Although right now, it's disorienting. It's mid-afternoon, but the Dust makes it appear like nightfall.

A handful of CogTV news crew cameras flash in my face. I spot Arden and glare at him, and he mouths an apology. They're not meant to leave the press room in the lobby.

The thin table runs the length of the room and can seat at least a hundred people. The table is dressed, with violet and silver candelabras, cutlery, and lashings of food.

Arden is sat in a seat furthest away from where I stand. There's an empty one next to him at the head of the table waiting for me. Opposite Arden is Israel. I note that Maddison hasn't made it, neither has Victor. But Titus, Nyx, a couple of professors including Kemble and Nyra, the Council secretary Nivvy Pushton, and a few junior members, as well as a handful of other Council members I have a vague memory of, are here.

The Council members stand, but I wave my hand signaling them to sit.

I might be a Fallon with my mother's lessons ingrained in me, but I'm exhausted, and I can't remember the last time I ate so I have no intention of waiting for pompous speeches before I tuck in. I sit down, pick up my fork and dig into the chicken and vegetables without waiting.

There's a few seconds of awkward silence, and a couple of muted coughs, then everyone tucks into their food, and conversational murmurs fill the room.

I am quiet most of the meal, preferring instead to listen and observe the Council members' interactions especially because we're being watched by news crews. Arden and Israel regale memories of my parents. I learn that Father and Israel were at school around the same time, and even shared a couple of classes. He goes on to tell me they were friends, and played pranks on the teachers together. I push the last piece of chicken around my plate, trying to imagine Father and Israel ever being friends but can't.

I give up on my food. "What happened to make you hate each other?" I ask.

Before he answers, Nivvy scans her CogTracker. Her eyes widen, and she stands up before disappearing from the room. I glance at Arden then to Israel. Just as they waited for me to arrive, they're meant to wait for me to leave too. Nivvy shouldn't have stepped out without permission.

Arden puts down his fork and says, "I should make sure she's okay."

I nod, and he leaves. Israel's looking at me; he wants to say something, but I'm not sure I want to hear it.

"Eden," he starts.

I look him straight in the eye, "Israel... There's nothing you can say to make this better."

"I know," he says, "I know." His face scrunches like he

can't decide what to say first. Then he rests his hand on mine. I flinch at the unexpected touch.

"But *I am* sorry, and I wanted you to know that although they were found in my house, I have nothing to hide. I'm helping Arden with the investigation. Although your father and I had differing views on politics, I respected him deeply. That's all."

He removes his hand, and I continue to stare at him, silent, stunned. Respect? I only ever saw them quarreling over Council tables and the civil war between our States. Did I miss something? I rub my face, tired, full of food, and confused.

Arden and Nivvy return, flustered, red faced, and sweating. Nivvy's eyes are even wider than before. Something's wrong.

Bulbs, lights, and cameras flash and pop. The news crews can sense the tension; it's peppered with a scandal.

Behind Arden, four huge men: two Shifters, and two Sorcerers, charge in wearing a black uniform crested in gold and covered with all five Trutinor State logos. They're from Datch, the Trutinor prison in Siren City.

The cameras click faster like gun shot.

I stand. My heart is beating hard and fast. Israel glances from Arden to the guards.

In my gut, there's a churning realization. Everything Israel just said was a lie. A twisted tale to make me believe he might be a good guy.

Arden coughs, then stands straight and says, "Shifter blood has been found in the poison that killed your parents."

It's automatic; hot black threads flow into my veins like silk. Imbalance, anger, hatred. It's controlling me. Or am I controlling it? My vision darkens, blurring as I round on Israel.

He steps back, "Eden, I didn't. I could never. You have to believe me."

But I don't believe him. I never have. Of course, he did it. There's years of animosity between him and my parents. Besides, he has a solid motive - the chance to take over the Council.

I want to hurt him. The cameras are still firing.

But I've lost control. What happens next is so fast I barely register it.

"Israel MacBey Dark, you're under arrest for the murder of Lionel and Eleanor East," Arden says.

Israel's figure drops to the floor, shifting into a wolf. I fly through the air, soaring like a flaming phoenix. As I dive towards his fur covered body, I'm flattened by Titus, and pinned to the ground.

When he hauls me up, it's over. Israel is standing, with special Faraday handcuffs attached that prevent him from using his power. Arden's shouting at the photographers who are snapping faster than ever. Titus drags me by the scruff of my neck out of the dining room and into a lift at the end of the corridor. He yanks the door shut.

The Imbalance has gone, my vision is clear, and Titus is shouting at me. Nyx is in the lift too, but she's bustling around us checking for injuries.

"Where are we going?" Titus shouts.

"What do you mean? We can't go anywhere because of the Dust."

"Forget the Dust; I'm your transporter, we're getting out of here. Now, tell me where we're going?"

I shake my head to clear my thoughts. Maddison said we were being Bound in a couple of days, and that I should go to the West. Well, screw Maddison, and Israel, and Bo for not replying to me and their stupid son. There's only one person I want to see, and the answer surprises me. *Trey. I want to see Trey.*

"The South. Take me to Siren City."

"Done."

The lift shudders, but instead of moving up, we jolt down so swiftly it makes my stomach roll. The lift stops, judders again then accelerates backwards as if we're moving underground.

FOURTEEN

'Aurora, Queen of the Mermaids, I hereby sentence you to an eternity of banishment, never to set foot on Trutinor again.'

From the Public Records Department – First Fallon's public sentencing, 11th October, 1100

NAKED marble statues stretch out in sleepy poses on the corner of every Siren City road. Sunset radiates a warm sheen off the sculptures, giving the marble just enough rouge it looks like skin. I half expect them to move, but they don't.

Titus, Nyx and I meander through the streets, each one

dripping with more opulence, creamy colored stone and mansions, than the last.

Titus reaches for my arm. "We should talk," he says, and he's right, we should. Nyx and Titus are the closest things I have to family now. I *should* tell them about the Imbalance, about how I'm dreading being Bound, and how upset I am that I haven't seen Bo. But not here, and not now.

"I know. We will," I say, and add, "I promise."

"What happened in the dining suite..." Nyx starts but falters. So Titus finishes her sentence, "Your eyes... They changed, they were so red, it was like you were possessed."

My lips press together, shutting my secrets away. "You need to be Bound, honey. This much Imbalance can't be good for you," Nyx blinks, slow and steady, like a drowsy cat. "Trey's bar is up there," she says, pointing to a street behind us full of bars and nightclubs. "Titus and I are going to pop into a parts shop down here before the shop closes."

"I need a new regulator handle, and the coupling rod's snapped. And handy for me, the best quality parts in the whole of Trutinor are made here. We won't be long, we'll wait for you in the bar. Okay?"

I nod, kiss them both, and leave.

As I reach Luchelli Lane, the street Nyx pointed to, my nose creases. The air smells like sour sweat and a cocktail of bitter drinks. Bars and shops line the streets with outside tables and stools littering the pavement. Keepers mill in small groups, laughing, chatting and exchanging lopsided grins. A young couple spills onto the road; their hands fly over each other's skin, lust driving their fingers. Their bodies fall against the wall, then the male's hand slips under the female's top. I wonder if they're Bound. Something about the furtive glances they're casting around the street tells me they aren't.

Trutinor law doesn't seem to apply in the South. Bo says she can't understand how Trey hasn't been hauled in front of the Council for continuous Balance violations under his reign. But he hasn't, and the violations are allowed to continue. I suspect it's because of his relationship with the First Fallon. A cog screen in a shop window catches my eye. Screens blare images of me, Israel and the Council dinner I just fled. I press my hands flat against the glass as if that will somehow stop the images from rolling. I watch the scene play out, my eyes deepening to red, Israel shifting, me leaping at him like a rabid dog and then his arrest. The images loop over and over like Groundhog Day. My parents would be ashamed of me.

I tear my face away and focus on the rich red glow emanating from some of the bar windows.

"Alright, love?" An enormous Shifter with a mop of brown hair appears in front of me. He looks like a bear with a face full of wild beard and mud-brown clothes that cling to his plump body.

"What's a pretty little thing like you, doing in a place like this?" He paces forward pushing me against the wall. His face is familiar, and I search my memory to place him.

"Just looking for someone. Excuse me," I say, and try to move past him. But despite his squidgy appearance, he is rigid as stone, and I bounce back against the brick. I look up, irritation hardening the lines of my face. I don't have time for this.

I spot some ink on his neck: the wolf symbol accompanied by the number 'six,' and I know why I recognize him.

"Angus Hathaway," I say, "Sixth House of the North, last member of The Six."

He grins, bearing a set of yellowed teeth, "That's the one, love."

If he's here then maybe Bo is too. Angus leans towards me and sniffs my neck as if I'm a meal he's salivating over. I straighten up, spreading my feet into a defensive stance, preparing to fight if I need to. The vault in my mind quivers, but I push it away, silencing it.

"I hear you've got yourself a nice shiny new leader."

His head snaps back, eyes narrowing.

"How'd you hear about tha'?" he growls. The stench of his breath makes my stomach swirl.

"You don't seem impressed."

"Would you be? You're an elite fighter one minute, and then boom. Your boss is a little stick insect brat, and you're a laughin' stock. Israel's takin' the piss, he is."

Poor Bo. She's given The Six, putting her dream of working on the front line in reach, and now they won't serve her. I wonder if that's why I haven't seen her yet; she's dealing with shmucks like Angus.

"Never mind," Angus says, pulling me out of my thoughts, "looks like I got meself a tasty little Elemental to make up for it."

Shadows slither over my face, the Imbalance kicking into life whether I want it to or not. But I hesitate and fight the vault because I know this road. I know where anger leads me, and I don't need any more news loops on repeat.

"I wouldn't do that if I were you, *Angus*," I say, drawing out his name.

He snorts, "And what's a poxy Elemental gonna do about it?"

I drop my fists, look him square in the eye, igniting one with electricity, and the other with fire.

"I'm not just any Elemental. Now tell me where I can find Trey before I burn your bloody beard off."

"Trey?" A sultry voice floats through the air breaking our standoff and distracting me. The fury dissipates as I scan the street to find the voice's owner. She's wearing tight fitting pale green robes made of smooth silks that cling to her body in all the right places. She flicks her golden mane of hair, and it tumbles down her back.

"Evelyn de Lest," I say through a tight smile, trying not to compare her immaculate figure to my crumpled fatigues and stained t-shirt.

"Eden East," she replies her words pricklier than is polite.

"Why do you want to see Trey?"

"It's private. Do you know where he is?"

She tilts her head to examine me. I shift, uncomfortable as her laser-sharp glare burns away my defenses, leaving me feeling inadequate. This time when she speaks there's no question her words are pointed like a sword, "I'm Bound to him, there's nothing private between us."

The thought of him talking to her about me makes my insides hot.

"I wouldn't be so sure about that. Are you going to tell me where he is, or not?"

"Not."

"Fine. Thanks for nothing."

As I leave, she scalds Angus, "Behave yourself, Hathaway. You might be one of The Six, but if you terrorize my customers, I'll kick you out of the city."

I smile to myself, at least I'm not the only one she's a bitch to. I spot a maroon leather door with chesterfield-like buttons pressed deep into the leather. In the middle of the door is the Siren's symbol: an ornately carved heart, with two hands either side controlling the heart's emotions. I push open the door plunging myself into darkness. When my eyes adjust to the lack of light, I move through a series of short, dim corridors. The walls are lined with black fabric and dotted with the same pattern of buttons as the front door. Slow music with a big base beat echoes through the walls. My legs twitch wanting to move towards it, like a Mermaid calling to me with her song. It makes me curious as to how much of the Mermaid's power the Sirens have retained.

I think back to my history class trying to remember what they said about her. Centuries ago, Aurora, the first Mermaid Fallon and Karva the first Siren Fallon, went to war with each other. Aurora thought their abilities were so closely aligned that she should rule over both the Sirens and the Mermaids. Karva thought differently. War raged, and thousands of lives were lost. I assume Karva won because Aurora was banished and nobody's seen a Mermaid since.

I enter an enormous circular room with a round dance floor sunk into the center. Around the edge are maroon booths, in the corner is a bar and at the back a set of stairs. The same red light from the street oozes around the room in a smoky haze. Aftershave and perfume drift through the air. I catch a hint of frankincense, and I know Trey is in here.

I search the room for him. Row after row of Keepers sit in booths with Sirens controlling them. They all wear the same vacant look in their eyes like they're lost, or dead. It's unnerving, eerie, like a sea of absent shadows.

"Eden? What are you doing here? Is everything okay?" Trey says from behind me.

"Hey," I say, facing him, "yeah, fine... Well, no actually. I mean, obviously not." My cheeks warm up with my rambling. "I was just..." I gesture at the room, and Trey smiles.

"You haven't changed your mind since the hospital then? You still disapprove of what we do?"

"It's not that I disapprove, it's just that I don't understand it. Our emotions ground us; they tell us we're real and alive. My pain reminds me that although my parents are gone, I am still here, and they would want me to keep living and breathing, and fighting. I guess I see my pain as hope. Because if I'm still hurting, I'm still feeling. And that means one day I'll feel happiness again. But these Keepers are having all that taken away. If they can't feel the bad stuff, how will they ever feel the good?"

Trey gazes at me, his eyelashes fluttering and soft. My stomach shifts and tightens.

"That Keeper," he says, pointing at a booth with a Shifter in it, "has uncontrollable jealousy. Completely unfounded, but it's ruining the Balance of his Binding." He points at another booth, "That Sorcerer there is called Sheridan, and this is a huge day for her. She has a severe case of agoraphobia. Felicia, the Siren opposite her, has been working with her for six months to cure it. At first, Felicia had to move into her house and work with her twenty-four hours a day taking complete control of Sheridan's anxiety. Eventually, she got her out her front door. Over time she's needed Felicia less and less. Today, Sheridan's controlling her anxiety by herself, and this is the longest she's spent outside her house in two years."

"Oh," I say, fidgeting with the hem of my t-shirt. A knot of guilt winds its way into my chest. I guess I never thought about them helping people, just controlling them. Maybe they aren't all bad, Felicia is helping Sheridan after all. But I still don't like the thought of being controlled or having my emotions taken away. Without pain, there is no happiness.

"This way," Trey says, and leads me to the back of the club and up a set of maroon stairs onto a mezzanine floor with a row of booths that look over the dance floor.

Kato is sat in the closest booth with the door open, surrounded by CogTrackers, screens and bits of wiring.

"Kato," I say, beaming. He grabs me and pulls me into a tight hug.

"I'll give you a minute, I'll be in the end booth when you're ready," Trey says and walks off to the other end of the mezzanine.

"Sooo, bravo on the awkward Council dinner," Kato says, grinning, "I caught a glimpse of it on CogTV. You know, you really should try out for the athletics team, you'd make an excellent long jumper."

"Too soon, Kato. Way too soon," but I grin as I say it. "You'd better watch your back, next time it might be you I try and knock out."

He pouts and raises his eyebrow, "Kinky. I might like it."

"You're disgusting. And because you're disgusting, you can do me a favor."

"Oh?"

"Can you take a look at my mom's CogTracker?" I pause, a lump forming in my throat. Mom's gone. I have to be able to talk about her, so I push the lump away. "She left an encrypted file on there for me, it's on the C-drive. But she didn't give me a password before..."

"I'll take a look," he says, the joking replaced with a softness that comes from understanding someone's pain personally. He might not have Inherited like Trey, but he still lost his parents. I hand him the tracker and head towards the booth Trey's in. He opens the door, and I glance at him. Is he joking? The booth is so small I'm not sure there's enough room for me to get in. There are maroon seats either side of the compartment and a small table between them, like a tiny train carriage. I climb in, scrambling around Trey as he seals the door shut. If it weren't for the table, I'd be sitting on his lap. But at least he's wearing clothes today, even if it is a skin-tight t-shirt that defines every inch of his body.

"Well, this is cozy," I say, unsure if the heat in here is me, or the compact size. I move my legs to one side of the table but knock against Trey's shin.

"Sorry," I say, and try to move it to the other side. But he moves his at the same time, and instead of avoiding each other, our legs interlock.

"Don't worry, it's fine," he smiles.

I try to laugh it off. But my heart is racing, and it sounds more like a cough.

"These booths are designed small for a reason. This is the only one without cameras. We're safe to talk in here. How can I help?"

I try to relax, but his body and voice are stiff, formal even, yet beneath the table, his left leg still touches mine. He could move it if he wanted to, but he doesn't, and neither do I. Is this a game?

"I, umm. I came because you said you'd be here for me if I needed you."

He nods, "Always."

I push a stray lock of hair behind my ear, and look him in the eye.

"Arden said there was an incident at your parents' Dusting. You lost control?"

He nods, the memories constrict his face.

"What happened?"

"I hurt a lot of people," he says, his eyes wrinkling. "It was an accident, I was just a kid, but that doesn't excuse what I did."

"You lost control? Did the Imbalance take over?"

"I tortured hundreds of people. Fear is a dark emotion. I also killed twelve people. Scared them to death with their own phobia-induced hallucinations. I can still hear their screams." He bows his head. I know he's taken his pain away because his face is blank and emotionless, and yet he's still haunted by the memory. I guess even if you can take the pain away it doesn't stop you from blaming yourself. I wonder how many times he's done this, and how big his personal memory ball must be. He must be so numb inside, and it makes me feel sorry for Evelyn.

"You can't hide from the pain forever," I say.

"One of them was a child, Eden. I killed a four-year-old, just a baby, and I let his nightmares kill him."

I swallow hard. *Could I live with that?*

"Ironic, isn't it?" he says, "I can control everyone's emotions but my own."

"And when you can't control them, you take them away?"

He looks through me, silent. The conversation is over.

"I hurt Victor today," I say changing the subject. "I lost control, and sort of sucked the air out of his lungs. I came because I need to know how you stop the Imbalance."

Trey moves in his seat, "Sucked the air out?"

Heat rises up my neck, and for some reason, I don't want to admit to kissing Victor. "I sort of sucked it out his lips."

Trey's eyes flash hard then soften. "It's easier once you're Bound; I guess the power and Balance of whoever you're Bound to helps to reduce the strength of the Imbalance. But it never goes completely. Not that the Council knows that. They think it disappeared when I was Bound to Eve."

"How do you stop it taking over?"

"I use a vault. A mental one. I kind of compartmentalize the Imbalance. It takes time and strength, but with practice, it works to an extent."

"To an extent?"

"Nothing's foolproof," he says, "as powerful as I am there are some emotions even I can't stop."

I want to ask which ones, I want to ask what memory or emotion is etching pain into his face, but I'm distracted. He's leaning closer to me. Close enough I can smell his aftershave: it's heady, powerful and draws me in. His hands are on the table, a millimeter from mine.

"Which emotions?" I force myself to say. I know he's not going to answer because I already know the answer. Love. The only magic stronger than all of us.

It's hot in here, and my mouth parts a fraction, but it's not the heat making it hard to breathe. Static electricity sparks off my leg and onto his as he presses it harder into mine. His hungry blue eyes slide over every millimeter of my face; words hover on the edge of his pink lips. There is something unsaid, something more, something he's not telling me and now I'm desperate to know what. The booth is reverberating, both of us giving off power we shouldn't. Just like he shouldn't be this close to me, or his leg locked around mine. But it is, and we are, and instead of moving away, something holds us in place. Something I can't quite reach. Like a ship at sea, searching for the faint beam of a lighthouse. Whatever it is, I can't recall it. It's too distant, too long ago, lost in the ocean of my other memories. I don't understand why I feel like this, why the raw intensity swimming between us is so familiar, so comfortable. I don't understand why I have the urge to kiss him or why everything else in the booth has disappeared. There is only us, the strange sensation of déjà vu, and the nagging feeling I've felt this way about Trey before.

FIFTEEN

'Civil unrest between the East and the North has raged since the beginning of Trutinor. It is said that the reason for war was forgotten. However, Professor Cuthberg from Stratera Academy's history department, suggests that it stems from the creation of Trutinor and the Fifth Law from the Book of Balance. Shifters deem their abilities superior to Elementals, thereby denouncing the decision of the First Fallon to have appointed the Elementals supreme Keepers.'

Excerpt from the History of Trutinor Vol. 4

A HARD WRAP on the booth's glass windows makes both of us snap back in our seats. Evelyn is staring, her green eyes piercing, cold and full of ice. She looks from Trey to me and back again making me feel like I've done something wrong. But nothing happened. Just a bit of misplaced static and a leg leant against mine. Knowing nothing happened isn't dispelling the knot of guilt in my chest.

Evelyn yanks open the door, spitting her words at me, "You disappeared, Eden. I was going to bring you to Trey."

Liar. I open my mouth to say something, but she cuts me off.

"You have visitors."

"Right. Of course, Titus and Nyx. I'll go see them then."

I stand to leave, but my feet are still wrapped in Trey's, and I stumble out of the booth straight into Evelyn's arms. Her fingers dig into my wrist as she catches me. Once I'm steady, she shoves me upright, but not before digging her nails in deeper. I pull my arm away and glare at her. She's staring just as hard. *What is her problem?*

I head down a few steps but stop short just out of their line of sight.

Evelyn barks at Trey, "This had better not be a repeat of three years ago. I thought you were over it."

A frown burrows into my forehead. A repeat of what?

"I am. Everything is fine, honestly."

"It'd better be."

Her heels clack against the mezzanine floor, so I hurry downstairs. As I reach the bottom Evelyn's hand grips my bicep, "Do you think I'm an idiot? I know what you're doing, Eden."

Her icy expression melts into a raging green fire. She hates me.

"I don't know what you're talking about," I say, and with

the exception of maybe sitting too close to him in the booth, and dancing with him at the end of year ceremony, which I had no choice over, I really don't.

"Don't play dumb with me, you little orphan bitch. You might've had his heart as a child, but he's Bound to me. *Forever*."

She squeezes my arm so tight my hand tingles. Then she leans in and whispers in sharp, cutting tones.

"So, whatever this little revival thing is that you have going on, it needs to stop. Before I make you stop."

My eyes narrow, I've never liked threats. I draw just enough Elemental energy to hurt and pump a burst of electricity through my arm. She yelps and lets go.

"I said I have no idea what you're talking about. Threaten me again, and I'll do more than make you stop."

She scowls at me then stalks off.

"Eden," Bo says appearing at my side. She's pale and disheveled, but what tells me something's wrong is that her red lipstick is missing.

"Bo, what's wrong? Where have you been?" I ask, pulling her into a hug. She pats my back like I'm a dog, her demeanor stiff, and edges away.

"I... It's complicated," she says, her eyes darting around the room.

"Do you want to sit down?"

She nods, and I gesture to a booth a few rows away from Titus and Nyx. The booth spotlight illuminates her face. She's a blotchy mess of red patches, smudged mascara and dark circles under her eyes.

"I'm so sorry about your parents, Eden. I was with you in the hospital. I stayed as much as I could. Then I got called away, and I've been trying to get back to you ever since." She's babbling, her words blurring together.

"Stop. It's fine. Really." I squeeze her hand. "Are you okay," I ask. I've never seen her in such a mess, and it makes an uneasy gnaw in my gut. This is bigger than a squabble between Victor and me, or a crossed word at Trutinor Council. Her father's been arrested, for killing my parents. This is life, death, and blood. Israel's arrest could be the thing that comes between our friendship. When she doesn't speak, I decide to confront it.

"Is this because of Is...?"

She pulls her hand out of mine and fiddles with the threads on the sleeve of her tight black jumper. After an age, she looks up at me.

"You need to let him go."

"What about the evidence? The Shifter blood?"

She flinches, her back rigid, leant away from me.

"Please?" she says, her voice cracked and hollow, "please just let him go, he didn't do it. He would never."

"You can't know that. Not unless you were there."

She chews on her lip, tears welling in her eyes. I think back to what Victor said after the Dusting. How convenient it was for Bo to disappear right before my parents died and how she was the only person that gained anything from their death. I shake the thought away. This is Bo, my oldest, most trusted friend. But the question still bubbles out, "You weren't...?"

"No. Of course, I wasn't," she says, turning her attention to the other sleeve.

"Sorry. I don't know why I even asked; obviously, you weren't."

"It's fine. I'm sorry it's taken me ages to get to you," she leans over the table and hugs me, "I'm so sorry, Eden. I can't even imagine what you've been through. I should've been there for you."

I squeeze her back, and she sits down. The air between us is thick, stagnated with unsaid words.

"If you knew something you'd tell me, wouldn't you?" I ask.

There's a pause, only a fraction of a second, but it's there.

"Absolutely." She smiles, but it doesn't reach her eyes.

One little word and it changes everything. I pinch my lips tight to stop them trembling, and once my heart slows, I say, "Okay, I'll ask Arden to release him once he's been questioned."

Her shoulders sag and a few tears spill out as she says, "Thank you."

Kato still has Mom's, so I take out my CogTracker and send Arden a quick CogMail telling him to release Israel once he's done and that I'll let him know why in person. When I'm done, Bo has her usual sparkle back and her mouth moves so fast it blurs. I think she's asking me about the Dusting and the scuffle with Victor, but everything is subdued; my eyes are fuzzy, and all I can think about is the fact she's lying to me. She knows something about my parents' death, and she isn't telling me.

Somewhere in my mind, a crack appears and the first shadowy wisps of Imbalance crawl out. My hands ball, fire licking the inside of my palm as I stand up, stopping Bo mid-sentence.

I have to get out of here. I close my eyes and try to form a vault around the Imbalance, but the threads of shadow and darkness are already murmuring to me, telling me Bo should be punished.

I blink, and I'm in the middle of the dancefloor. I don't know how I got here. Even through the smoke and haze I can feel the eyes of a dozen stares.

"Are you okay, Eden?" This is Titus; he's stood in front of me, his voice soft and warm.

"Your hands are on fire."

I look down, he's right, they are.

"She's lying," I mumble.

"Who is?"

The fire dances around my hands, swimming up my forearms; it wants to consume me. I can feel its hunger, or maybe it's my hunger for it.

Titus takes a deep breath and then holds my hand in his.

My eyes widen. He'll get burnt.

"No," I say, snapping awake. But it's too late. Like a stampede, the Imbalance thunders through my veins.

His navy uniform jacket must be flame resistant: like a magnet repelling fire, the flames lick around his sleeves. But his hand is not protected and already yellow blisters are bubbling on his skin.

"I can't stop it. Let go," I plead.

"You can. Just focus." His face is scarlet against his blond dreads. Sweat pours from his forehead and a piece of skin on the back of his hand peels up.

I slam my eyes shut, concentrating. *I will not hurt him.* I make the vault bigger, wider, chase the dark threads into the box. Sweat pours down my neck as I fight to control myself. When the last wisp of Imbalance is gone, I open my eyes. Titus is pale, clammy and wobbling on his feet. I grab him and rush him to a booth. Nyx is next to me, her hair wild and on end like a startled cat.

"I'm sorry, I'm sorry," I keep repeating to myself as if that will make his hand better.

"You controlled it, that's what matters, Eden. It would have been a lot worse if you hadn't."

He pulls himself upright. "I'm fine; I just need to see a Dryad, they'll fix this up no problem. Nyx, get a portal cog from my bag; we'll take the lift in the back straight to the Ancient Forest." He tries to stand but loses his footing.

"Bo," I shout across the bar, "go upstairs and get Trey and Kato."

She disappears and returns with them. They help me lift Titus to the lift in the back of Trey's bar.

"I'll be fine," Titus says using his good hand to cup my cheek. "I knew you could control it. I wouldn't have held your hand otherwise."

I manage a limp smile. He might've known, but I really didn't.

SIXTEEN

'Unbound Baby – *The birth of a highly Imbalanced baby caused by the lack of Bound parents.*'

Excerpt - Myths and Legends of Trutinor

STRANDED in the South without Titus, Trey and Kato offer me a room in their mansion for the night. I consider saying no because Bo will no doubt be staying with Kato and I still don't know what she's hiding. But I have no choice, so I accept.

Kato takes us to one of their living rooms. Photographs and paintings hang on the walls and underfoot a plush, cream carpet swallows your toes as you walk across it. Three huge maroon and black sofas curve around a coffee table. On the table is my mom's CogTracker and the left-overs of a late dinner. Trey, Kato and Bo have cleared their plates, but mine is still full; after the Council dinner earlier, and what I did to Titus, I've lost my appetite.

"I managed to decrypt your mom's C-drive. I tried not to read anything, but I did catch sight of a few things while I was in there. I don't know what your parents were investigating, but there are some serious accusations in there," Kato says and flicks a few buttons on his CogTracker which makes Mom's light up. "Do you want to see?"

"Sure," I say and glance at Bo, wavering on whether she should see the contents. I decide I was overreacting in the bar. Just because she's hiding something doesn't mean it's about my mom and dad. After seventeen years of friendship, she deserves the benefit of the doubt.

Kato taps a few more buttons and Mom's tracker projects the image of its screen over the coffee table. He places it down and picks up his own, which he uses like a remote to control mom's. My heart pumps fast. If my mom's investigation files are in there, there might be a clue that points to their killer. Two folders appear. I suppress the tang of disappointment; I'm not sure what I was hoping for, but I guess it was more. Solid evidence? A piece of them? I'm not sure but something more than two folders.

The first folder is called 'Cassian Black – Unbound Baby.' But when I see the next one, I freeze. 'Eden's prophecy.'

"Prophecy?" Bo says, "What prophecy?"

"Do you want to start there?" Kato asks.

I nod and he opens the file. I expect to see ancient script or a photograph of parchment paper. But instead, there's a CogMail trail between Mother and Arden.

Kato expands the projection so we can all read it. As I

do, Mother's soft voice echoes in my head as I scan the
words, and I have to swallow down a hard lump.

30th May, 2017

ELEANOR.EAST@FALLONCOGMAIL.COM
   Subject: The First Couple
   To: **Arden.Winkworth@FallonCogMail.com**

ARDEN, I'm worried. Have you found evidence to suggest
the rumors are true? Is this prophecy genuine? I want
unequivocal proof that Eden is one half of this First Couple
before we tell her. Have you any news on who the other
half is?

I'M sorry to bombard you with questions, but time is short,
you need to get unequivocal proof from RA.

I'M sure you're aware there's an increase in Balance violations of late. Not least of which, is a very serious case: a
suspected Unbound baby that needs immediate investigation. Frankly, it begs belief. I don't think in all my years I've
heard such a ridiculous accusation. Unbound babies are a
myth! Or so I thought, but the evidence is suggesting there
might be some substance behind it. We're leaving for the
North tomorrow; we suspect its parents are Shifters. I've
sent you my encrypted files on the case for Guild records.

LET me know as soon as you can about the prophecy. If it's true, it will change everything. There will be war, and I'm not sure if we can win.

LOVE ALWAYS, E.

I RE-READ THE WORDS 'LOVE ALWAYS,' wishing I could hear her say them out loud. What if one day I forget the sound of her voice? My throat aches so much I daren't talk, so I gesture to Kato to keep scrolling down.

30th June, 2017

ARDEN.WINKWORTH@FALLONCOGMAIL.COM
    Subject: RE: The First Couple
    To: **Eleanor.East@FallonCogMail.com**

ELEANOR,

IT'S true and it's definitely Eden. Hermia has proof. Can't send it by CogMail though. As yet, I don't know who the boy is, but I have my suspicions, and I am certain it's not VD. Which leaves a question hanging over all the Potentials.

WE LOOK up at the same time, all wearing confused expressions.

"VD? Victor Dark?" Kato says.

"Makes sense given he's talking about Potentials. But if there's a prophecy about me and another, and it's not my Potential then..."

"Then who is it?" Trey finishes my sentence and we look at him, the same question on all our lips.

"I don't get it," I say and stand up. Frustrated, or curious, or maybe both. I pace the living room as a million questions flood my brain. I thought mom told me about those files to help me? Not to confuse me. I stop and turn to the others, "I'm going to be Bound to Victor. So how can there be a prophecy about me with anyone else? And who the bloody hell is Hermia?" I say.

"Hermia is the First Fallon's personal messenger. I grew up around her, she's like an aunt to me," Trey says.

"Oh," I say, and sit back down feeling deflated.

"Keep reading," Bo says pointing at the screen.

I SUSPECT CA knows and is keeping it quiet. I, too, am very concerned about war. Even more concerned than I am over the validity of the Binding process. Let's keep this to ourselves and the LL, for now. I want to protect my sources, and I don't trust the Council. Let's meet in our usual spot two days from now. I should have confirmation of the boy by then.

BEST, Arden.

"KEEP SCROLLING," I say, nudging Kato.

27th June, 2017

ANONYMOUS@UNKNOWNCOGMAIL.COM
   Subject: Cassian Black
   To:**Eleanor.East@FallonCogMail.com**

ELEANOR,

IF YOU WANT to find Cassian, he'll be at the Camden Cage Fighting Club on 9th July, 2017.

BE SWIFT, the First is aware, and she won't let him live.

YOUR ANONYMOUS FRIEND.

"IS THAT IT?" I ask, "that can't be it, give it to me." I take the tracker and try scrolling up and down, but there's nothing else, no other emails. Heat fills my chest. I shove it down and slump back into the sofa.

"What was the point of mom telling me about these files if it's all mystery and anonymity? How could she keep all this a secret?"

"She was going to tell you," Bo says.

"What do you mean? How do you know that?"

Her eyes widen, "No. I don't. I umm. I guess I mean that she probably would have told you eventually. We had the big ceremony and stuff. You and your mom were close. She wouldn't have hidden it from you."

She squeezes my arm. I glare at her trying to work out what the hell she's hiding from me. She chews her bright red lip and when my expression doesn't change, she smiles and adds, "We will figure this out. I promise."

"Fine, who is CA? And who on earth is the anonymous friend?" I ask. No one answers at first, but then Trey says, "Well, CA is Cecilia Arigenza."

"And who is that?" Bo says.

Kato's eyes are wide, "No, Trey. Come on. It can't be?" Kato picks up his tracker and makes mom's scroll back through the email again as if he's expecting to see a different acronym.

"Is someone going to enlighten us?" I say.

Kato looks up at me, his eyes wide, "Cecilia Arigenza is the First Fallon..."

"She has a real name?"

"She does," Trey says, "and I can't think of anyone else it could be. It makes sense because Cecilia... Sorry, the First Fallon holds all of the prophecies in the Binding Chamber."

"And how do you know that?" I ask.

"After I Inherited, she mentored me for a bit, helped me get control and stuff. That's how I got to know Hermia."

"But if it's the First Fallon suppressing a prophecy," Kato says, "then we're all in way deeper than we realize."

"She can't be. She's the epitome of everything that's good and Balanced," I say folding my arms. But even as I say it, I recall her blank face on stage and how it made my insides cold.

"We don't have another explanation," Bo says, and leans

over Kato to tap his screen. "Let's keep looking. Open the other file, K."

The words 'Cassian Black – Unbalanced baby' appear in the projection and then a string of documents. Kato flicks through them at a pace. We scan Balance tracking reports, profiles, birth records and a ton of other documents in silence. Except for his birth certificate, which looks fraudulent, the records only go back seven years, to 2010. That year feels familiar, but I can't think why. I keep scanning the documents, by the looks of the handful of photos collected, there's an older woman with him, but there's no clear image of her, only her back. He's been on Earth and living in Camden ever since. School attendance is perfect, he doesn't get sick, and if he's ever been in trouble, he was clever enough to cover his tracks because he looks like the model citizen.

"I don't buy it," I say, "no one's that perfect."

"Only one way to find out. According to your mom's CogMail in the other file he's still in Camden," Bo says, "but I've been thinking, isn't that weird? Why hide him on Earth? Wouldn't a Balance violation that size be picked up?"

Kato moves through another set of documents, and a description appears.

NAME: Cassian Black
    Height: 6"4
    Hair: White-blond
    Age: 19 years old
    Eyes: Black
    Occupation: Professional Cage Fighter

"I'M GOING TO FIND HIM," I announce. "It's the ninth tomorrow, and we have the details of where he's going to be. I'm not missing this chance. My parents died trying to find his parents. So I'm going after him."

"I'm not sure that's a good idea," Bo says, her face creasing.

"I'll take you," Trey cuts in. "But in the morning. It's too late now, we all need some rest."

"But what about the Binding Ceremony? It's in a day's time," Bo says, tugging her bottom lip.

"That's a bit rich, given you missed the last one," I say, and then regret it. She recoils in her seat, her mouth pressed shut.

"I'll get her back in time," Trey says, "I promise. Magnus is fast."

"Be careful," Kato says, "we don't know what we're dealing with and if you're right and the First Fallon is covering something up, then we're all in way over our heads."

After we agree to meet for breakfast in the morning before Trey and I head off to Earth, Bo and Kato say good-night and leave. Trey leads me to a room somewhere deep in the center of his mansion. He opens the door, lets me through and pauses in the doorway. "You look exhausted," he says.

"Thanks," I say, "you're not looking so fresh either."

Lie.

He always looks fresh; tonight, he's wearing tight dark trousers and his usual white string vest. I try not to look at his brown shoulders. His tousled hair is tied in a knot at the back of his head, and his beard is trimmed short.

"I've just got a lot on my mind."

"I heard you arguing with Evelyn earlier."

"It's nothing. She's just paranoid."

"Maybe. But she hates me, that much I do know."

He sniffs; I'm not sure if he's laughing, indignant or both.

"She's harmless."

Harmless? I rub my arm where her nails marked me.

"I'm not sure about that. Are you sure she will be okay with you coming to Earth with me?"

"She'll be fine. And anyway, she's my problem to deal with."

He's staring at me, with those intense eyes, taking me apart piece by piece.

"I should go," he says, stepping inside my room.

"Yeah, you should," I say, my heart thudding harder with each step forward. My feet urge me closer. Then pause. I'm not exactly in Evelyn's good books. What if she walks past?

I step back, thinking better of it, but his hand catches mine and holds on tight. His blue eyes scan my face and I wonder if he's trying to read me, or if it's me trying to read him. Part of me wants him to hold me. He's the only one that knows what I'm going through. When I'm around him, I don't feel so lost or isolated. But as soon as I think it, Victor's face flashes through my mind making my chest swim with guilt. I'll be Bound in one day's time. I shouldn't be doing this. I inch away, but his grip on my hand tightens. Then I am in his arms, my eyes shut, and I lean against his chest. I fit. Perfectly. Like the moon in the arms of a thousand stars. Everything about Trey is so familiar. Evelyn's words flit through my head 'You might've had his heart as a child, but he's Bound to me. *Forever*.'

"Why don't I remember you?" I say, the words spilling out before I can stop them.

His back hardens, and he lets go of me.

"Bad memory, I guess." He's in the doorway with his back to me, "I have to go."

"You know, don't you?"

He turns to look at me, his silent expression the only answer I'm getting.

"Goodnight, Eden."

Then he's gone.

SEVENTEEN

Arden Winkworth, Private Journal.

13TH AUGUST, 2010

MY GUILD SORCERERS have been studying Trey's Inheritance. I am concerned with the amount of attention the First Fallon is giving him. I fear this is an indication that the prophecy may have some truth to it. I will investigate further. The Council must not be informed.

TREY, Bo, Kato and I are standing on platform one of Siren City's central station.

"Listen, I know we've said it already but, seriously, you both need to be careful; we don't know what we're dealing with," Bo says and pulls me into an arms' length hug. She's stiff, and it's obvious the gap between us is more than just physical space.

"And make sure you're back tonight. We don't need anyone else missing the Binding Ceremony tomorrow... *Bo*," Kato says, nudging her in the shoulder.

"Hilarious," she says, and rolls her eyes.

Trey and Kato pump fists, then shoulders before Trey ruffles Kato's blond locks and pinches his cheek making baby sounds. Kato slaps his hand off and glares at him, "Ruined it."

Trey laughs "You'll always be my baby brother."

"And you'll always be an asshole." He punches Trey in the shoulder then swings his arm around Bo's neck.

Maddison and Israel appear at the end of the station platform. They must have released him already. Bo looks from me to them and back again.

"Thank you," she whispers, and squeezes my arm before dragging Kato off to talk to them.

Trey's train is dark maroon with black and brass cog fixtures decorating the outside. Shiny brass tubing criss-crosses the length of the train until it reaches a huge chimney billowing steam at the front. The emblem of the South: a heart surrounded by two hands is emblazoned in highly polished brass on every carriage.

"After you," Trey says and places his hand on the small of my back guiding me into the train. His fingertips skim against a patch of skin poking out of my t-shirt making my face heat up. It doesn't help that I'm wearing one of his vests. I had no clothes with me and my t-shirt was filthy so he leant me a clean vest. I managed to rinse my underwear in my bedroom sink and left it to dry overnight.

The inside of his train is just as regal as the outside, and reminds me of his bar in Siren City. The same red and black

Chesterfield seating, low lighting and heady mix of perfume and incense drift through it. A brass bar stands at one end of the carriage, and behind it rows of optics filled with bright colored liquids.

"Drink?" Trey says and walks behind the counter.

"Sure," I say, and perch on a bar stool. "Although I don't think I can squeeze much more in after your Siren breakfast. How do you guys eat so much and stay so trim?"

He shrugs, "Gifted, I guess." He pours various liquids into a metal beaker; he shakes it, spins it and loops it around his hands. He pours the purple liquid into a tall, thin conical glass with one hand and drops ice in with another.

"Show off."

He bows as he passes me the glass then presses a button on the edge of the bar and says, "To Earth, Magnus."

"Earth, sir?" a rumbly voice filters through small square speakers in the corners of the carriage. Magnus must be his Steampunk Transporter.

"London. Camden Lock, specifically," I say, and take out my CogTracker. I show Trey the location of Cassian's cage fighting arena, and he punches the details into his tracker sending them to Magnus.

"Sir? Pardon me, but that doesn't sound like Evelyn."

"It's not."

"Oh."

The speakers crackle and cut out.

"Is he always that welcoming?"

"Pretty much," Trey says, as the train shudders forward.

The air cracks, and a loud bang makes me jump and spill some of the purple juice onto my fatigues. A puff of dark blue smoke appears and when it clears, an Elf, in the First Fallon's navy double breasted uniform, is standing in front of us. Her orange hair is untamed and bushy, and her big green eyes blink unnaturally slow.

"Your Majesties," she says, bowing so low her hair touches the floor. "I am Hermilda Endlesquire," she says to me, "messenger, tracker and announcer for the First Fallon."

I flick my eyes to Trey, panic creasing my brows. What if she tells someone where we're going? Trey shakes his head at me dismissing my worry.

"Hermia, hey. It's been a while. Can I get you a drink?" Trey asks.

"Would you mind? I'm desperate, it's been a right day already, and breakfast is barely over."

She pulls out a transparent ball which floats above her hand. At first, I think it's empty and then I see what's inside and the color drains from my face. A speck of Dust.

Trey mixes and pours another glass and hands it to her. She finishes it in one gulp, places the glass down and opens a scroll.

"Fallon East, I am duly here, by order of the First Fallon of Trutinor, to inform you that the Dusting is complete. The last piece of Dust," she nods to the floating orb, "has fallen."

"Is that?"

"It is. I like to collect them, you see. It's something special. The last piece of someone's essence. Besides, it's powerful stuff that Dust. Shouldn't be wasted."

"Thank you, Hermia, that's very thoughtful."

"I'll have it transported to your quarters. In Element City." She coughs, straightens her jacket and turns to her scroll again, "I hereby formally end the Fallon reign of Lionel and Eleanor East. Your coronation will be one month from today. This..." she hands me a small navy cog with a circle of gold around the inner hole, "...is a direct line to, and from, me. You know, in case the First Fallon ever needs to summon you. Or in case you need me. Emergencies. That sort of thing. Trey will explain, won't you, dear?"

Trey nods as the speakers splutter to life again, bringing Magnus' voice with it. "Approaching the fabric, sir."

"That's my cue to leave," Hermia says bowing again. "Long live Fallon East, may your reign be Balanced." And with that, there's another crack and she's gone.

As the train lurches forward gaining enough speed to break through the barrier between Trutinor and Earth, we take a seat in the booths and reach for a handle to hold on to.

We hit the fabric and every world converges in on each other. Obex is the realm within the barrier that we pass through. It's a gateway of sorts: a world between worlds, both living and dead, nothing and everything, a place where time doesn't exist and our souls reside after we die. It's also the source of all Imbalance.

Motion, like time, slows as we break through the fabric. Everything blurs like we're underwater; my body is a leaden weight locked in a dreamy prison. Strands of my hair come loose and float through the train. I lift my hand off the rail to push the hair behind my ear, but I'm too slow and we pass through to Earth. Motion stabilizes in a jerk; I lose balance and fall off the seat, taking Trey with me and the pair of us collapse in a tangled heap on the floor.

Laughing, I find myself lying on top of Trey. He sits up grinning with me still sat on his lap. Our faces are millimeters from each other. His crooked teeth are smiling at me making my stomach bloom in butterflies. He edges closer, and for a second I'm certain he's going to kiss me. But once again, Magnus' voice booms out of the speakers.

"Approaching the Camden coordinates, sir. Anywhere, in particular, the mystery girl wants to be dropped off?"

Trey lifts me off his lap and eyeballs the door to the engine room.

"As close to Camden Cage Club as we can get, Magnus. And for your information, it's Fallon East."

There's a pause. "Fallon East? But, sir, I thought you weren't suppo..."

There's another crackle and then silence. Trey's finger is hovering over another switch on the arm of the booth. He's cut him off.

"He just likes rules, ignore him," Trey says.

When we leave the train, Magnus casts an invisibility spell over it so the humans don't find him and he gives us an hour to return. As we walk off, he drapes his enormous figure over the engine, flings his waist-length dreadlocks behind him and starts muttering like a bitter old woman about rules and the First Fallon.

"Is he always that uptight?"

"Mostly. But what can I do? He's been around since before Titus."

I flinch at Titus' name and pull out my CogTracker. I go to message them, but there's already one waiting for me. Titus and Nyx have sent me a cheesy photo, both smiling like idiots at the camera. He's giving me a bandaged thumbs up. The message says:

See, told you the Dryads would fix me up. Right as rain, I am. Oh, and long live Fallon East. Love you. Be safe. See you at the ceremony tomorrow. Titus and his kitty cat x

A bridge stands above us with bright yellow letters across it that read 'CAMDEN LOCK.' We pass under it and make a left into the market, walking under a huge set of canopied stalls. The smell of hot fresh food hits us as we pass a row of food sellers. Noodles, meats and vegetables overflow on their stalls and queues of people wait in front of them. After a few minutes of searching, we reach an oak door with medieval studs in it and a small tatty sign that says 'Camden Cage Club.'

"Ready?" I ask.

"Ready."

The door opens into a dark stuffy corridor. I'm not sure if it's the heat of the hallway or something else, but I'm aware of Trey's every move behind me and I have to concentrate on not releasing the static building inside me. It doesn't help that his hand keeps brushing over mine.

There are various doors with glass panels on either side of the corridor. Some of them are gym rooms with sports equipment and clusters of sweaty people sparring against pads or punch bags. As we reach the end of the hall, the last door hangs open. There's shouting and cheering coming from inside. I peer around, and in the center of a room is a huge caged ring that reaches almost to the ceiling. There's no mistaking him. Cassian is inside the cage with another brown-haired fighter.

"Got him," I say, and nod to the cage. "Why don't you see what else you can find? There must be records in the offices; maybe you can find some information or his home address?"

Trey looks at me, his blue eyes pouring into mine, making me feel as though he's undressing me. "Fine, but be careful." And this time, when his hand brushes mine, I'm sure it's on purpose because he holds his finger against mine for a fraction longer than an accidental bump. I bite the corner of my lip, and try not to think about what that means.

I stand at the back of the crowded room observing the fight. The place is crowded; coaches, managers, parents and fighters of all different ages mill around. Some are practicing against sparing bags in the corners, but most of the room is watching and shouting at the fighters in the cage.

"They're giving it some for a warm up fight, eh Mike?" says a young lad with spiky blue hair to my right.

I want to get a better look at Cassian so I squeeze into a space near the front. Cassian is enormous. Muscles bulge from every limb and inch of his body; his eyes are dark wells that seem to suck me in like an endless night; his hair is the palest blond I've ever seen, and a stark contrast to his eyes. He raises his hands to protect himself, then lunges out jabbing and punching his competitor across the jaw. His opponent staggers for a moment, steadies himself and wipes the sweat from his rosy face before clicking his neck and hopping from foot to foot. They move around each other like animals hunting. Cassian's opponent is smaller than him, but by the looks of it, faster. Legs fly out, elbows crash into heads and both fighters bounce off the netted cage walls as they reach and claw for any piece of flesh they can get.

And then I see it. Cassian swipes out with one hand, covering his other hand from view and jabs it under his opponent's ribs. If I hadn't been paying attention, I'd have missed it. The hand that jabbed into the ribs flickered and changed for a millisecond. One second it was human, the next a snake head protruded from his wrist and bit down on his opponent's waist. Who takes a stupid risk like that? He could have been caught by a human. I look at the rest of the crowd, but no one seems to have noticed. Cassian's opponent is struggling to breathe; poison, no doubt. Cassian's won. Not because he deserved it, but because it was an unfair fight to start with. He's a Shifter, that's for sure, and he's not afraid to show it. I step back and bump into a woman with flowing brown hair and bright blue eyes. Something sharp catches my hand. I wince and she apologizes, rushing off.

Trey is waving by the door and tapping his wrist. It must be time to leave.

"I got his address," he says, as I reach the door.

"Okay, good," I say, and rub my hand.

"What happened?" Trey says, examining the injury.

A small dot of blood oozes from my hand, "I don't know. Some woman caught me."

I look for her, wondering what cut me, but she's vanished.

EIGHTEEN

Trey Luchelli, Personal Journal.

I HAD no choice and still, I regret everything. She's gone. I'll never get her back. Tonight, my heart is broken.

EVERYTHING outside the train window is a streaky mess of raindrops and greenery. Clouds billow black and gray across the sky as night falls, and the train groans against the force of the wind.

I tuck my feet under my legs and sit in the same big maroon booth I sat in on the way. The seat is huge, but Trey slides in next to me - his leg touching mine. Again. I rub my hand, poking the bruise as a distraction.

"Can I ask you something?" I say.

"Always."

"What happened to your parents?" I've wanted to ask since the night on the rooftop in Element City. I held back because he didn't offer the information and despite our shared Inheritance, I didn't think we were good enough friends then. Now it's different. Maybe it's the way he looks at me, or how close he sits to me, but things feel different now, safe, enough to ask anyway.

Trey pulls his hand through his brown locks and takes a deep breath.

"I don't know..." he says, his shoulders sagging. "Supposedly Kale, my dad, died in a training accident on Earth ten years ago."

"You mean the professor that died? That was your dad?"

"Yeah, but it was hushed up, like everything, so I don't know all the details. I didn't Inherit the extra power and Imbalance until Lani died. She just disappeared. One minute Mom was there, the next she was gone. If it wasn't for the fact I Inherited her powers, I'd never have known she was dead."

"I'm sorry," I say, reaching out to touch his hand. His face crumples, the memories stitching wrinkles into his brow. I know that heartache, my chest is full of raw wounds too, and I wish I could make it better for him. But as he looks at me, I notice the pain hasn't reached his eyes. I recoil; he took his pain away, again. Is there anything he's actually felt?

The speakers rumble to life, "Approaching crossover, sir."

I let go of Trey's hand and reach for the handle, but he snatches it back as we hit the barrier, time and movement slow, and I'm unable to let go. Then the train goes black.

My breath echoes, hollow, ringing and loud in my ears. Light flashes, and a white face smeared in blood appears. Its red eyes flick from Trey to me. It smiles, detached lips peeling away from its gums, displaying sharp teeth. I know this creature. I saw it in the sim.

"It's him," the creature says to whoever is standing next to it.

"Now we have them both."

Darkness fills my vision, and we're yanked out of the gloom back to the train as it continues to pass through the barrier. Our hands are still clasping each other, only now our knuckles are white and our faces pale. The train lurches, knocking me forward. I drift, slow and steady towards his arms. Then the barrier breaks and I slam into his chest, but this time I'm not laughing.

"Did you see that?" I ask, sitting upright.

"Yes."

"I saw the same creature right before my final sim exam. But Victor didn't see anything. What with everything that's happened I'd forgotten all about it. What is it?"

"It's not a what. It's a who."

"You know who that was?"

He nods, "Rozalyn Arigenza. The Last Fallon. But I don't understand how she appeared. I mean, we were crossing the barrier, yes. But she's trapped on the other side in Obex. That's like someone from Earth penetrating the barrier crossing."

"Hang on," I say, waving my hand, "go back a step. The Last Fallon is alive? I thought she died."

"She's not dead. Never was. Why do you think there's still so much Imbalance?"

"But... But then why does everyone get taught she died when the First Fallon banished her to Obex thousands of years ago?"

"Because of panic... And control. If all the Keepers knew she was alive, it would cause widespread panic, uprising even. The Council decided the only way to live in harmony was to teach everyone she had died. You'd have found out eventually. It's one of the secrets Council members swear to keep."

"One?"

"There are parts of the Council you haven't seen yet, that even I haven't seen yet. Things are often hushed up, kept quiet for the benefit of Keepers. The Council is not what you think, none of this is. But now isn't the time. After your ceremony, once you're more stable, I'll tell you everything."

I rub my face, a headache forming in my temples.

"What do you think Rozalyn wants? When she appeared in the sim, she said 'it's her' and this time she said 'it's him.'"

I sit bolt upright, my eyes wide. "This is to do with the prophecy. It has to be. In Mom's CogMails to Arden about the prophecy, they were looking for a boy too. It has to be the same thing. But then... Why would we be in a prophecy together?"

"I don't know. But what I do know, is that we'll never find out if we don't get into the Binding Chamber, that's where the prophecies are. We've got no hope unless we break in."

"How are we supposed to get inside? Aside from Datch it's the most heavily guarded place in Trutinor."

"I don't know. But that's where the most important artifacts are kept, including prophecies."

"Have you seen it in there?"

"No. Hermia told me that's where they were kept years ago. Cecilia was examining one of them in her Council office in the Ancient Forest, and gave it to Hermia to put back when she was done. I'm telling you, this is the only way we'll know for sure."

"Right. Sure. Break our way into the Binding Chamber, which happens to be guarded by ten thousand angry Keepers and a hundred booby traps. Easy."

Trey falls silent, opens his palm and draws up a spinning ball from the center. It's dark and purple, smeared with violet and reminds me of the memory ball he had in the hospital. He studies it for a moment and frowns.

"The prophecy," he breathes, more to himself than me. He looks up, "Eden, I..." His big eyes focus on me. Today, instead of shallow water blue, they're as dark as ocean beds.

"What it is? You can tell me," I say.

He leans back into the booth studying me, then gestures for me to sit closer. Even though I think better of it, I do. He wraps his arms around me pulling me in close. I shut my eyes and lose myself in the warm scent of his skin. The memory ball he was playing with spins behind my ear, its quiet whir lulling me into my thoughts.

Tomorrow all this will be over. Victor will be my soulmate and his will be the only arms that hold me for the rest of my life. No matter how right Trey feels, it isn't our fate. There's an ache buried so deep in my chest I don't think it will ever leave. Whatever this is, should stop. But he's moved closer; the heat from his body wraps around me and his breath trickles over my skin. I tell myself that after the ceremony, Trey will just be a silhouette, an instant of 'almost,' that was never meant to be. This moment, our moment, whatever it is, is over. I open my eyes; he's millimeters from me. Our lips edge closer until my air becomes our air, and I know we're going to kiss.

The train shunts forward and I lurch sideways. Trey catches me with both hands, crushing the memory ball between his palm and my bicep.

Everything stops. The air rushes out of my lungs, and I am frozen by memories. So many memories. They stream into my body making my head dizzy as it floods with emotions. Flashes. Scenes. Images. Each one familiar and yet distant. Then I realize, they aren't just anyone's memories. They're mine.

"Trey? What have you done?" I ask, tears filling my eyes.

A moment from my childhood, of playing with Trey and Kato, comes back to me. His Inheritance, his disappearance. Then The Pink Lake in the Ancient Forest appears. The same one from my dreams. Over and over it emerges, and always from a night of my birthday. And every time, every birthday, Trey is there. The fog that's clouded my mind every time I've tried to think of him clears.

I spent years thinking Trey had vanished, my childhood friend gone. But he never left. I remember now: he was prevented from seeing me. So, he snuck out on my birthday each year to find me. Even when he wasn't with me, I knew he was. Until the evening of my sixteenth birthday. That night he took my memories but not before he took my first kiss.

I gasp and press my fingers to my lips, the sensation of his kiss tingling my mouth all over again. His eyes are wide and he pulls his hand away, "No. No. No. You weren't supposed to see. You're not meant to know."

I'm breathless, as the memory of my sixteenth birthday forms. Traipsing through the Ancient Forest at midnight encircled by the calls of night bugs and the crunch of foliage. I break through the trees to The Pink Lake's shore. Trey is already there, waiting for me surrounded by star light and the glow from the blanket of rose colored lilies smothering the water's surface. I run to him and fling my arms around him. It has been an entire year since I've seen him. We've sent encrypted CogMails and photos, of course. But I haven't seen him, felt him, had his skin press against mine. I drink him in, desperate to savor every moment together because I've already made my mind up. The next day, Victor is to be formally named my Potential. Trey was Bound to Evelyn nearly two years ago. We have to stop.

His hand touches my cheek.

"Eden..."

"Wait..." I say, pressing my hand against his, stopping him mid-sentence.

"No. I don't want to wait anymore; I love you. Only you. Always you."

Then he leans in, his breath trickling over my lips as he presses them against mine. Soft, warm, hypnotic. He pulls me close, his mouth moving over my lips making my heart shatter into a million fragments. He is everything. And it has to end.

"Stop," I say, pulling away.

"Don't," he shakes his head. "Don't do this."

"We have to. We can't keep chasing this thing that can never be. We are not fated, Trey. You know that as well as I do. We can never be."

"I don't believe that."

"You know it has to end. I can see it in your eyes."

He shakes his head again, "Cecilia. I wasn't going to tell you. But she found our encrypted mail. She's furious, threatened all kinds of things. But I don't understand why.

Kato and Bo are seeing each other, and she's done nothing to stop that. Why us? She's hiding something. I know it."

"Either way," I say, and my chest aches so hard as I say the next words I think it will collapse, "this... Us... We can't..." *Love each other,* I think, but I can't say those words. I can't tell him how much my heart aches for him because if I say the words then they become real and if I love him, I can't live without him.

"I know," he says, his crystal blue eyes watery, "but I don't want to be without you."

He presses his lips to mine again, harder this time, more urgent, then he whispers two words against my mouth, "I'm sorry."

The air rushes out of my chest, forcing my eyes closed as a sucking, pulling sensation, grips my mind, rattling my brain until my memories fade and blur and mix together into a foggy slush. When my eyes open, I am alone, standing next to The Pink Lake in the middle of the Ancient Forest, with no idea how or why I'm there. Tears streak my cheeks and my chest is in agony like I'm broken, wounded, dying. Except there's no blood, and I'm not injured. As I drag myself back to school, I am empty except for the throbbing pain in my chest. I cry myself to sleep that night, with no idea why the tears are coming. Day by day, the pain eases, but the emptiness never leaves. I loved him. I loved Trey. With every piece of my soul, my heart and my body. The ache I felt on the train a few minutes ago was real. The shadow of a love my mind had forgotten. Trey knew I had feelings for him and yet, he still took my memories. But my memories weren't the only thing he stole that night: he took my heart too. He told me he loved me. I was going to tell him, even though I knew better, I was going to say the words, but I never got to. Now, I never will.

"How could you?" I breathe, focusing on him.

"I had to. The First Fallon found out. She forbade it. She said you weren't my fate. Evelyn was. That I had to give you up because I was creating Imbalances. After my parents died, she took me under her wing, taught me about the vault and how to control it. She forced me to Bind early to Evelyn because I wouldn't give you up. The Council wanted me to wait until I was sixteen, but she forced it at fourteen. Now I realize it must have been because of the prophecy."

"But you kept coming to see me?" I rub my chest, the memories still reforming, aching and hurting.

He nods, "The first year was easier, she assumed I was obeying because I was calmer after being Bound. And in her defense, Evelyn did make me more Balanced. But that just made it easier to hide what we were doing. We'd meet in the forest, by the lake..."

"And then on my sixteenth birthday, I told you we had to end it."

He puts his head in his hands, but I continue as the memory sharpens.

"Victor was going to be drawn as my Potential, and you were already Bound to Evelyn. I couldn't cope knowing you were hidden away with her. That you were someone else's soulmate."

He looks up, this time with tears in his eyes.

"She's not my soulmate."

I sniff, "I think the Council, let alone the First Fallon, might disagree with you on that."

"I'm so sorry," he reaches out to me, but I pull away.

"Don't touch me. You know how much I hate the thought of having my pain taken away. I said it in the hospital, in the bar. God knows how many times I told you growing up. You knew you'd taken my memories away and you still lured me back in with your bloody Siren charm. You should have let me grieve properly so I could move on. Instead, I still had to grieve, but I ached and cried myself to sleep night after night with no idea why. And this whole time... This whole time you knew, and you said nothing."

He opens his mouth to speak, but I continue.

"You told me not to touch the memory ball in the hospital. Well, now I know why. You said you loved me and yet, because of you, I was in agony for months and I couldn't fix myself because I didn't know what was wrong. I could have forgiven the lie, but betraying me like that..."

"I didn't betray you, Eden, I swear. I just couldn't watch you in pain after we ended."

"THAT'S THE POINT, TREY. I WAS IN PAIN ANYWAY."

"I thought I was protecting you and stopping you from having to hurt."

"You mean, *you* were stopping your pain. You never dealt with your parents' death, and you couldn't face the fact we weren't soulmates either. How ironic..." I stand up. My voice, cruel from his hurt, "The king of the Sirens can't deal with his own emotions. So instead, he steals everyone else's. No wonder Evelyn hates me." I recall her words on the stairs in the bar 'Whatever this little revival thing is that you have going on, it needs to stop.' I had no idea what she was talking about. I looked like an idiot, because of him.

"I thought it was better that way; you'd live a free and happy life without me and the memories of me."

"That wasn't your choice to make," my voice cracks, tears flowing fast now, reliving all the pain.

"Eden, please. I loved you. I still lov..."

"Don't," I bark. "Don't you dare say that."

He gulps the air and then starts again, "Look, after I was

Bound to Evelyn the Council decided I was Balanced enough to return to public Fallon duties. Every inch of me wanted you. I couldn't hide the way I felt, so I took it away. It was easier. Or I thought it would be, until I saw you again at the dance..." He reaches for my hand, but I slap him away.

"It's too late. Don't touch me. Don't talk to me. How can you say you love me? Love is the most powerful of all emotions and you can't even deal with the smallest ones. I'm done. Done with this. With us. With you."

NINETEEN

'While it is not a violation of the Balance to love another prior to being Bound, it is deemed inappropriate and risky. Moreover, the conception of an Unbound baby is a violation of the Balance.'

Teachings of the First Fallon

I STORMED out of Trey's private cabin last night, and locked myself in the furthest passenger carriage away from his, spending the rest of the journey in and out of fitful sleep. At some point in the middle of the night, we arrived at the Keepers School station in the West. I pull the train's glass window down and scan the platform left and right, to make sure he isn't around. Then I sneak off the train, out of the school station and into the grounds.

I push open the towering iron gates and I'm filled with a sense of awe and warmth. No matter how many times I arrive here, it always shocks me. Keepers School's enormous sandy colored mansion rises up like a desert mountain stretching out and back into a horseshoe shape. Triangular thatched peaks skirt the rooftop - upper floor bedrooms for seniors. I spot Rita in one of the peak windows and she waves as I stroll through the courtyard towards the entrance passing a fountain sculpture of the First Fallon. Around the edges are neatly pruned gardens that make the yard smell like sweet perfume. The Sorcerer's have a species survival programme for the exotic and endangered plants in the Ancient Forest. They like to display the most successful cases where everyone can see them.

Glancing up, I spot Nyx by the oak studded door. She's waiting, smiling and blinking those slow cat blinks that make me feel tired.

Binding ceremonies are the event of the year. In fact, they're the event of our entire schooling and the only thing anyone talks about once the date is announced. But today, the atmosphere is flat, subdued and cold. There is no excitement this time. Eyes follow me all the way to the Fallon changing room; pair after pair bore into my back like arrows and I wonder if they blame me for ruining their original ceremony.

Like the atmosphere, the vibrant colors of my classmates' gowns and finery seem dulled. The anticipation of seeing each other's outfits for the first time is gone.

"Here's your dress," Nyx says handing me the mended violet gown as we enter the Fallon dressing room.

"Oh, what did you do to your hand?"

"Not sure. Someone scratched me, it's nothing," I say, kneading the bruise that's flourished into an array of purples and greens.

"I'll see you in there," Nyx says, "I'm going to get Titus and make sure we get good seats."

I take my khaki fatigues and top off as the door creaks.

"Trey?" I ask, wondering if he's come to apologize, again.

"Trey?" Victor's drawl answers.

"Victor? Umm, can you give me a minute, I'm not dressed yet."

"I don't mind," he says, and walks in. I swivel around holding my dress to my body.

Despite his pawed hand, he looks good. He's let his hair down, it's washed for once. Instead of grease brown, it's creamy blond and flops below his ear. His black uniform is neat, ironed and tailored to his body, which is surprisingly triangular. Something I'd never noticed.

"What do you want?"

"You, as it happens. I thought we should talk."

"And that couldn't wait three minutes?" I nod to my semi-clad body. "What's so urgent?"

"You know as well as I do we're about to be Bound."

"Let's not nail that coffin yet; there's still hope."

He kneads his chin, which seems more chiseled than pointy today. I shake my head clear, "What is it, Victor? This isn't exactly a good time."

"It's just... It's just that..." he pauses, shifts his footing and glares at the floor.

"Seriously, I need to get dressed. What's the problem?"

He rubs his hands down his uniform, straightens up and looks me in the eye, "Look. I know we've had our differences."

"That's an understatement," I snort.

"Are you going to let me finish?"

"Are you going to spit it out?"

"I'M TRYING. God, you're annoying. I can't believe we're going to be Bound."

I shift the hip I'm leaning on and fold my arms over the dress. "Go on..." I say. Even if he is my soulmate and we're going to be Bound, no amount of First Fallon magic is going to make us fall in love with each other.

"What I'm trying to say... Is that, I know you don't want to be Bound to me, but... I *do* want to be Bound to you. I think we will be amazing together. Revolutionary even. We can unite the North and the East in a way that's never been done before. We could even end the civil unrest... For good. You and me, Eden, we can work. Be a team. Build an empire and change Trutinor for the better. Don't you see? We were always meant for each other."

I can't help it. I laugh. He's joking. He must be joking. For seventeen years, we've hated each other: fighting, breaking each other's bones, killing pets, electrocuting and biting each other and most recently, suffocation. But he's not laughing. As his brow furrows, and his lips press together, I realize he's not joking either. I stop laughing. Silence fills the space between us. Then he steps close to me, making me inch back and hit a chair behind me. His fingers tip-toe across my exposed shoulder, making me lean even further away.

"Look," he says, glancing at the naked parts of my flesh. "I admit, there's been some friendly rivalry in the past. But what happened after the Dusting, I guess it made me realize some things."

"Friendly? I don't call killing my dog friendly."

He ignores me and continues.

"But I've always known you were the one. It's obvious. It's not like I can be Bound to Bo and you're the only other Fallon close in age. Don't you see? We're meant for each other..." He pauses for breath, unfurls my arms and holds my hands making my dress slip to the floor so I'm standing in only my underwear. His giant figure peers down at me, his eyes roaming across my bra. My skin writhes, but I can't move, transfixed by Victor's bizarre admission.

"We're going to be together, whether we like it or not. I guess I've come to accept that faster than you. Not just accept it... But want it." He bends to my ear, and whispers, "In every way." He takes my lobe in his mouth and gives it a soft suck. I flinch, which he takes as a positive sign and grins. But inside I'm shriveling up like a dead spider.

"I guess that's all I wanted to tell you... Well, that and I know I've not exactly been nice to you, but..." He turns to leave. "But it's because I didn't know how else to be around you. I'm going to do right by you, Eden. I promise." He scans my bare skin one last time, his tongue sliding over his lips like a snake, then he's gone.

I'VE BEEN WAITING in the foyer outside the Great Hall, for a while. Stepping from checkered tile to checkered tile, I pace, think, pace. My classmates fill the space with their dresses and their anxiety. I try to shut down my Elemental powers and block out the air, but it's not working. I keep going over and over the last day. The prophecy, the memories I got back. Trey and now Victor. Who seemed so genuine, but it's Victor. He can't have meant it, surely? I shrug the thoughts away, but I'm still clouded by the awareness that last time I was here my parents died. I tell myself it will be fine, that this is nothing other than a simple Binding, but the nerves don't shift.

Evelyn walks past me, then stops and back tracks. She picks up the shoulder of my dress with her elegant fingers. Her nose wrinkles like she's smelt something rotten.

"Aren't you the sweetest little girl, all grown up now. That color *almost* suits you too."

I bite my tongue hard; my mind rattles, the Imbalance, or maybe it's just me, desperate to lash out. I want to teach her a lesson or better, make her hurt. I smile sweetly, bright and full of venom.

"And you *almost* suit Trey."

Her eyes flash dark; she drops my dress, and stalks off up the stairs in the corner of the foyer. As she reaches the open landing at the top, Trey appears. He glances at me seconds before she throws herself at him. With her arms around his neck, she fires a pointed stare at me, daring me to watch and stupidly, I do.

She smiles at him, then presses her lips to his. My stomach coils with emotions. She is his. Forever and always, fated soulmates destined to Balance each other out for all eternity. She will always be his. I remind myself he's a liar and a thief. That he's not the sort of person I'd want to be Bound to and that I'm better off with Victor. But the churning doesn't dissipate, and I wonder if I'm really the liar and he's just a thief.

Evelyn pauses for breath, glaring at me from the landing; a sneer crosses her mouth and she locks eyes on Trey.

"I love you," she mouths, clear enough I can see it. Then she kisses him. I try to look away, but I can't. I'm locked in place, staring at them. They both know I'm watching. They've both seen me. Which is why what happens next feels like a knife in my chest: Trey kisses her back. Hard and furious, opening her mouth and slipping his tongue inside. His hands roam her body, and she smiles under his kiss as he pushes her back against the landing wall and out of my sight. My stomach froths and rolls and churns; I'm not sure if I'll throw up or scream. I'm so confused. He lied to me. I should hate him, but he isn't the only one betraying me, my heart is too. On the train, I stopped him saying he still loved me. Now I'm glad I stopped him. He can't love me if he kisses her like that. I might be betraying myself. But at least I know I was right about him. Trey is a liar and a thief.

TWENTY

'The Balance Scriptures are a powerful fate reading device capable of being read only by the First Fallon.'

Teachings of the First Fallon

MADDISON KNOCKS past me as I loiter outside the Great Hall, and feigns an apology.

"Eden, do excuse me, I wasn't paying attention. I'm glad I bumped into you though…" She glances at my hand and says, "Oh, what happened there?"

I stare at the patch where the woman in the gym pricked me and notice that it's blackened and covering most of the back of my hand.

"Oh, it wasn't that bad to start with. It was just a spot;

someone knocked into me. I guess whatever cut me must have gone deeper than I thought."

"A bruise or magic. Where did you get it?"

"Earth."

"Oh," she says abruptly and shakes her head. "Can't be magic then, silly me. I'm sure you'll be fine."

Rita Runskall appears next to me and says, "Are you coming? They're about to start."

I nod and turn to Maddison, "Excuse me, I should go. What was it you wanted?"

"Oh, nothing, nothing," she says glancing at my hand again, "it can wait."

She walks into the hall, Rita and I following behind. *That was weird,* I think, and then falter as I see the hall. The room looks like ground zero of an apocalypse.

"It's hideous," Rita says, looking around the room. "What the hell happened?"

"The magic that created the décor in the ceremony room must have deteriorated because it's been a while since we were here."

Flowers adorning the chairs in the West have wilted, drooped or snapped. Petals lay crushed and strewn over the floor, and the limestone chairs are crumbling and derelict. The lake in the East is half drained, and the fire chairs are more like smoldering heaps giving off an ashy stench. Even the rocky mountain seats in the North look like the rubble remains of a demolished tower block. This is not what a Binding Ceremony should look like.

I sit at the front with Rita and wait for the last Keepers to filter in. This time there's no formal procession, no music and no sparkle. No doubt the Council want us Bound fast, and the drama of last time hushed up.

Trey sits on the Council table in front of the stage. Our eyes meet, his pleading, mine furious.

Next to him sits Israel, Maddison, Arden, Charlie the chief Dryad and a few other Council members. As the last Keeper traipses into the hall, the doors close and the First Fallon appears on stage.

The same three Sorcerers as last time, guide the Balance Scriptures into the center of the stage. The feeling of deja vu makes an unease creep over me that I can't shake. This should be a celebration, the best day of my life. Instead, my eyes flick to the door and my feet itch like they want to run.

"You okay?" Rita whispers, "your leg keeps tapping."

"Sorry. Yeah, I'm fine..."

She turns to me and raises an eyebrow, "Sure you are. You're as fine about being Bound to Victor as I am not being Bound to Tiron."

I've been so wrapped up in anxiety over the last ceremony that I'd forgotten her Potential, Tiron had been Bound to someone else.

"Sorry," I say, "I've just..."

"It's fine. We've both been through a lot. Today will be better."

She gives me a weak smile and squeezes my arm. I glance at the seating in North. Victor's there, of course, wearing a strange expression: nerves, but underneath, he's smiling. Was he telling the truth in the dressing room? He genuinely wants to be Bound to me?

The First Fallon opens her arms signaling for silence.

"Welcome, Keepers and Fallons. This time, I shall keep it brief. Look not to our surroundings but the symbolism of these Bindings. I know many of you will be disappointed you've had to wait, but these Bindings still represent the most significant day of your life. And the most important act you'll undertake both for Trutinor and the Balance. From today, you will be Bound, at one with the Balance and able to keep the fate of us all."

She waves her hands over the cogs and they grind into motion until the five colored wisps of smoke appear.

"May you all have Balanced Bindings," she says and plunges her hands into the mist.

She pulls face after face out of the smoke. As if to torture me, each Binding is slower than the previous one and all of them make my stomach twinge. Waiting for the inevitable is so much worse than not knowing. At least if I wasn't sure who I was going to be Bound to, I'd still have hope. But with every passing Binding, the chances of Victor being my Balancer grow bigger.

When Rita's face appears, she grips my hand and her face pales.

"It's going to be fine," I lie. I have no idea if it's going to be fine, but it seems like the right thing to say.

Then, Trat's face appears and Rita drops my hand to look at me, "Not what I expected, but man is he handsome."

A grin peels across her face, the pale fear that washed her out replaced by a warm glow. To my surprise, she wants this, him, and by the number of teeth Trat's displaying, he's just as excited. Perhaps they were always destined to be with each other.

I scan the crowd looking for Bo. She's sat on a crumbling mountain ledge, gazing at Kato. The mental wards I've put over the vault flutter. I should be happy for her and in a way, I am. She and Kato are perfect for each other. But I can't help compare; she's about to get everything she's ever wanted and I, on the other hand, am getting Victor.

The smoke on stage shivers and rolls until her face appears. My knuckles turn white where I'm gripping the seat. I shut my eyes, unable to look. If Kato's face emerges, my fate is sealed.

Then I scold myself. Even though I know she's hiding something from me, Bo is my oldest friend. I should support her no matter what. She deserves her happily ever after, even if I don't get mine. Seconds tick past and my heart thuds out a drum beat counting me down to the inevitable. And then the First Fallon speaks, "Fallon Kato Morello Luchelli."

I squeeze my eyes shut harder, trying to push the stinging away. It's over. I *will* be Bound to Victor. My insides writhe with jealousy and the vault rattles, but I refuse to be bitter for Bo's sake. Once the tears recede, I take a deep breath and look at the stage, smiling and ready to cheer her.

Bo leaps on to Kato's front, and he carries her off stage while she smothers him in kisses. I'm sure her parents won't be impressed with such a public display, but there's nothing they can say now she's Bound to him.

On stage, violet smoke ripples into the shape of my face. This is it. I stand. Dazed. The First Fallon yanks out the last wisp of smoke. The room falls silent, except for the throb of my heart beat.

From across the room, Trey's eyes fall on me, his jaw flexing back and forth and his hands clasp into fists on the table. For one tiny instant, I wonder what it would have been like to have been Bound to him. Then I force myself to look away. The smoke convulses. Shifts and turns black. The only movement in the ceremony room is the black smoke on stage. Then a face emerges. I blink, once, twice, three times; the same face hangs there.

"Fallon Victor Archibald Dark," I whisper in unison with the First Fallon.

On stage, our smoky essence faces hover mid-air reflecting every expression as though they're a live recording. Our faces couldn't be more different. Victor's beaming while my jaw is hard, my face blank and eyes emotionless. Inside, I am teeming with resentment.

I walk past the Council table. Israel is sat in my father's seat, chest puffed out, eyes twinkling. In my mind, I slap the smug look off his face. Maddison is chewing her nail and glancing from me to Victor. Trey's face is as hard as mine. I don't need to be a Siren to work out that he's as much of a mess inside as I am.

I climb the stage stairs and stand in front of Victor, searching his face, hoping to find something, anything that will convince me this will be okay. That he is my perfect soulmate. But I find nothing other than a queasy sensation in my gut.

"Your essences," the First Fallon says clasping our hands with her claws.

A small wolf puppy appears in the palm of Victor's hand. It circles and digs at Victor's furry palm until it finds a spot its happy with and sits its bottom down. Stifled laughter spreads through the hall, and I cough to hide the twitch of my lips. *A puppy? Really?*

"Silence," Maddison barks from the Council table.

A smattering of coughs replace the laughter, and the room is silent again.

I cock my head to examine the pup. Victor must have read my mind because he rolls his eyes and nudges the dog. It responds with snarling, yapping and a mouth full of razors. *Better than nothing, I guess.* But as a Fallon, I still think it's odd his essence isn't more predatory.

I put my hand out, and four elements appear. Projections of fire, earth, air and water all spin in front of me and then merge together and form an angry violet cloud spitting out bolts of electricity. My essence is air, just like Mom.

"Ready?" the First Fallon asks.

I'm not ready. But then I'll never be ready to be Bound to Victor. I give a weak nod, and she joins our hands. Our essences lurch towards each other, springing up and attaching themselves to the necks of our floating faces. This is it. No more stalling, no running away, no escape. This is the moment my freedom vanishes, forever. The tendrils, one black for Victor, one violet for me, float from our necks towards us. When they're millimeters from connecting to our arms, I flinch. Heat erupts through my hand where I've been cut, and a searing sensation flies up my arm. The skin around the injury wriggles, then the bruised black skin peals away and floats out of my hand forming a tendril of black smoke: essence. Just like Victor's.

"Stop," the First Fallon breathes.

Both mine and Victor's essence tendrils halt and pull up as though responding to a drill sergeant. *This can't be happening. Am I ever going to be Bound?*

A collective gasp rips through the audience as the third thread of essence slithers through the air towards mine and Victor's heads where it attaches to our necks. Victor and I freeze, neither of us knowing what to do. A third face appears from the Balance Scriptures. It ripples as it forms and attaches itself to mine and Victor's essence heads. Then the third tendril that latched onto our necks fires forward until it's parallel with our essence tendrils.

"What the...?" I say, and stare at my hand. It's healed. What did that woman do to me? I turn to the First Fallon. "What is going on? Are you doing this? Three people can't be Bound."

The First Fallon takes a step back; her serene complexion cracks like an eggshell, "This isn't me."

The smoke morphs into a face. Part of me hopes the face hijacking our Binding is Trey's. But as I glance at him, shock peels across his face and all I see is the memory of his hands flying over Evelyn's body. The smoke crystalizes, and the face takes shape. It isn't Trey. But it is a face I recognize: a cage fighting Shifter called Cassian Black.

TWENTY-ONE

'Double Binding – Myth, a Binding that
occurs between three Keepers.'

Excerpt - Myths and Legends of Trutinor

VICTOR TWITCHES ONTO TIPTOES. He wants to
run. I do too. Before either of us can, all three essence
strands spring at us like darts, pushing our hands together,
locking my palm to Victor's wrist. The three threads of
essence, an impossible combination, loop around our forearms like rope, squeezing and pinching our grip tighter.
Then they pierce our skin; hot and needle-like, the two
black strands and one striking violet slice through our skin
like slashes in a wound. Victor whimpers as the tendrils
bury deep into his muscle fibers. Cassian's smoky face gasps

for the same breath I'm struggling to catch. Both of their essences coat my lungs like hot tar: suffocating; sweltering; choking.

Victor's eyes and mouth purse shut as if he's straining not to cry out. Then my vault cracks, a thin fissure but enough for Victor's eyes to snap open and make him stagger back. His nostrils flare. He can feel it, the darkness, the anger, the Imbalance, seeping and slithering its way into his body, and he knows it's coming from me. It takes every ounce of strength I have to seal the fissure shut in my mind. As I do, the tendrils break off and we're flung apart crashing to the floor.

Victor's breathing fast and staring at me. As I pick myself up and extend my hand to him, he flinches and shakes his head, but he doesn't turn away. Does he think I'm a freak? Or a danger? Or maybe that look curving his eyes is because he's glimpsed the power I wield, and now he wants a piece for himself.

Three disembodied heads, connected by a plaited neck, float across the stage and disrupt my view of him. *Three heads. Three? How did this happen?* I turn to the First Fallon. But she's not by my side; she's at the front of the stage.

The whole room is silent. At first, I think it's because the Keepers are as shocked as I am. But as I focus, I realize they're not just silent, they're motionless too. Frozen. A sea of dropped mouths and inert eyes. Everyone, that is, except the Fallons. Bo, Kato, Trey, Arden, Maddison and Israel stand at the bottom of the stage, staring at the chaos on stage.

The First Fallon's shoulders heave in time with her haggard breathing. Her hands are facing the auditorium. A single wisp of maroon smoke trails from the center of each palm and dissipates over the audience. *She's compelled the Keepers.* Her shoulders stop, her hands drop and she turns to the Fallons standing by the Council table. Arden moves, but the First Fallon holds her hand out and he stops.

"What did you do?" she says, staring at Trey. *Trey? What's Trey got to do with this?*

I almost miss it, but her eyes dart to Maddison. Is she deflecting?

"Your Majesty, with respect, this is nothing to do with me."

Behind me, there's a shuffle and everyone focuses on Victor.

"Are we going to die?" Victor squeaks.

The First Fallon stalks over to him, snatches his hand and pulls it this way and that, examining the double black and violet scar imprinted on our forearms. All the while, Victor shakes and twitches at her touch.

Then she picks up my hand, her violet eyes zeroed on mine and I'm certain they're full of hate. *What did I do?* She examines my arm then drops it, "You might."

"Might? What kind of a comment is might? Death is kind of black and white." The words are out before I think about what I'm saying.

She glares at me, her focus hot and furious, yet her pale skin is hard as marble. My cheeks heat, but I'm not blushing. She's trying to compel me. A wave flows over my body, honing on my throat like a choker, forcing my voice box to work. Then a word forms in my mind. *Apologize.*

The compulsion makes the vault quiver and crack, sending Imbalance flowing into my veins, defiant, angry, rebellious. "No," I breathe, through gritted teeth.

Then Trey is next to me. He places one hand on the First Fallon and one on me. Where his skin touches mine, a cool sensation like swallowing an ice-cold milkshake dampens the First Fallon's hold on my throat.

"Your Majesty," he says, smooth, silky and calm. "She didn't mean it; she's in shock. This is unprecedented."

She stands straight and smiles, the fury in her eyes gone. *Did he compel the First Fallon? Is that even possible?*

"It appears that while the heads have connected, the imprint on your arm is not sealed. Therefore, your Binding is incomplete."

"What does that mean," Maddison says, moving towards the stage. "Is my son going to be okay?"

"It means, Maddison, that this Binding will continue to shrink until it's gone. If they do not seal their Binding before it's gone, they will all die. However, if two of them manage to seal their Binding, then only one will die."

Maddison's hand clasps her mouth, and she shakes her head collapsing into her seat.

"Either way, someone dies," I whisper.

"Either way, someone dies," the First Fallon says.

"How do we seal the Binding?" Victor says, standing for the first time.

But I already know. And the glint in the First Fallon's eye confirms it. "Binding magic is powerful," she says with a hint of a smile tracing her lips. "There's only one thing strong enough to fix something that powerful..."

"...Blood," I finish for her.

"Blood," she says, smiling at me like I came top of her class. "And on that note, I'll leave you to it. Trey, clean this mess up. I don't want them knowing what's happened." She gestures to the still frozen audience, and then vanishes in a puff of navy smoke.

"So, we're killing that boy?" Victor says, wafting the smoke away.

"NO," Maddison shouts.

"No?" Victor says to his mother. "What do you mean, no?"

Yeah, what does she mean 'no'? And then my mind starts putting the puzzle pieces together.

"I just mean we should bring him back here, study him first, make sure he hasn't damaged you in any way."

The way she snapped at Victor, that instinctive reaction to protect. It was same reaction after the Dusting when I was suffocating Victor. I glance at the heads drifting across the stage: the blond hair, the chiseled jaw line, so familiar. But it's the eyes that give it away; dark, endless pools. Just like Maddison's, just like Bo's, just like Victor's. Then I remember Bo's insistence Israel didn't kill my parents. And now I know why. My mother and father were hunting for Cassian's parents and found them. They died in the Dark's house because Maddison is Cassian's mother and she killed my parents. And Bo knew about it. That's what she's been hiding this whole time.

The vault snaps wide open. There's no time to control it or stem the flow. Gray spots my vision as my entire body heats up; flames burst to life in my chest and the palms of my hands set alight.

Trey is next to me and must sense the change. He grabs my arm. I'm expecting a flood of cool, calming vibrations. But that's not what I get. A warm, yearning ache fills my body and touches my soul. It collects around my heart and pours into my stomach, my legs, even my toes. It fills me with a deep sense of sadness, a sense of loss. A longing for something.

No. A longing for someone. Me. The surprise shuts the vault down. *What was that? Did he mean to share it?*

"Not now," he whispers. I'm not sure if he's referring to Maddison, the vault, or the feeling he just shared with me.

"Arden," he says "could you prepare a holding cell in the West? We'll need some Sorcerers from the Guild of Investigations to question him and it's easier for us to bring him there than you drag a dozen Sorcerers to Datch. Bo, alert The Six we will need a guard. Kato, could you sort the room out and ensure the Keepers enjoyed their pleasant, uneventful ceremony. Victor, Eden, we will go and collect the boy."

We all stand in silence. The air is heavy with secrets, unspoken truths and the knowledge that something bad is brewing. Everyone looks at each other, and I wonder if they're as worried as I am. We're meant to be a council, a team, fighting Imbalance together, ensuring fate is carried out. But somewhere down the road, we got lost. And now each of us is harboring a secret. Maddison's a murderer and together with Israel, they're parents to an Unbound baby, something they've hidden for years. Bo's the daughter of a murderer, and traitor to her best friend. Trey's a thief and liar. Arden's suppressing knowledge of a prophecy that could change everything. Not even Kato's innocent as a CogHacker. Then there's me. Imbalanced, vengeful and lying to myself about my feelings. Maybe... Probably.

What happened? As Fallons we're meant to be more Balanced, purer than our Keepers, purer than anyone, because our bloodline is closer to the First Fallon. Yet, we're the cause of so much of this mess.

Then all of our CogTrackers shriek simultaneously.

I pull mine out and flip it open. Alerts fly across my screen. Imbalances are popping up faster than I can track them, and they're all in Trutinor.

"Shit. It has to be the Binding," I say.

"Go," Bo says, "just go. I've got this. I'll split The Six. Arden, you take half of them and go sort out a Faraday cell in the West. Like Trey says, we can hold the boy there. I know those cells are to stop magic, but maybe if we get him inside, it will slow some of the Imbalance outbreaks too. I'll take the other half of The Six and try to stem the outbreaks. Can you spare some Sorcerers? We might have to seal off the area if the outbreaks continue."

"I'll call the Guild now. Bo's right, you three need to hurry. Get the boy back here as fast as you can. Go. Now," Arden says. He flips open his CogTracker and starts dialing.

Trey, Victor and I look at each other and set off running towards the station.

TWENTY-TWO

'Jugo – Unlike a binding, which seals souls and magic, a Jugo connects two lives. If one lives, so does the other. If one perishes, they both do.'

Excerpt from the Manual of Dangerous and Forbidden Weapons

TREY SENT Magnus a CogMail as we made our way to the station so, as soon as we arrived, we boarded Trey's train and left. As the train speeds towards Earth, it rocks from side to side making me queasy. The instant we sat down, Trey's CogTracker rang. It was Evelyn, so he moved to a maroon booth on the other side of the carriage. That was half an hour ago; he's still sat there because she hasn't stopped screaming. Even with the volume down, Victor and I can hear every word she's saying and the more she shrieks, the more awkward it gets with Victor.

"How dare you, Trey. You swore to me this would stop. She's Bound now. Why are you even helping her?"

Victor looks at me, then Trey. His face grows darker the longer she rants.

"It's not what you think," I say to him, although I don't know why I'm defending myself.

"There's nothing going on. I promise," I say, and give him a quick smile. He doesn't look at me, instead he kneads his paw-hand.

"She's an old friend, Eve. Just leave it," Trey says.

"See?" I shrug at Victor.

He nods, satisfied until Evelyn shouts, "You know as well as I do, you were never '*just friends.*' She's a manipulative, conniving little bitch..."

"That's enough, Eve. We're just friends, and that's the end of it. I'm helping her because this is official Council business and it's threatening the Balance of Trutinor. This conversation is over; I need to work."

He slams the CogTracker shut and stands up.

"Eden. A word please."

"Anything you want to say to her, you can say to me. We're Bound now," Victor says, standing up.

"Not this," Trey says.

Victor's face shudders, as if he's holding back from shifting; he doesn't, however, stop his wolf teeth from lowering.

"Victor," I snap.

"I don't think you understand, Eden. WE are Bound now, you and me."

"This won't take a minute," Trey says, guiding me toward the next carriage, but Victor's in front of him in a

172 SACHA DE BLACK

flash. His teeth bared, both hands shifted, claws gripping Trey's arm.

Trey takes a deep breath, and picks Victor's paw off his bicep. His eyes blaze fiery blue.

"I said, this will only take a minute. SIT."

Victor's face is dark with fury, but unable to resist, he sits in the nearest booth.

"There's a good puppy."

This time, Trey takes my hand making sure Victor can see and pulls me through the connecting door into the next carriage. Victor's scarlet as he glares after us.

This carriage is plainer than Trey's. Although it still has the maroon chesterfield booths and incense filling the air. Once the door's shut, I'm ready for some pathetic apology about kissing Evelyn or stealing my memories, but instead, Trey says, "Maddison."

And I instantly forget our argument.

"I know. I thought the same. She has to be Cassian's mother."

"Agreed."

"Do you think Bo knows? She was holding something back in the bar about who killed my parents. She made me release Israel. Do you think she was protecting Maddison?"

"Possible. But I'm not sure. Bo's pretty loyal to you; she's taken your side over Victor's countless times."

"I know. But this is her parents."

He nods, and thinks about it for a while, "You need to ask her."

"I know." But that's the last thing I want to do, because if it's true and she's lied to me, then I'll lose my oldest friend forever.

"Listen...," he says.

The tone of his voice snaps my attention back, and I remember I'm meant to be angry with him.

"What I really wanted to talk about was the foyer. Before the ceremony... I was..."

"Don't. It's fine. You're Bound to Eve. I'm Bound to Victor... And apparently, Cassian too. But whatever. It's not important."

"No, that's the thing. It is."

"Drop it, Trey. For once, listen to Evelyn. You might have stopped me killing Maddison in a very public way back there. But that doesn't mean we're even. You still lied to me. You still betrayed me and just because you decided to show me that you can feel, doesn't change anything."

He shifts on the spot, "So, you umm, you did feel that then?"

I stay silent, just like he does when I want an answer to something. I'm not answering that, so I change the subject, "Why did you stop me from attacking her?"

"Because we don't know for sure it was her."

"Oh, come on, you saw the way she reacted. We both know Cassian is her son. And my parents were found in her house. What more proof do you want?"

"Absolute, undeniable proof. Maddison is one of the highest ranking Fallons on the Council. If you're going to take her out you better make sure you're right."

"How am I supposed to do that? She's not an idiot; she'll have covered her tracks."

"*If* she did it, then yeah, I agree, she will have. But there's one place even a Fallon can't hide the truth."

I look up, my eyes round and wide, realizing what he's saying. "The Binding Chamber – her essence head will have a record of every moment of her life, including when she killed my parents."

"Exactly."

"Then we have two reasons to break into the Binding Chamber. Our prophecy, and the heads."

Trey nods, "We'll have the perfect opportunity once we're back from Earth. The Faraday cell will be in the West and everyone will be distracted with Cassian."

"Okay," I say, nodding.

"Okay," he says, reaching for my hand. "Then we have a plan."

I pull away, "We?"

When I look at him I see his betrayal. And yet, there's another part of me that remembers the aching and yearning he showed me. Like a shadow, it still lingers inside me and it's overwhelming. I inch further away, making sure he knows I haven't forgiven him. But as if to protest, my insides squeeze.

"Two minutes from Camden," Magnus' voice rings out through the speakers.

"We should..." I say.

"Yeah. We should." He opens the carriage door and we return to Victor, who is still sat where we left him, scowling.

THE THREE OF us are standing outside the Camden Cage Club.

"Trey, you'll need to keep the room suppressed. There will be enough testosterone in there because of the cage fights as it is, let's not risk anymore because of us. Victor, you guard these doors in case Cassian tries to run."

"What? No. I'm coming with you. I'm Bound to him as well remember."

"Fine. Then guard the arena door. But one of us needs to so that if he tries to run, he can't escape."

I pull the door open and we walk down the same dark corridor we were in just a few days ago.

It's dim; the hall smells like stale sweat and plastic. When I peek inside the rooms on the left and right there's new equipment in them, and the training sessions are fuller than last time.

"Let's keep this quiet," I say to Trey and Victor, "there are a lot more people in here than last time."

As we reach the arena at the end of the corridor, Cassian bursts through it. The three of us freeze, there's no time to guard doors or suppress anything.

Cassian's face is swollen with a purple eye and cut lip that's weeping blood. He's smiling and holding a large black belt with several gold embossed circles on it. Behind him are a couple of fighters wearing the same shiny blue training pants he is. He's topless, but they're wearing tight t-shirts with a white stripe down the side. He pulls off a pair of puffy blue gloves, and hands them to one of the fighters next to him. His Binding scar trails up his arm, but the other fighters don't pay it any attention. Maybe they think it's a tattoo. When Cassian sees us, he pauses, his eyes flicking to my scarred arm, then to Victor's.

He leans down to one of his friends, whispers in his ear and both of them disappear leaving Cassian alone with us.

"Eden East," he says approaching us, "I wondered when you'd find me."

I glance at Trey, who's tilted his head like he's trying to work Cassian out.

"How do you know my name?" I say.

"We're Bound, aren't we?"

My eyes narrow, "How do you..."

He cuts me off, "I was hidden in Trutinor until I was thirteen. I wasn't brought here until then. I know all about you and your world."

"So, you know why we're here?" Victor says, his arms folded, voice chilling.

"Because of this?" he says, raising his scarred arm.

"Because of that," Victor nods.

"Okay," Cassian says.

"Okay?" I ask, "that easy? You're just willing to come with us?"

"You might not have known this was coming, but I've known for a long time."

He's Maddison and Israel's son alright; he's as arrogant and annoying as Victor.

Then Cassian, Victor and I drop to our knees grabbing our Binding scars. A pinching, burning sensation grips the inside of my forearm. Victor groans and as he does, the upper inch of my scar melts away, disintegrating and drifting off into the air. It's shrunk. Just like the First Fallon said it would.

When I manage to stand again, Cassian's expression is wide, but when he sees me watching him, he pulls himself together.

"What just happened?" he says.

"We're not supposed to be Bound to two people," I say, and then I get distracted by a woman in the arena behind Cassian. Her wavy brown hair swishes behind her as she heads for the exit in the back of the room. I rub the back of my hand; the bruise or Cassian's essence or whatever it was might be gone, but I want to know what she did to me.

"Excuse me a minute. Trey, Victor, take him to the train."

I jog through the arena after her and out into another

street in Camden. The street is cobbled like Keepers school, only these cobbles are stained and dirty. I scan the street left and right, and clock her a little way ahead of me. "Hey, you. Stop," I shout.

She hears me and glances over her shoulder. Her bright blue eyes widen. There's something so familiar about her. It's the way her wavy hair rests on her shoulders, the bronze of her skin and the curve of her eyes. I can't quite place it. Before I can decipher who she reminds me of, she runs.

TWENTY-THREE

'Unbound babies have been deemed Imbalanced and immoral. On the rare occasions they have been created, they have been terminated. Therefore, studying such creatures has been extraordinarily difficult. It is, however, arguable that should a baby survive to maturity, it could be Bound and essentially, Balanced.'

Excerpt - Unbound Babies – Myth and Mystery, An Essay by Professor Cuthberg

---

IF THE TRIP to Earth was awkward, the way back is cringe worthy. I'm not sure who Victor hates more, Cassian or

Trey. Trey suppresses Cassian so Victor can handcuff him. But Cassian is twice as wide as Victor's scrawny stature, and he's well aware of the fact.

Cassian moves suddenly while Victor's putting the cuffs on; it makes Victor flinch and Cassian snort with laughter.

"Laugh all you want; you'll be dead soon anyway," Victor spits.

Cassian's face falls for a second, then the glint in his eye returns as he leans back into the booth, "Oh yeah? Big strong boy like you going to kill me then?"

"If I don't, she will," Victor nods at me.

"No one's dying. We will find another way to fix the Binding and if we can't, then we'll find a way to slow it down until we can stop it."

"Slow it down?" Cassian asks.

"Bindings are only meant to hold two Keepers, not three. With three of us, it couldn't seal. And now, it's shrinking. If we don't find a way to seal the Binding before it's gone, we're all dead."

"And the only way to fix it is to kill me?" Cassian says.

"One of us must die to fix the Binding. Unless we find another way. Which is what I plan to do."

"And what are the chances of that?" Cassian asks.

"Slim to none," Victor says, smiling. "So, when I do bleed you dry, I'll enjoy watching the smile wipe off your face."

Cassian shunts forward fast as if he's going to headbutt Victor, who recoils into his seat.

"We'll see about that," Cassian laughs.

"No one is dying," I repeat. But, as I say it, I'm not sure I believe it. If it does come down to a fight, Victor's got no chance, not even against me, and I've got no intention of dying for him.

The train jolts as we break through the barrier. We're thrown into slow motion, but something's wrong. Passage through the barrier is always slow and fluid. But this time, the train jolts, rocking in violent swings like we're going off course and Magnus is fighting it.

As we break through to Trutinor, it's not the West where Arden's preparing a cell that we land but into the East and the middle of the desert.

Everyone looks at Cassian; we're all thinking the same: his imbalance caused the redirection.

"Don't blame me. Not my fault your transporter can't drive," he says folding his arms.

Trey grits his teeth, but I shake my head at him; it's not worth arguing over.

The air is arid and penetrates the walls of the train as we cross the desert. Magnus tries to control the train. I run to the gangway and pull down the window. Ignis is rising in front of us with a huge translucent green dome over the entire city. The Sorcerers must have locked it down already.

"We've been pulled into the East. We're approaching Ignis, the Fire City, according to my CogTracker," I say, pulling it out and flipping the screen around to show everyone, "it's the primary source of the Balance violations since our Binding. We should stop and help."

"Another nail in Earth boy's coffin. This is obviously his fault," Victor says, pointing at Cassian. "Bring an Unbound atrocity into Trutinor, and we're going to have problems. I told you we should just kill him."

"And I told you we're not killing anyone. We're both Bound to him, we don't know this is his fault."

I scroll down the CogTracker, and scan Ignis. Bo's essence is in there and some of The Six's too.

"Eden's right, we should detour and help the city before heading back to the West," Trey says.

"Your funeral," Victor says.

Trey frowns, "Give me your arm, Eden."

"Why?"

"Because I think the shrinking is speeding up."

He pulls a marker out from behind the bar, and I raise my wrist for him. He draws a black pen mark around my wrist and the top of my Binding.

"This is to measure how fast it's shrinking. It's four o'clock now, let's check the Binding in a few hours," he says, and underneath his breath he adds, "Cassian's hiding something."

I turn my back so I'm facing away from the others, and mumble, "Yeah, he was far too willing to come with us."

Trey picks up Victor's wrist and marks it, then Cassian's as the train slows, and pulls to a stop.

"You stay here, Cassian," I say.

"But I can help."

"Help get us killed," Victor says.

"If you leave me here, I'll escape."

"Awesome threat. You'll escape into the middle of a desert with no water and no transport; you'll be dead by nightfall. Actually, that's a great idea. We should leave you here."

Trey and I glance at each other. If Maddison is Cassian's mother, there's no way she'll let one of her sons die. I suspect she knows we're back in Trutinor and is tracking our every move. The last thing we need is him disappearing.

"He's coming with us," Trey says, taking the words out of my mouth.

"I'm taking the handcuffs off because you might need to defend yourself, but if I think for one second you're trying to escape…" I light one hand with electricity, one with fire, "…Take your pick."

"Got it, sweet cheeks," he says, winking at me, "no running."

Dick. For brothers who grew up apart, they are so similar. I let a bolt of electricity off, and it hits him square in the chest. He yelps and the smug grin disappears.

"Oops, sorry, sweet cheeks," I say, and saunter off the train.

Through the transparent green dome, a column of smoke plumes in the center of the city with the occasional wisp evaporating through the dome's peak like a smoky osmosis.

Victor notices the smoke too, and says, "I hope Bo's okay. This is the problem with Sorcerers quarantining a city; we're blind going in."

"Better that, than an outbreak of Alteritus."

"What's Alteritus?" Cassian says.

"I thought you knew everything seeing as you lived here for thirteen years," Victor says.

Cassian looks at me, "It's an extreme form of Imbalance. You only get it in Trutinor, humans have their own set of problems. But for us, it induces a kind of crazed hysteria where all you want to do is maim, kill and destroy."

"This should be fun then," he says as we reach the edge of the dome. I raise my hand to the shimmery boundary, and stop. My wrist heats up again; Victor and Cassian are both wincing as more of our Binding disintegrates. When the pain fades, Trey's wearing the same hesitant look I am.

The domes quarantine people with Alteritus. I swallow hard. I'm not infected with Alteritus, but I do have some kind of Inheritance-Imbalance lurking inside me. What if it doesn't let me in?

"Are you going to cut us a hole or what, Eden?" Victor says pushing me aside. "I'll do it. We haven't got all day with the rate our Bindings are shrinking. Let's get in, get out, and get Earth-boy into a Faraday cell, so the Council can determine what to do with him," he says, glaring at Cassian.

"He's right; we don't have time to mess about. At the rate it's shrinking we might only have a couple of days before it's gone."

Victor places his palm out, and summons his wolf puppy essence. The dome creaks like old leather and the surface swells, cracks then ruptures. He pulls it aside and lets Cassian and Trey through.

But he stops me, placing an arm on my shoulder, "I told you. I'm going to protect you. We both know what's inside you and that if you'd tried to open the dome it might have rejected you. I felt the darkness inside you during the Binding. But I don't care. I want us to work. No matter what."

He walks off, and I step inside the city sealing the dome behind me. I summon my own air essence and the dome responds, swelling and rupturing as it did for Victor. Whatever is inside me is more complicated than I realized.

Victor stops to wait for me, a smile on his lips. He seems genuine, but for some reason, I can't swallow the kindness.

As the dome seals, it's like stepping into a nightclub. Noise vibrates around the streets. Screaming. Explosions. Cracks of lightning. Bolts ricochet off the dome's roof and rebound onto the buildings blasting chunks of brick into the streets. An enormous ball of fire rolls past the street in front of us.

"This is bad," I say, grabbing Cassian by the wrist and pulling him behind me. Which seems ridiculous because he's a foot taller than me and wide enough to shield two of me from anything we encounter.

"Victor was right. You shouldn't be in here."

"Too late now," he says, "besides, I can handle myself."

"Not by the looks of your face you can't," Victor says, his lip curling.

"Enough," I snap. "This isn't the time for petty ego-fights. Everyone we encounter in here can infect us. This is my city, my Keepers so we play by my rules. No one kills anyone. Immobilize them until the Sorcerers can administer an antidote. Got it?"

All three of them nod.

"Now, let's find Bo. If I know her, she'll be in the center of the trouble trying to protect as many people as possible and given that ginormous column of smoke..." I point towards the city center. "I guess that's where she is."

Victor, Trey, Cassian and I jog through the bright streets. Towers in Ignis are splashed with orange and yellow flames, homage to the city's dense population of fire Elementals. Although the city is rectangular and made of thousands of towering skyscrapers like Element City, the streets here are much wider. Wide enough we can all walk side by side.

As we get closer to the city center, I notice that the dome's ceiling is dotted with thunder clouds. Clouds, I suspect, that are left over from lightning fights. Beneath the snowy puffs, rain falls in patches that I can't help splashing through. We pass a ransacked newsstand. Newspapers are strewn across the pavement and rustle as we hurry through them. The closer we get, the more debris we have to dodge. Metal bins, bits of broken furniture and shopping trolleys litter the streets. A couple of armchairs in the middle of a road are smoldering as a result of a cracked fire fountain which is spewing orange lava over the street. I pause, hold one hand over the chairs and aim the other at the fountain, dousing both with a jet of water.

We stop on a street that joins the main road through the city center. The shop windows on this street are broken, and the street lights smashed. The smell of fresh coffee fills the air, as if it's a normal work morning and nothing is wrong. To our right is the source of the smell, a looted coffee shop. Beans scatter the pavement like a cartoon sketch waiting to trip someone up.

Several Keepers charge past our street. Their eyes blaze red, a sign of Imbalance. As we cross into Main Street, they smash into another group of Elementals. A brawl breaks out, limbs hurtle towards body parts. Lightning, fireballs and waves of water circle above the group. Every so often one of the balls dives into the brawl like a spear, and someone moans. In the distance, a flash of blond hair attached to a petite figure shifting as fast as she moves, jumps through the air.

"We need to split up. Cassian you're with me. Trey, Victor, see if you can use the parallel street and make it to the top end. It looks like that's where most of the trouble is, and I think I see Bo."

Victor nods, and drops to the ground shifting into a larger version of his wolf essence. Trey follows.

"You ready?" I say to Cassian, "just stay out of the way, and I'll protect you."

He rolls his eyes at me, "Yeah, right. Do you know how rarely I get to shift properly?" His body vanishes as he drops to the ground and reappears as a wolf three times the size of Victor's. His furry shoulder stands at my head height; his sleek white fur is interrupted only by dark eyes, and a slip of black that streaks his coat from tip to tail.

"Woah. You're even bigger than Israel," I say, and have to stop myself stroking his glossy fur. I'm sure his wolf mouth pulls into a smile.

"No biting, Cassian. I mean it. Do not hurt anyone."

He howls an acknowledgment, and we enter Main Street as another couple of Keepers run past flinging a variety of Elemental weapons at each other. Then they join the growing group of brawling Keepers.

I kneel on the ground, put my palm on the road and let my mind channel through the tarmac into the soil below. It's bad soil. Hard, redundant, left under the road for eons. I push my mind a little deeper until I find some good patches and pull them to the surface. The street quakes. Some of the Keepers fighting on the outside of the group trip as the road cracks and fissures appear.

Cassian sees them fall and chases after them, growling and circling them. I probe deeper underground, drawing as much dirt as I can into worm-like strings hauling them all to the surface.

Tarmac explodes as dozens of dirt worms surge through the cracks.

Each worm zeroes in on one of the Keepers and loops around their bodies tightening around their torsos like a noose. When everyone is trapped, I pull my hands away from the pavement and fling them out sideways. The Keepers' bodies swing out and slam against the nearest building's walls. On contact, the mud oozes loose connecting with the dirt particles in the bricks and mortar. I twist my wrists and the mud solidifies, cementing them to the wall until one of the Sorcerers can inject them with the antidote.

As the Elementals fathom that they're trapped, screeching breaks out. They kick and lash at the dirt restraints until they realize they're stuck. A dozen gaunt faces stare at me. Their only expression is an angry hunger, as though it isn't Keepers I've trapped but a pack of zombies.

A hundred yards up the road Trey and Victor, still in his wolf form, are darting around the street trying to herd up other Elementals. I place my hands on the ground again. Sweat runs down my back as I pull more dirt worms into the air. They attach to the Keepers surrounding Trey and Victor, and I fling them against the wall then fire another worm at the Keeper preoccupying Cassian.

"I think you got them all," Trey shouts as the last two Keepers crash against a bright red building covered in orange flames.

Cassian and I run up the street to Trey and Victor, hopping and jumping over the debris.

A shadow above my head catches my eye. I glance up, thinking it's Bo in falcon form. But before I can determine what it is, a body smashes me into the ground.

I cry out as pain erupts across my shoulder. More bodies crash into me, pinning me to the ground. Muffled shouting, and thuds of fists to body parts come from above. Someone lands three electrified punches to my ribs. My hands are trapped palms down on my stomach. I can't use them to free or defend myself. A leg moves, freeing my face in time for me to see Cassian's wolf jaw and blood red eyes sinking his teeth into the neck of one of the bodies on top of me. The Imbalance inside him must have taken over.

"Cassian, NO," I shriek, but it's too late. Blood flows from the victim's throat and drips onto my cheek as he drags the limp body from the pile. He drops it on the floor, still twitching. It's a young man, with dark hair and straight teeth. He can't be much older than me. The body quivers then goes still, a pool of blood forming around his head like a red halo.

The rest of the bodies are pulled off me. The weight eases enough for me to free my hands and push a gust of wind out to help shove the last two away. I expect to see Trey's face, staring back at me, compelling the Elementals off me. But to my surprise, it's Bo who's standing hands on knees panting over me. She throws the last body against the wall; the mud holding the others in place slackens and engulfs the last Keeper. Then she gives me a hand up.

Cassian's standing again, back in his normal form, his eyes blinking back to black. "I'm sorry," he says, his eyes wide and head shaking, "I'm sorry, I didn't mean to, it just..."

"It took over. Yeah, I know the feeling. Let's talk about it later. Right now..."

Trey appears next to him, and I nod, indicating he should cuff him again, which he does.

I take Bo's hand and pull myself up. My shoulder is sore, a bruise already forming, but at least it isn't broken or dislocated.

"What's going on?" Bo says, "why wasn't he cuffed?"

"Figured he might escape if we left him on the train, and he needed to defend himself in here."

Angus, the Shifter who tried to intimidate me outside Trey's bar, and Obert, Trat's father, appear sweating and smeared in dirt and blood.

"How's it going?" I whisper to her, but my voice sounds forced. I take a breath; Trey is right, I can't make assumptions. I have to be sure before I accuse anyone of anything.

"Not great. They think I'm weak and hate that I'm so young, let alone a girl."

"Kick their sexist asses; they'll soon change their mind."

She laughs, and it feels like it used to between us.

"I'm working on it," she says.

"The city is secured," Obert says, as they reach us. He wipes his forehead; his brown hair crinkles and curls at the edges where the sweat pools, and reminds me of the curly mop Trat has.

"The uninfected Keepers are confined to their flats. They know they can't leave until the outbreak is contained." Angus adds, "And it looks like you just got the last of the stragglers, Eden."

"That was Bo," I lie, and smile at her. Angus nods, seemingly impressed and she mouths thank you at me.

"Angus, Obert, can you stay here just to ensure there aren't any more breakouts?"

They give Bo a stiff nod, and she turns to me, "Kato already left so can I hitch a lift back to the West with you guys?"

"You can," I say. "But it will cost you."

"What do you need?"

"Escort Cassian to Arden with Victor. I need to do something this evening."

I look at Trey; he nods, acknowledging that I just bought us the time and privacy to break into the Binding Chamber.

"Deal," she says, and we head back to the train.

TWENTY-FOUR

Eleanor East, Private Journal.

20TH JUNE, 2002

ARDEN HAS TOLD me of the Libra Legion – he is creating an army of like-minded Fallons and Keepers. He believes we are being deceived at the highest echelons. Trutinor is not as we thought. War is coming, and I am afraid for Eden.

———————

AS WE REACH the West State, nightfall is creeping over the sky, rubbing out the streaks of pink and replacing them with charcoal.

Bo has spent most of the last couple of hours chipping red paint off her nails and looking from Cassian to Victor. I am certain she knows who he is, and it makes anger bubble in my gut. If she knows about Cassian, she must know about Maddison and my parents. Trey nudges me until I take the hint.

"Bo, can I have a word?"

She flinches, "Umm. Yeah, okay, sure."

I close Trey's carriage door behind me, and gesture to a maroon booth, "We should talk."

"Talk. Right. Yep. We should." Her eyes shift to the door then back to the only nail with polish left on it.

"Are you okay? You seem wired."

She stops picking and looks right at me, "Do you think Cassian's my brother?"

I sink back in my seat, unsure if I'm shocked, relieved, or confused. I thought she was hiding it, but that was a question, and by the strain in her eyes, I don't think she knows the answer.

"I do."

"Shit. So, do I," she says, putting her head in her hands, "but that means my mom and dad..."

"I know. It makes sense though; my mom was following a lead on Cassian's parents and ended up in the North..."

"You mean in my house...?"

I fold my arms, "You really didn't know?"

"That Cassian was my brother?"

I nod.

"No, of course not. This whole trip, I've been thinking and piecing it together. The pair of them, Victor and Cassian, sat next to each other. They're so alike."

"Bo..." I cut her off, and the coldness of my voice makes her head snap up. I have to know if she's protecting the killer. If she's lied to me this whole time. I have to know, and yet I don't know if I can handle the answer.

"Did your mom poison my parents?"

The question hangs in the air, blunt and solid, like I could pluck it from the air and wallop her with it. There's no turning back: one way or another, she has to answer.

She looks down, and tears plop onto the carriage table. When she looks at me again, a couple run down her cheeks and she rubs them dry with the sleeve of her jacket.

"No. She didn't."

"You swear to me?"

She nods.

"But you know who did?"

She turns away from me, wiping her face as the tears fall faster and then she whispers, "Yes."

"And you're not going to tell me?"

She turns to me, and grips my hands, "I can't. Not yet, I swore. You have to understand. If you want to know what happened, you need to get into the Binding Chamber and find your parents' essence heads. It's the only way."

I yank my hands away, "You know who killed them and you're refusing to tell me?" Tears prick the back of my eyes, but I refuse to let them out.

The train grinds and judders as it pulls into Luna City's central station. Bo's standing, her face pale, makeup smudged under her lids. "I should take Cassian to Arden," she says, her voice quiet, withdrawn.

I can't look at her so I stare out the window, my eyes burning with tears.

She moves to the carriage door, then stops, "Find their essence heads, Eden. Find them, and you'll understand everything." Then she's gone.

I'M NOT sure how long I sit there, watching the light fade, but by the time Trey's hand touches my shoulder, it's pitch black and I haven't been able to see through the window for ages.

"Are you okay?" he says.

"I don't know. Bo says her mom didn't kill my parents but she was really cryptic."

"We will find out what happened, I promise. Do you still want to do this?" He asks.

"I do."

"Then we should go."

I pull my hair into a knot, stretch and stand up.

"Where is everyone?"

"Bo and Victor took Cassian to Arden; I suspect Maddison has some explaining to do. I've been getting supplies and checking the rotas. Lucky for us, there's a night guard shift change at nine, which is in fifteen minutes, so we need to hurry. It's the only chance we'll get."

"Let's go then."

As we cross the school gardens, an eerie silence swallows the grounds like someone's flicked mute.

I step closer to Trey, a chill running down my back.

"You okay?"

"Yeah, it's just a bit quiet."

"We've got this," he says, smiling. Something rustles in a bush in front of us, and I yelp. He laughs as a rabbit hops past.

"Let's just get this over with."

"The entrance is down there," Trey says, then checks his watch and pushes me into a bush.

"We have to wait."

His chest presses against my back, his breath trickling

down my neck. I close my eyes and focus on blocking out the heat that always pours from him.

Two guards wearing the First Fallon's navy uniform stroll past. Trey wraps his arms around me, and pulls me closer to him and further out of the guard's line of sight. His lips brush my ear, sending a shiver through me. "This is it. Are you ready?" he says.

I nod and peel myself out of his arms.

We scurry down the side of the school through a set of gates with a huge 'no trespassing' sign and parallel to a sandstone wall. Then, a solitary dark green door appears.

"My contact said it would be locked," he says.

I take the handle, focus my mind and push ice through my palm, colder and colder, until the handle is brittle and I snap it off.

Pushing the door, I take a step, but Trey grabs me. "Wait."

He takes out a small bronze double cog, twists the base and slides it onto the bottom of the door frame. It clicks and then shoots out a translucent field that fills the doorway.

"The doorway has an inbuilt scanner; the cog makes it think we're guards."

"You must share these contacts of yours."

"Never," he says grinning.

I roll my eyes, "It was Hermia, wasn't it?"

"That obvious?"

We're both smiling as I enter the foyer, and I have to remind myself that I hate him and haven't forgiven him. The foyer has the same sandy colored brickwork and checkered tiling on the floor as the rest of school. But the high arched windows are missing, instead, there's another single door.

"Is this where those guards would have been?" I ask.

He nods.

"Though there will be a guard every few meters or so along the corridor leading to the chamber. I'll go first and compel them asleep. If I fail, electrocute them till they're unconscious. I'll have to do a memory wipe on the way back."

"Wow, it really is that easy for you to take someone's memories."

"Seriously? Now is not the time to have a fight about that." He opens the door silencing me and steps down into a set of winding, circular stairs. Flaming torches hang from the central pillar at random intervals. As the light grows Trey stops short and points around the bend; there must be a guard there. He presses a finger to his lips and disappears. There's a thud, then the scratch of fabric sliding over stone before he appears again.

"One down, four to go."

We creep through the corridor, me staying in the shadows and Trey slipping out at the last minute to catch the sleeping guard as they fall to the floor.

There's two at the doorway to the Binding Chamber, so this time I hold Trey back and push my sleeves up. I have to hit them at just the right spot on their head with just the right amount of electricity, or I'll kill them instead of knocking them out.

I still my breathing and then fire. The first guard drops, making the second panic. As he bends to grab the first, I hit him with a bolt and they collapse in a pile.

I place my hand on the door, but the handle melts in my palm and the metal reforms around my hand cuffing me in place.

A voice rings out from the door, almost as if it is the door.

"State your intention in the chamber."

I crane my head around to Trey and he nods, urging me to answer.

This is a test and I suspect if I lie, it will know. There are so many reasons I am here: justice; retribution; knowledge, but there's one I care about more than any other.

"I want the truth," I say. The handle melts and the door clicks open.

The stone chamber is bigger than either of us imagined. Both of us ogle in silence as we scan the vacuous chamber. It stretches further than I can see making it look like an endless black hole. The same flamed torches hang from the walls in here, only dozens more than in the corridor. It produces just enough light to see the thousands upon thousands of phosphorescent essence heads drifting around the room. They hover several feet in the air floating like balloons. Their Bound tendrils dangle from their necks at just the right height to brush our scalps as we walk through them. I shudder as a cool, silky tendril skims my forehead. It's like a forest of bodiless ghosts.

I flip open my CogTracker, but there's too much interference from the essence heads for it to work.

"We should try and keep the door in sight. The trackers are useless if we get lost in here," I say.

"It looks like it's sectioned," Trey says, pointing to different parts of the room. "But I don't see any Fallon heads. I think there's another chamber through there though."

In the corner of the room, I can just make out an arch with a cool glow inside.

We edge around the top end of the room trying to stick to the walls and keep our bearings.

I stop in front of the archway; it's open. There's no door,

no security. "It's too easy," I say, "what if there's a silent alarm or something?"

"I don't like it either. But what choice do we have? The prophecies are inside that cog."

I crane my head and see a large silver cog that stands half my height; it has a huge hole in the middle, and a silvery light emanates from it.

"I'm going in."

I step into the room and pause, "I guess it *was* that easy."

Trey follows me in, "Maybe, but I still don't like it."

The room is small, the size of an office and empty except for the enormous cog and another arch in the back corner, which Trey sticks his head through.

"The Fallon essence heads are in here."

"Prophecy first," I say, as I lean over the rim and look into the hole. "It's right here."

Silvery liquid spins in the middle, creating a small whirlpool in the middle. Inside the whirpool's funnel are several silver cogs.

"How do we know which one is ours?" Trey says.

"There's an inscription on the rim of the cog."

PURISSIMI ANIMI soli fidelissimomfatum quarere possunt.

"WHAT DOES IT MEAN?" he asks.

"It's Latin, an old Earth language. I think it says: The purest hearts alone can seek the truest fate. But my Latin's rusty. It's an instruction. If I don't seek the truth for a good cause, my guess is, I won't get my hand back."

"Sounds more like a warning to me. Maybe we should leave it and just find Maddison's head."

"Look. If I don't fix my Binding, I'm as good as dead anyway. This prophecy might not give me a solution, but it might tell us something. Everything's wrong and messed up, you must feel it too. I'm certain it's connected. We're linked by an Inheritance that the whole of Trutinor thought was just a myth. There's a prophecy about us, and the Last Fallon just happens to have been looking for us? My parents are dead because they chased after the worst balance violation in centuries, a boy who I just happen to be Bound to, and you don't think it's all connected? I'm getting that bloody prophecy even if I lose my arm for it."

I plunge my hand into the silvery liquid. It's cold, but to my surprise, it's drier than I expected: congealed and gloopy.

I peer into the liquid; I can see dozens of cogs, but when I reach for them, my hand swipes through them as if they aren't there.

Please show me the prophecy? I just want to know what my parents died for and how to stop this mess before it destroys everyone I love.

I swish my fingers through the liquid again but still nothing. Then the liquid thickens and pulls my hand deeper into the gloop. Goosebumps track down my back, and I'm convinced it's going to swallow me whole. My fingers touch something solid. As soon as I grab it, my hand is spat out of the liquid. I open my palm, and there's a small shiny silver cog sat in it. "Got it," I say, grinning, and then my smile fades. "There's no opening, or button to make it play." I flip it over in my hand.

"Don't worry about that now. We can figure it out once we're out of here. I don't want to be in here longer than necessary. Let's find Maddison's essence head and get out of here."

"Not Maddison," I say, remembering Bo's comment on the train. My head wants to ignore her; logic tells me she's betrayed me, purposefully holding back information about my parents. But despite all our differences, our family history, she's never given me a reason to mistrust her before. Trey's right, I do have to be one hundred percent sure because, for me and Trey, Imbalance still lurks inside us, and faulty assumptions can be deadly.

"No," I say again, "my parents' essence heads first."

"Eden, we don't have time."

"It's fine. If Maddison killed them, we'll see her in their memories anyway."

"Fine," he says, "but quickly, we need to get out of here. The guards won't be out much longer."

He leads me through the arch in the back corner into another chamber, this one, much larger than the Prophecy Room. It's lit by flaming torches and is far more regal than the first chamber. The ceiling is inlayed with the five State symbols, all in gold.

We wander through the room. Unlike the first chamber, most of the essence heads in here are faded because the Fallons died centuries ago.

Arden's head floats past me. His face is stark white on one side and where it rests next to his dead wife's, it's lifeless and dull, like hers. How is he alive with a Binding that damaged? I can't imagine struggling day after day with what must feel like half a soul. I reach up to touch it, but out of the corner of my eye, I spot my mother's pallid face hanging limp next to Father's. My blood turns to ice. Trey must sense my shock because he's beside me asking if I'm okay. But I can't hear him because I'm consumed by the recognition that I'm about to find out who killed them.

I push past him, hands out as I march towards their faces. Then everything is black, and I am head first in a hard chest. I stumble back, "What did you do that for?"

"I just want you to be sure."

"Trust me. I'm sure."

He holds me by the shoulders, his face soft, kind and warm, "We might be able to influence fate, but we can't change the past. That's why we're not allowed to look through these memory traces. This won't bring them back."

"I know..." I look down, taking huge shuddering breaths to ease the tightness in my chest. "...I know."

"Okay then, if you're sure because you can't unsee this."

"You're right. I can't," I shift under his grip, "would you...? I mean, you don't have to. But maybe in case I lose control or something?"

He squeezes my shoulders before letting go, "Of course I will. I know you're still angry with me, but that doesn't change how sorry I am or the way I feel about you. I told you, Eden, I'll always be here for you."

He turns, pulls my parents' Bound plait, and tugs on the essence strands, passing me one and keeping the other.

"Ready?"

I nod, and we touch the threads to our Binding scars, and everything goes black.

TWENTY-FIVE

The greatest sacrifice, is the one you make for another – Balance Proverb

---

LIGHT. Colors. Smells. Snippets of memory flash across my vision until they settle on a scene in Luna City's central station. It's dark, the station is quieter than normal, but those arriving off the steam trains are carrying luggage and dress bags. *This is recent. It must be before the end of the school ball. Just after my parents left.*

MY MOTHER'S hand rises in one fluid motion. She's pointing to someone in the dark, under a platform arch. *Well, this is weird...* I am inside Mother's body; she's much more petite than me, and her wiry frame is odd to move in.

To my right, is Trey, except he's my father and he's shot into the darkness. Mother moves, quickly, light on her toes, and rushes after Father. I have no control over her body; the memory plays on its own, like a film.

"Were you followed?" Mother says as she drops into the gloom.

The man in the dark pulls forward. It's Arden. "I was," he says, "but I lost them twenty minutes ago."

"Who was it this time?"

"Shifter. She always could brainwash them the easiest." Mother nods.

"And Hermia? Did she get to Obex?" This is Father speaking.

Arden's lips press together, and he touches Father's arm.

"It's not good news, is it?" Father asks.

Arden gives a single shake of his head.

"You said in your CogMail you had absolute proof," Mother says, "has Rozalyn confirmed it is Eden and Trey?"

"She has," Arden says, "Hermia just got back. The Last Fallon made the confirmation just yesterday. But she's having trouble tracking Trey. Hermia's going to offer her tracking assistance. Once Rozalyn gets a lock on them both, she can observe their progress and protect them. I'm so sorry, Eleanor."

Mother stands straight. "We knew it might come to this. Trutinor is at war, and our Keepers don't even know it. Nothing is more important than the Libra Legion, not even a life. Not even a Fallon's. We must win, Arden. No matter the cost."

Arden nods, but his eyes are bloodshot, and he's shaking.

I don't understand. What Libra Legion? What war?

Why is Mother saying Fallons' lives aren't important? I want to shake Arden and tell him to make them stay, but I'm stuck in my mother's body moving only as she did.

"You'll need to make it look convincing. At least until Eden is Bound properly. Arrests. Questioning, the works," Mother says.

"I'll throw everything I have at it."

"Good," Mother says, "good."

"Look after..." Father says.

"...As if she were my own," Arden says, pulling him into a tight embrace.

The scene dissolves and races forward. When it settles, we're standing in the penthouse suite of Eris Castle in the North State. Bo's house. As we enter, we have to step down into their living room. Despite the castle's black exterior, their living room is pure white: sofas, walls, and decorations, made brighter by the back wall which is made entirely of glass windows and throws shards of light into their room. Both my parents move to the window. Snow-capped mountains stretch out in every direction. The rock beneath the snow is dark and craggy like the remains of burnt lava.

I remember the report in Arden's files. They died in this room. My heart pounds inside my chest. I'm not sure if I can watch any more. Trey was right.

Mother turns around, and my heart stops. Bo is standing on the steps that lead down into the living room.

"Mr. and Mrs. East? Hi," she says, her gaze flitting between Mother and Father. "Is Eden with you?"

"No, sweetheart, she doesn't know we're here. Did Arden send you?" Mother says.

She nods, "Yes, he caught me at the end of the ball, told me it was an emergency and to fly straight here. What's going on? The Binding Ceremony is in a few hours. We should get back."

Father nods, "You must, yes, but we have to do something here."

"What's going on?"

"We need to ask you to do something very difficult. Something you won't want to do," Mother says, walking to take Bo's hand and sit her on the sofa.

Bo's sculpted eyebrows pinch together, "What do you need?"

"Two vials of your blood."

Bo laughs, but when Mother's face doesn't change she stops.

"You're serious?"

"I am."

"But it's poisonous and not just a little bit, it's deadly. Last time someone used my blood... You know what happened to Trey."

Trey? Did his mom die because of Bo? I want to turn and ask him if he knew, but I can't.

"I know about Trey."

"Then you want it to kill someone?"

Mother nods.

"Who?"

"I think you already know the answer to that."

Bo stands up, her face red, tears brimming under her lids "No. No way. Absolutely not."

"I know how difficult this must be for you. But you must understand, this is bigger than any of us. I believe Maddison told you about the war, that's why she's giving you The Six?" Father says, gesturing for Bo to sit down again.

Bo paces around the room, tears flowing down her cheeks as her head shakes a rhythmic 'no' at my parents.

"Bo? Sweetheart." My mother stands and reaches for her hand, but Bo yanks it away. Mother tries again, cradling her this time and Bo sinks into her arms sobbing into her shoulder, "She called it The Libra War, the fight for Balance and said she was giving me The Six because we need an elite army to fight it."

Bo pulls back, wiping her face, "And because of who I am, who I'm related to, she thinks I can bring the Mermaids back to help us."

Wait. What? Bo is related to a Mermaid? How?

"Indeed. It will take all of us to win."

Mother touches Bo's shoulder, "We were planning to tell Eden after the ceremony tomorrow. But there's no time now. There's been a development."

"What kind of development?"

"When the time comes, your elite soldiers will take their armies into combat and win the battles. But there is a much greater force that only immense power can defeat. Like Trey, Eden must inherit our essence too, or together they won't be strong enough to win the war."

"I can't," she says, and falls to the floor, tears flowing down her cheeks again. "Please, Eleanor, please don't make me."

"Your blood is the only source of Mermaid magic we have. It's the only way we can guarantee she Inherits."

"She'll blame me. I can't lose her."

"This isn't your fault. You're saving her. You're making her stronger. She's going to need you."

She puts her head in her hands, her whole body is shaking, then when she drops her hands, her face is still, emotionless, and I know that's the moment she decided to give it to them. "What do I tell her?"

"You don't," Father says. "She needs to hear this from

us. She needs to see our essence heads and our memories, so she knows this was our choice. That we made you. When she's had some time to heal, tell her to go to the chamber and find our essence heads."

Bo nods, wipes her face with her sleeve and says, "There's no other way?"

Mother shakes her head, "We could fight... Use your armies, even pull soldiers from other realms, and we would win battles. But she will never stop, and none of us are strong enough to take her down. Thousands would die for nothing. This way, only two lives are lost and we give you, the Libra Legion and the whole of Trutinor a chance at survival, a chance at winning and repairing our world. It *will* take all of you and more to win this war. You need Eden to Inherit, otherwise she won't be strong enough to make the final blow. She will die and then all our hope is lost. This is the only way we give her a chance, the only way we give all of you a chance at winning."

"Okay," Bo nods, "okay. I'll give you my blood."

And that's when mine runs cold. I remember Arden's words, '*Shifter blood has been found in the poison that killed your parents.*'

The scene races forward again, quicker this time; we are still in Bo's living room, but she has gone. Maddison is in front of us, hunched over a table by the back window, mixing ingredients. On the table are two vials of dark maroon liquid. Blood. Her eyes are as puffy and as blood-shot red as her hair. She drops her tools, and they clatter to the table as she looks up at Mother and Father.

Mother holds her hand out, "Maddison. We've been through this."

"I know... But I just wanted to say that we will win, you know? I promise you. Whatever it takes."

"I know, Mads." Mother walks over to the table and squeezes Maddison. When she lets go, steam rises from two conical glass jars. Maddison takes the vials of Bo's blood, and pours one into each which makes the smoke puff harder.

"I need a drop of blood from each of you," Maddison says. Mother and Father extend their index fingers. Maddison pricks them, and squeezes a drop into each jar.

"And you're certain that once you release Cassian from the Binding, she will be Bound to Trey?" Father says.

"If the binding seals, yes. Then the Last Fallon can sense the Imbalance it creates and she will ensure it is corrected."

"How sure are you it will seal?"

"Sure. The only thing that can prevent it now is if the First Fallon finds out and sabotages it. I have a contact that will smuggle Cassian's essence back to Trutinor via Eden herself."

My hand? That woman from Earth? She knows Maddison?

"Then we're ready."

Maddison hands each of them a jar, and hugs them once more.

"Until the next life," Mother says.

Maddison smiles through tear-streaked cheeks, "May your death be Balanced," she says, squeezes Mother's hand and leaves, sobs already rocking her shoulders.

Mother turns to Father, "Thank you for giving me everything I could ever have wanted, Lionel. A perfect life, a beautiful child, and more love than I could have dreamed of."

"This isn't goodbye. We will be together in the next life,

and the next, and every one until the universe draws its last breath."

"I'm scared," she says. "Not of dying, but for Eden. What she has to do, it's a burden greater than any Fallon should have to carry."

"I know. But she has the heart of a warrior; your heart," Father pulls Mother into his arms and kisses her. "She will save them, Eleanor."

"She has to," Mother says leaning against Father's chest.

"Are you ready?" he says, looking out at the mountain range. The sky is clear, the snow caps have shrunk in the lunchtime sun, but in the distance, thick white clouds are forming, ready to replace the melted snow. A Peregrine Falcon, with a streak of white down its back, swoops and dips between the castle turrets. It lands on one with a clear view of the window and then, a second later, Bo is sitting in its place watching my parents and sobbing. *Bo was there, right to the end.*

"I love you, Lionel."

"I love you too, Eleanor."

They drink the liquid in their glass jars in one go, wrap their arms around each other and kiss, deep, intense and filled with a love entrenched in their souls. Darkness clouds my vision. The threads detach, and the weight of her body falls away from mine. I remain standing. My lips, as Mother's were, are pressed against Father's, only now Father is Trey, and my lips are on his. I pull back, letting out a wailing cry as I collapse on the floor.

"I thought..." I say, but the words catch in my throat and stumble out between broken sobs, "this whole time... I thought they were murdered."

My chest spasms as the tears flow down my cheeks.

"I wanted to blame someone, to get revenge. But I can't,

and they're still gone and there's nothing I can do about it," I cry into Trey's chest.

"I know," he says, kneeling and wrapping me in his arms, "I know."

"I don't understand what they died for. I've never heard of any war. Who are they even fighting?" I say.

"That would be me," the First Fallon says, as she steps into the chamber and my blood curdles.

TWENTY-SIX

'The use of dark magic is prohibited for a reason; it has a way of betraying you.'

Excerpt – The Annals of Sorcery

I STAND UP, backing away from her until I hit the wall. My face drains of color leaving a slick of cold sweat on my brow.

Trey hasn't moved, he's standing tall like he's not afraid. Her milk-white face is hard, her violet eyes dark and protruding.

"Why are they fighting you? You're the First Fallon," he says.

"Strange, isn't it? You shouldn't listen to them, Trey

darling. They don't understand. I *am* Balance. I bring Balance to Trutinor. Without me, this world and Earth would descend into chaos."

"Then why are they fighting you?"

"Let's call it semantics."

"What's she talking about?" I breathe.

Her head snaps to the side, her gaze focusing on me, "So she speaks..." Her eyes fall to my arm, "Not much left of that little bracelet of yours, is there? Shame you couldn't seal it for my dear sister."

Her lips part as she bares perfect white teeth then she flicks her hand and my forearm sears with heat. I fall to my knees clutching my wrist as an entire inch of my Binding disintegrates into the air.

No, no, no.

"You'd better sort that out before it disappears. My sister would be so disappointed if you were to die... If *both* of you were to die."

Trey moves fast, hauling me to my feet and shouting, "Run."

"I'm not leaving you," I say.

"Run." This time it's a command, and his eyes burn like fire.

"No," I shout, but he is compelling me, forcing me forward towards the door. As he turns on the First Fallon, his grip on me fails.

"Cecilia... Cecilia... Listen to me." Trey's voice is spellbinding. His words slip through the chamber like silk, wrapping a hypnotic blur around all of us and filling my consciousness with commands.

Cecilia's face softens, her cheeks rounding.

I frown, glancing between Trey and the First Fallon.

Her body relaxes; her stance is docile, calm like she's a puppet and Trey the master. *I was right, he can compel her. But how?*

He shakes his head, telling me not to ask. So, I don't. He slides up to her, stares at her eyes which are glazed, unfocused, then he touches her cheek. "Forget," he says, and as he does, her eyes white out and her head slumps forward. The color drains from his skin making him wobble. I run to him grabbing his arm as his knees buckle.

"Hermia," he breathes, "Hermia."

At first, I don't understand; then I remember the train and the navy cog Hermia gave me. I dig into my pockets until I find it and press the gold middle.

"Hermia? Trey needs you," I say into the cog.

Within seconds, there's a puff of navy smoke in the middle of the chamber and Hermia appears. She scans the room her face hardening. Did I make a huge mistake calling her? Hermia's the First Fallon's closest companion, and Trey just ripped out part of Cecilia's mind.

"What happened?" she says, coming to my aide, and I breathe a sigh of relief as she helps me walk Trey to the exit.

"She..." I pause, thinking through the last ten minutes, "I can't believe I'm going to say this, but I think if Trey hadn't stopped her she might have killed us."

Hermia nods, "Now that she knows someone's been plotting to fulfill the prophecy, she's furious. None of you are safe. Did Trey wipe her?"

I halt, and turn to her across Trey, "Yeah, but how...?"

"Not the first time, won't be the last. Listen. You must get to Rozalyn. She's the only one that can help you now. You must seal that Binding; it's the only way you'll get time to regroup. Trey won't be able to compel Cecilia forever.

Eventually, she will discover what he's been doing all these years and then the real war will start."

"How are we supposed to get to Obex to find her?"

"I'll take you," she says as we break out of the chambers and into the school grounds. "Tomorrow. In the morning once I've sorted Cecilia."

She glances at my Binding scar, and then says, "Perhaps we should make that a couple of hours. I'll find you; I can track you using the cog I gave you."

With that, there's another puff of navy, and she's gone. Then, Trey collapses on the floor.

I kneel at his side, brushing stray hairs away from his face. His skin is so pale, like essence heads drained of life. The thought of losing him makes my chest constrict.

"Are you okay?" I ask.

He nods and pulls himself to a sitting position.

"How did you compel her?"

"She doesn't know I can do it. It was an accident the first time. I was so cross with her because she forbade me from seeing you, then it just sort of happened. It was like I had all this extra power but not from the vault; this was different, it wasn't dark. It was protective. I tried again, and it worked. But each time it would cost me so much energy because she's so powerful. It took everything I had. So, I couldn't be careless with it, I wasn't sure if the effect would last, or if she would find out what I was doing. Cecilia didn't, but Hermia did. I thought she was going to tell her what I'd done, but instead, she made me swear to use it sparingly because it was a gift and I'd never know when I might need it. Hermia's on our side, she always has been. From then on, I only used it when I wanted to see you. That's how I got to the lake each year."

"Are you okay now?" I say, as I help him up, noticing the color's already returning to his cheeks.

"I'll be fine. The older I get, the stronger I am and the quicker the exhaustion passes."

"Trey?" Evelyn's voice cuts through the night air. She and Victor are standing on a path that leads back to the school entrance. "Where have you been? Arden's been looking for you two."

"Eden, excuse me," Trey says standing up. Without so much as a glance at me, he heads towards the school entrance with Evelyn. I glare at their backs. I was just starting to forgive him, but she reminds me of what he did, and what we will never have. Try as I might to suppress it, an acid tang of resentment settles in my chest.

"Eden?" Victor says.

"Victor. Hi," I say, feeling guilty I hadn't even noticed he was still there.

His pale features look worse than usual against the evening light. In fact, as I take him in, I don't think I've ever seen him look this sick. His skin is translucent, lifeless and faded like a corpse. He surprises me by taking my hand in his.

"Eden..." he starts, "have you checked your Binding? Mine shrank suddenly in the last half an hour."

I flash back to the First Fallon ripping part of my scar away and shudder.

"I know, me too," I say, and decide not to tell him it might have been my fault for antagonizing the First Fallon.

"There's less than half left, we haven't got much time to sort this out," he says. "I know you don't want to kill anyone, but really..." he squeezes my hand, "we don't have much choice. We can't let that half-human, whatever he is, get in the way of our future."

I scan his face, but his expression remains blank. *He still doesn't know who Cassian is?*

"Victor, have you spoken to your mother recently?"

"No, she was with Bo and Cassian last I checked. I was busy with the F... Umm, well I was busy."

"Well, there's something you should know."

"Wait," he says, "just wait. About what I said before the ceremony... You know I mean it, right?"

"The whole, 'we'd make a great team' thing?"

He nods, "I protected you from the dome, didn't I?" he says.

The dome was going to let me through anyway, I think. But I let him take the credit.

"But we can't be together or be a team unless we fix our Binding. Me and you, Eden. Tonight. Let's just sneak into the cell block and end him."

I rub my face; this isn't the sort of thing I should be telling Victor. Maddison should.

"It's more complicated than that. You can't just kill him, Victor."

"Why not?"

Why is he so stupid?

"Seriously, have you seen the resemblance between you? How you have the same eyes, the same hair? He's just a bit bigger and taller and..."

"And more handsome? Is that what you were going to say?"

I shift on the spot; that was what I was going to say, but I don't want to hurt Victor's feelings.

"No, I was going to say, 'and he's your brother.'"

His mouth drops and he takes a backward step. His face darkens; he grabs my hand, pulls me into a corner where two school walls meet, and steps in front of me, blocking me in.

"Eden," he says, stroking a few loose hairs behind my ear, "we're meant to be together, you and me. I don't care who that human rat is. He's still going to die. You're mine. You're meant to be mine. And you're going be mine whether I have to kill my estranged brother or not."

I swallow hard. My legs scream for me to run, but Victor obstructs the way. His hand slips up to cup my neck and where he touches my skin it feels hot, dirty, diseased.

"Victor, don't," I say, placing my hand on his chest.

"Don't what? We've been waiting for this for seventeen years, to give ourselves to each other. To continue our Fallon line."

"Not like this. Not out here."

He steps closer, leans in and kisses my neck, his dog breath trickling over my skin. "You need to understand we're meant to be together; I'm not going to let anyone else have you. This is the only way you'll see."

"Victor. Stop. I said no."

"And I said yes. Not everything is about you. I've waited a long time for you... For us to be together. And now we are, I'm done being patient."

He pulls both my hands above my head, and inhales the scent of my skin. I tug my hands down, but his fist has shifted into a clawed paw. His grip is so tight I can't release myself.

"Victor, I SAID NO," the panic is sharp and clear in my voice.

"I love you, Eden," he says. But his words are hollow and at that moment, I know he's lying. When you hear those words for the first time, they're meant to fill you with tingles and warmth and summer roses. Real love leaves a signature on your soul, a piece of the other person that stays with you, even when they're gone. But his words fill me with fear. I saw it when we were being Bound, the moment he understood what lurked inside me. The power it gives me, the power it could give him. He doesn't want me. He wants what's in the vault.

When his mouth finds mine, fear grips me. I try to force him back, but with my arms locked above my head and my palms pressed flat against each other, I can't use my power against him. His remaining hand roams across my chest. Bile rises in my throat, a wave of bitter sickness rolling around my stomach. He pushes his lips over my mouth again and again.

He squeezes at my breasts, and his hand slips to my trouser button and instinct floods my system with adrenaline.

I kick his shin as hard as I can. He flinches, but stays upright and knocks my legs out sideways wedging his feet next to mine, so my legs stay apart and I can't use them to defend myself.

When he pushes his lips over mine, I bite down, hard. He yelps, releasing my mouth, so I scream, loud and fast, hoping he's still in earshot. "TREY, HELP?"

"Oh, yes. Trey. So, Evelyn was right. There is something between you two?"

"You've been speaking to her?"

"We have a mutual interest, something we could both benefit from," he says, squeezing my wrists.

"I have this little relic, a forbidden magic kept by the First Fallon," he pulls out a black tube. It's rigid at first, and then flops. Despite its black texture, it's silky and shines under the spot lights attached to the school building.

"What is that?"

"A Jugo. One of the only ones left in existence. Unlike a Binding, our lives aren't linked. If I die, you'll still survive and be Bound to the rat. But not if we use a Jugo." He flicks his wrist, and the Jugo cracks into a spear, each end pointed like a needle. "When I showed Evelyn, she suggested I Bind my life to Trey's. That way you would be forced to kill Cassian and spend an eternity with me, while she was with Trey. But I don't care what she wants. I have a much better idea. I'll just Bind myself to you. You can't kill me then and my life is your life. Which means your life is mine."

"You mean my power?" I breathe, a cold tightness gripping my chest.

He grins then stabs the spear into his neck making half of it snap off. His eyes roll back as the dark shiny liquid seeps into his skin.

"NO," I shriek, and wriggle harder under his hold.

Trey appears, with Evelyn by his side. Her lips pull into a sneer as she spots the black liquid on Victor's neck.

Trey runs over and pulls him off me. The liquid on his neck is dissolving and he's come to his senses. He punches Trey, hitting him in the jaw, which sends him stumbling back. Then he rounds on me; one hand grabs my neck, the other holds the remains of the Jugo spike and aims it straight at my artery. He grabs my face and kisses me.

"No," Evelyn shrieks pulling out her wand and aiming it at his head, "you swore, Victor."

Victor's head snaps back at a strange angle and a wisp of green magic originating from Evelyn's wand loops around his scalp.

"I said, no," her voice is deep, full of his betrayal.

Trey's hand is on Victor's throat; his piercing blue eyes have vanished, replaced with blood red ones. His shoulders heave with ragged breaths and deep lines cut rage into his face. I know that look. The wild, uncontrolled anger. Trey's vault is open. Eve flicks her wrist. I fire a bolt of electricity at her, but it's too late.

The green wisp releases Victor's head and attaches to the Jugo spike. But as she drops to the floor unconscious, the wisp flies straight into Trey's neck making his red eyes roll back.

TWENTY-SEVEN

Eleanor East, Private Journal.

12TH FEBRUARY, 2009

LIONEL and I have been watching Eden play today. She's drawn to the Luchelli's eldest son. Dear, sweet boy he is. But I am worried; there are already intense rumors that Eden's Potential is Victor. Not Trey. Yet I see the way she looks at him. She is unaware, of course, too young to understand, but there is already love in her heart. I know, because it's the same way I looked at Lionel. I've told Arden of my concerns. He revealed something startling. He believes the First is meddling with the Bindings, picking and choosing who she thinks fits best. If it is true, then her desire for Balance has gone too far. I am confident she will not Bind Eden to another because there are some 'loves' stronger than all of us, even her.

I ZAP VICTOR, knocking him unconscious and pry Trey's hand from his throat, letting him drop to the floor. The liquid on Trey's neck has almost gone. There's nothing I can do to stop the link now, so I take his hand and pull him into the edge of the Ancient Forest surrounding the school.

Strain pulls at Trey's forehead; his blood red eyes are hard with fury. But he doesn't resist me dragging him away. The trees thicken, fast. It's late, maybe eleven o'clock already and with such dense trees, what little moonlight there is, dims, plunging us into darkness. I slow to a walk and throw a ball of fire out, making it hover above us, illuminating the path.

After ten minutes of walking, I stop at the base of a tree that's so large I can't see the top. I run my hand over the dark brown cavernous ridges wondering how many years it's stood there watching Trutinor and how many secrets it must carry. When the light dims, I wave my hand and stop the ball of fire floating off. It returns and hovers above us projecting dark shadows over Trey's face. I lean back on the tree, making the foliage underfoot rustle. I check Trey's neck, the Jugo's gone. My jaw flexes; I was too slow – Evelyn made sure Victor's life is linked to Trey's and I didn't stop her in time. Other than a bruised cheek, Trey seems fine.

"Are you in there, Trey?" I say, knowing how lost I get in my own mind when the vault opens.

I reach out to touch him, but he steps back. His breathing is back to normal, though his face is still rigid.

"I shouldn't have lost control," he says shaking his head.

"It's fine; it happens all the time to me."

"No. It was... I don't know. I've never lost control like

that before." He squeezes his eyes shut, tugs his hand through his hair and takes a deep breath. When he looks at me again, the softness has returned and his red eyes have vanished.

"Well, you've had longer to practice controlling it. I bet it's always like that; you just can't remember because it's been a while."

"No...," he says, stepping closer to me, "this was different. It was like you were in my head. The vault snapped because it wanted to protect you. Normally, it only breaks because I want to hurt someone."

He reaches for my hand, then stops and looks up at me, as if asking my permission. I suck my lip in. Have I forgiven him? I want to be angry with him. But no matter what I do, I'm pulled towards him like an anchor to a ship. The way my heart's racing tells me it still aches for him like it has my whole life. My mother said I needed Trey, that we could only win this war together. Before she left me that last time, she told me to follow my heart. Can I ignore that?

Even though I think better of it, I thread my fingers through his.

Trey's body relaxes as he wraps my hands around his waist and pulls me into a hug. At first, I'm stiff, the last pieces of his betrayal nestling inside the bruises on my heart. But when he says, "I've missed you, I thought I'd lost you," and leans his cheek onto my head, my resolve fails and I snuggle into his arms. I've missed him too, but there's something I still want to know.

"Why did you kiss Evelyn the way you did before the Binding ceremony?"

He pulls back so that he can see me.

"I don't have feelings for Evelyn. I never have."

"Then, why?"

"You really don't know?"

I shrug. "Because I was hurting," he says, "you said you were done with me, with us...I couldn't handle the thought of never being with you again. Then when I saw you, saw you looking at Evelyn...I just. I don't know. I'm sorry. There's no excuse; I was an asshole..."

"Yeah. You were."

"You make me feel things I can't control. I'm not used to that, I...I..."

"You take it all away?"

He's silent and can't look at me. It's the closest thing I'll get to a confession. He never dealt with any significant moments in his life. Not his mom's death, his Inheritance, being Bound to Evelyn, or losing me. He's never dealt with anything that makes him feel something.

He looks at me, a yearning in his eyes that reaches into his heart. His smile is soft, as he grasps my cheek and pulls my chin up towards his lips. Butterflies make my stomach flip as they dance around my insides. His hand is warm against my cheek and soft against my skin. The trees around us rustle as a breeze passes through the forest. Somewhere in the distance an owl hoots and animals rustle in the undergrowth.

He sighs and says, "Yes. Because I take it all away. Everything except you. You're the only thing I've ever felt. The only thing I can't stop feeling."

His breath trickles over my skin as he moves closer to my lips.

"Trey, wait. We can't," I say, pulling myself together. "If you kiss me, it will change everything."

"Everything's already changed. As soon as I saw you on

stage, I knew we were meant to be together. Then your double Binding. Your mother even said it in her memories - we have to work together."

The mention of my mother reminds me I have the prophecy cog in my pocket. I pull out the smooth silver cog and show it to him.

"How do we open it?" he says, turning it over.

"My guess is blood. It's always blood," I say, thinking of my parents.

Trey searches the ground until he finds a sharp rock. He uses it to cut his index finger and smear the blood over the cog, then he hands me the stone, and I do the same.

The cog rattles in my hand and plummets to the floor. A cone shaped shaft of light projects up from the cog, lighting up the forest. Strange letters and shapes appear in the middle scrolling through what looks like dozens of old languages until it settles on one we understand. It projects text, which scrolls as we read.

Where there is Balance, there is Imbalance.

The oldest law of the universe.

Two sisters. Two halves. One of light, the other of dark. Sisters born to protect the universe, sworn to keep it Balanced; equal parts, Balance to Imbalance.

Where there is Balance, there must be Imbalance.

*But the sister of light will fail; in her search
    for Balance, she will create disparity in
    the universe. Bringing with it, not utopia
    but the crumbling of fabric between
    worlds and universal destruction.*

*A new pair, one of the East and one of the
    South will be born, fated to be Bound
    and bring Balance to the universe once
    more: the First Couple, two halves of one
    soul. Equal parts Balance to Imbalance,
    light to dark, and able to Inherit power.
    Together they will unite with the sister
    of darkness and wage war on the sister
    of light.*

*But they will face a grave choice. Their
    decision will lead either to the defeat of
    the sister of light and restoration of
    Balance to all the realms or the end of
    the universe and all life within it.*

THE PROJECTION DISAPPEARS, and the cog goes dark. I pick it up and return it to my pocket.

"She knows," Trey says, "the First Fallon knows, that's why we're not Bound to each other." He pouts his lips and folds his arms, all smug. "I told you we were meant to be together."

"Really?" I say, using my best impression of Trey's voice, "you choose now to pull the 'I told you so' card?"

He laughs and pulls me back into his arms, putting his lips right where they were before I pulled the cog out.

"Come on, seriously. The prophecy is wrong. How can it be talking about us when you're Bound to someone else?"

"Details, details," he says, brushing his lips over my cheek.

"Yeah but, details that kinda matter."

He swaps sides, grazing his lips over that cheek and down my neck.

"You can't take back a first kiss..." I say.

He laughs in the crook of my neck, then inches round, placing his lips so close to mine they almost touch.

"Technically, this isn't our first kiss. And if there's one thing I am certain of, it's that it definitely won't be our last. Bound to Evelyn or not, my soul will spend eons kissing you. I might not feel a lot but that, I know deep in my bones. I ache for you, Eden. My insides yearn when we're apart. I know I've spent every lifetime that's ever been with you and I know I'll spend it with you in every one to come because I'll live each life searching for you. For that one moment when my soul is Bound and united with yours, and I get to hold you. As mine, only mine. For that perfect moment when I get to kiss you again."

He closes his eyes, and I sink into his arms. Finally, his lips meet mine. Hard at first, as urgent as his words, then they slow and soften, sending shivers sweeping over my body. His guard drops, opening the floodgate to his emotions, and like the hospital room and the Binding Ceremony, they project on to me. Heat, lust and love, and a deep hunger that pours over my body making a strange silky electricity pulse at my fingertips. The world slows, our kiss stretching over a thousand lifetimes. And I know I've been waiting for this moment too. His kiss is as familiar as it is new. That's when I realize he's right. We are meant for each other; we were always meant for each other.

I lose myself in his arms. And the forest, the chirping of night insects and the fireball crackling above us all disappear in the depths of his touch.

TWENTY-EIGHT

True love touches even the coldest souls –
Balance Proverb

WHEN WE DISENTANGLE OURSELVES, everything's different. There's an unspoken connection between us. A knowing determination; someone, *and I think Trey's right, the First Fallon's*, wronged us. We're meant to be Bound; I know that now. I don't know how to undo the past or the Binding that's been forced upon me. But what I do know, what we both know, is that neither of us will stop until we find a way to fix this.

As we break out of the forest and back into Keepers School grounds, I check my CogTracker. It's close to midnight and the gardens are empty except for the occasional rustle in the bushes. The chill of the West's spring night blows a draft under my t-shirt making me shiver.

"Do you think we should go find them?" I say, glancing at the patch of grass Victor and Evelyn had collapsed on.

"Probably," Trey says, "But first..." He nods in the direction of a lone figure walking out of the school entrance and down a cobbled path towards an area out of bounds to students, which I assume, is where he set up the Faraday cage for Cassian.

"You want to ask him about the prophecy?"

"No. About the war, the army. I'm on the Council, why don't I know about it?"

He picks up his pace until he reaches Arden and taps his shoulder. "You lied," Trey says.

Arden's eyes skip between us. I expect him to ask Trey what he means, or maybe deny it, but instead, he flattens his green robes over his stomach and says, "I've lied about a lot of things in my life, Trey, for many different reasons. Which lie are you referring to?"

"The Libra..." Trey starts, but Arden cuts him off with a sharp look.

"Not here. Come with me." He continues heading down the cobbled path towards a small cottage made of the same sandstone as the school. When we step through the front door, Arden locks it and waves his wand around the door frame, sealing it with magic. We're in a single room. It's small, dim and empty. In the center of the room is a hatch in the floor. He opens the hatch and a set of stairs appear winding downwards.

"Once we're through the hatch, it's safe to talk," Arden says and gestures for us to enter.

The stairs lead to an entrance hall, a kitchen, a couple of living rooms, a couple more closed doors, and another set of stairs that lead down instead of up.

"It's an upside-down house," Arden says, as he seals the

hatch shut. "And it's magic proof. No powers work down here, not even the First Fallon's."

"Which means no one can listen in?" I ask.

"Exactly. We use it as the Libra Legion's main safe house."

He leads us into a living room, takes off his robes and sits, fussing with his jeans belt and repositioning it under his belly to get comfortable. I always find it odd seeing Arden out of official robes. Jeans don't suit him.

"Have you eaten?" he says.

I shake my head, even though I'm not that hungry. He pulls out his CogTracker, taps a few buttons and a few minutes later a Sorcerer brings a couple of plates of food and drink in. The sumptuous smell of warm salty chicken and garlic changes my mind and suddenly, I'm ravenous.

"You must have questions," he says.

"How long has this been going on?" I ask, reaching for the plate.

"There have been whisperings about the First Fallon for centuries. Secret groups, investigations. But no one could prove anything until Trey was born. That's when the prophecy first appeared. Call it chance, or maybe fate. But I was working in the Binding Chamber as Lani was giving birth. The moment he was born, the prophecy was created and it floated to the surface of the barrel cog they're held in. I stopped what I was doing and took it out. More out of curiosity than anything because I'd never seen movement in the prophecy cog. I used my wand to slice my hand and draw blood to open it. That was the first real proof we had that the First Fallon wasn't who we thought she was. That our world wasn't as we thought. I had to be careful at first. I wasn't sure who to trust. But over time, we built a small network of people. Lionel, Eleanor, Lani, Kale, Maddison,

Israel and Hermia. There are others of course, but we are the founding members."

"If this has been going on for nearly twenty years, why haven't you stopped her already? Or if you can't take her down, then why haven't you taken her power and told the whole of Trutinor who she really is?" Trey says.

He stretches his arms into a yawn, takes a band off his wrist and pulls his hair back into a loose knot. It shows off his chiseled jaw, making his eyes pop and my cheeks burn. I push my plate away and wait until my stomach stops flip flopping.

"We tried. With small groups of people at first, loved ones, relatives. But you have to understand. Trutinor is founded on an institution that is thousands of years old. The First Fallon is ancient; she's engrained her beliefs into everything we do."

"They rejected what you were saying?"

Arden nods, his lips pinching for a moment before he says, "It caused uprising between family members. Fights, revolts, outright disconnection from us. So, we stopped trying. A revolution takes time. We had to gather members, evidence, hard irrefutable facts that the First Fallon was rigging the Bindings and lying to us about what our true purpose is."

"And now?" I ask.

"Now our ranks have grown substantially but not enough to declare war on the most powerful being in Trutinor."

"So, what now?" Trey says.

"We need to fulfill your prophecy."

"So, it is true then?" I say, fiddling with my hands, a flicker of hope rising in my chest.

"Without a doubt."

"How do we fulfill it?" I ask, "we're Bound to different people, my Binding is shrinking, and I'm going to die if we don't fix it."

He nods, "I know I can't help you but the Last Fallon can."

I cast Trey a sideways look, knowing the myth and danger that surrounds Obex.

"That's why Hermia wanted us to go?"

He nods again, and I wonder where she is. "She's coming for us. She took the First Fallon back to her quarters and said she would meet us here."

There's an explosion. The house above shudders making the plates shake on the coffee table.

Maddison runs into the room, her face white, her hair wild and harried. "Victor is here," she says, panting, then her eyes focus on me.

"Please, Eden. Take Cassian to the Last Fallon, find a way to save them both."

My arm throbs. I grab my wrist as another burning sensation charges through my wrist and the Binding scar shrinks another centimeter.

"Eden, please. There isn't time."

"Okay," I say standing, "okay, I'll try."

"Maddison, release Cassian and take him out the rear exit," Arden says drawing out his wand, "Trey, Eden, we'll go out the front. I'll try to talk Victor down and cover so you two can make a run for it."

Another explosion booms above us.

"Go, now," he says, and Maddison disappears.

Arden unseals the door, and pulls it open a fraction. Something explodes to the side of the door and he jerks back. When he's recovered, he cracks the door open a bit more and grits his teeth.

"They've been in the Guild," he says, pushing his sleeves up. "Stolen element orbs."

"He's throwing fire bombs? How the hell did he make them? I didn't know you could harness element magic."

"You can't... Couldn't. Franklin Seffi is studying element magic to see if we can weaponize it against the First Fallon."

"Right," I say, touching Arden's shoulder and I squeeze past him. "I'm going, I can counter their attacks. You get my back and, Trey, you sneak around the back and cover for me when I make a run for it. Oh, and Arden...?"

"Yes?"

"If you need to, go for Victor's pawed-hand. It's the weaker of the two."

I poke my fists out the door first, firing off a jet of water from one hand and pulses of electricity from the other, enough to stun, not to kill.

Victor, Trat and two more of his Shifter friends are standing in the middle of the school grounds, on a green slope in front of the cottage. They're laughing at me as they bounce the fire orbs up and down. Behind them, the sandy school mansion looms dark and foreboding, unlike its usual homely feel.

Victor stops laughing when he sees me, his eyes narrow and I'm sure I see him mouth the word 'bitch.'

The two friends break off and run at me, dropping to the floor and shifting as they hit the grass. One's a wolf, the other a Doberman.

Trey disappears around the side of the building. Arden's on my left flank, firing green threads of magic like arrows at the boys.

The Doberman's fast; he leaps at me, and I barely

scrabble out of the way. I shoot a pulse of electricity and clip its front leg hitting him off balance.

Victor throws another fire orb straight at the front of the cottage. It bounces off, and explodes to Arden's left against a wall. Bits of stone and grass fly into the air and when Arden stands, the flames reflect in his eyes; he's furious. He discharges five fast strands of dark green magic – whatever spell he's using is going to hurt. Victor and Trat duck and dive, but Trat slips and one hits his shoulder sending him reeling back. Victor reaches out to catch him as a second strand clips his hip and knocks him to the ground.

"Go," Arden shouts at me, "I got this."

Cassian and Trey are standing a way to the side of the building. Next to them, Hermia's orange hair burns bright in the darkness. I turn to run, but a stabbing bites into my calf. I snap around; the Doberman's teeth have sunk into my leg. I pump him full of electricity and he yelps, whimpering off.

I set off, trying to run, but my leg is streaming with blood and I can't do much more than hobble.

Trey runs to me and lifts me into his arms. Hermia grabs hold of the three of us, and a plume of navy smoke fills the air as she portals us away.

TWENTY-NINE

'The Last Fallon died three thousand years ago, may she rest in peace. She had a terminal case of Alteritus and fought a hard battle for two thousand years. My heart broke the day she left us.'

Teachings of the First Fallon

THEY RUN. Fast. I hobble as quick as I can to keep up. My ribs burn as much as my wrist, which has shrunk again. There's less than a quarter of our Binding left. Hours of time, not days, and the more it depletes, the quicker it seems to shrink. My leg throbs, but the blood has at least dried.

"Where are we going?" Cassian asks, panting and breaking the silence I hadn't even realized we were in.

"North," Trey says, "then out."

"Out?" Cassian asks as we enter Lunar City's station and run straight to the main platform where Trey's train is sitting. He pulls the door shut then heads straight to the engine room and seconds later, the train is moving. Minutes after that, Hermia arrives in a ball of smoke in the middle of the carriage. Her hair is in disarray and her uniform on the slant.

"I hate moving targets," she says, "but I got what we needed."

She ambles behind Trey's bar, where all I can see is the top of her bright orange curls bobbing up and down to the clink of glass. When she reappears, she's holding two glasses full to the brim with a green liquid sloshing around the rim. Cassian edges his hand forward as if to take one, but Hermia frowns at him and steps back downing the liquid in one. Then, still glaring at him, she proceeds to guzzle the second, before sliding the empty glasses across the booth table, making Cassian's cheeks an amusing shade of pink.

Hermia ignores him and squints at my forearm, "You're running out of time."

"I know."

"The First Fallon said one of us had to die to fix it."

"But you want another solution?"

"If there is one, yes."

Her lips press together as if she doubts there is another solution.

"Well if anyone knows, it's Rozalyn. But I can only take two of you. I don't approve of hitchhikers, and I only grabbed two barrier pills."

I shrug an apology at Cassian, who grimaces, "Just find a way for us all to stay alive."

"I'll try."

"That's all I ask," he says.

"Good. You two take these..." Hermia says, and hands Trey and I a black pill each.

"What is it?" I ask, eyeing its shiny coating.

"Time works differently inside Obex. It will stop your bodies going into slow motion and help you move freely. It's what all the Steampunk Transporters have to take during training."

"Sounds like there's a 'but'?"

"There is."

"Go on..."

"Normally, when you pass through the barrier, you don't see anything. With the pill, you will. You'll see *everything,* between every world, good and bad." She rubs her throat.

"So, the but is that, once we see Obex, we can't unsee it?" I say, glancing at Trey. That was his same warning in the Binding Chamber, which makes me dread what I'll see in Obex.

In a strange way, my parents' deaths feel bittersweet. I'm relieved they weren't murdered, but I can't decide if the truth is worse. I rub my wrist; there's only a couple of inches of scar left, I can't turn back unless I want to die too.

"Last chance to change your mind," Hermia says.

"I'm going."

Hermia looks to Trey.

"Then I'm going too."

We swallow the pills as Hermia says, "Excellent. You should know Obex is where the underworlds, the shadow-lands and all the worlds 'between' converge. Stay close to me because getting lost is a real possibility. Those streets are all identical and infinite. But more than anything, there are creatures in there you do not want to get lost with. Stay close, okay?"

We both nod, and my stomach tightens.

"One minute to the barrier," Magnus says through the speakers.

The train lurches forward, increasing its speed to break through the fabric.

"Be safe, and don't move," I say to Cassian.

He rolls his eyes, "Like I could if I wanted."

Then we hit the fabric, and I'm thrown to the floor with Trey.

"Oh," Hermia says, chuckling to herself, her orange locks bouncing with her shoulders, "I forgot to say hold on."

Glaring at her as I pick myself up, I catch sight of Cassian's face. Even though his eyes are blinking in slow motion, he seems still, like the smooth surface of the ocean with a raging current hidden beneath.

It takes me a minute to realize that while he is stuck, I'm not. I can't help but flap my arms and legs just to check they all move as normal. They do. Outside the window, the white mist quivers and throbs with things that are just out of sight; we're still in the barrier.

"Do I want to know what kind of magic was in that pill?" I say to Hermia.

"Not really."

"Okay, good. Let's keep it that way."

The train stops and Magnus' voice drifts through the speakers.

"Good luck, sir," he coughs, clearing his throat and adds, in a much quieter tone, "and umm, you too, Fallon East."

"Aww, look. You're finally growing on him," Trey says smirking.

Hermia opens the train door and as the seal breaks, steam hisses into the carriage.

"I see the resemblance to Kato now," I say, glancing back at him as I walk off the train.

Outside our vision's obstructed by dense fog. The air is damp and thick with a cold that burrows into my bones.

Hermia pulls out a small brass tube and presses a button on the edge. The tube whirrs and sucks the mist inside it clearing our view.

As the mist vanishes, the air changes. It's hot, and still, and even the stray particles of dust are frozen mid-air. It's like everyone upped and left suddenly, discarding this place to rot centuries ago. Only it didn't rot; it remained unchanged. A sheen of sweat clings to my skin. I glance over my shoulder, expecting to see Trey's train and a platform, but the train is gone and we're in the middle of a street.

"I told you, things work differently here. The streets might be infinite, but that doesn't mean they stay still," Hermia says as if answering my confusion. "Don't lose sight of me; it's quite a walk. This is the good end, but Rozalyn is in the bad. Oh, and before I forget, welcome to Obex." She stalks off at a pace I struggle to keep up with.

A gloomy orange hue kisses the skyline. It's darker than twilight but not quite nighttime either, and it casts shadows over everything. The shadows seem to crawl and it makes my stomach uneasy.

I scan the street as we jog to keep up with Hermia. It reminds me of some old sepia photographs I saw in an Earth history class a few months ago. The pavement is lined with black iron railings like Victorian London and has rows of terraced town houses that stand side by side and stretch far into the distance. Each house has a set of peaked windows and silky-white marble pillars supporting grand porches.

When I think she's far enough in front she can't hear, I lean into Trey and ask the question that's been bugging me since she turned up in the Binding Chamber.

"Isn't she risking a lot playing double agent between you and the First Fallon?"

"She's risking everything," Trey says.

"Then why?"

"Because Cecilia took everything and everyone from her as punishment. She's never told me what she did to deserve it. But whatever it was, it made Cecilia angry enough to kill her son and husband for it."

I pause and swallow hard, seeing her in a new light for the first time. I wonder if the real reason she comes to Obex on behalf of the Libra Legion, is because she's hoping, however unlikely, to find her family down here.

"But why stay and work for the First Fallon if she did that to her?" I say.

Hermia stops and turns to face us, "The same reason we all do. Fear. Repression. And overwhelming hope that one day there will be someone strong enough to beat her. You don't win a war with a single battle. We're all meant to make choices and sacrifices, Eden. This is mine. And one day, you will make yours."

I stare after her as she stalks off. I've already lost my parents, how much more can I lose?

Hooves click-clack against the street cobbles snapping me out of my daze. Trey urges me into a jog, and as we catch up to Hermia, an empty black carriage with red trimmings appears on our street, pulled by two horses. When they draw near, I lean forward to get a better look and it makes me lose my footing. As I steady myself, I grip Trey's arm and my mouth runs dry. The horses have no heads, just a neck that protrudes out and up, and then... Nothing. They clip-clop past, and my hand automatically covers my mouth. There are dark lacerations across the horses' backs and legs. Each one is weeping an abundance of green ooze that smells like soured meat. From their neck stumps, a continuous drip of blood falls to the floor, leaving a trail after them.

"Come on," Hermia says, tugging me away and guiding us down a set of stone steps onto another street. "We're in luck; there's a short cut today."

This street looks identical to the last, but instead of town houses either side, there's a park on the right. It's gated with the same black spiky iron railings as before. Only these sweep into the sky like outstretched fingers. Random boulders scatter the park.

I turn to Hermia to ask her what the rocks are, but the hairs on my arms quiver. Out of the corner of my eye, one of the rocks moves. Only, it isn't a rock, it's a person, of sorts.

Masses of black fabric drape over its back and as it moves, its head pokes out, which makes me grip Trey's arm so tight I dig my nails in. Its skin is a soft silver, a web of purple veins dappled over it. Its head is bald, eye sockets empty and its mouth hangs so far down its jaw can't be connected.

"What are they?" I whisper.

"Them? Oh, they're nothing, just Alteritus sufferers from before we had a cure. But it's not the creatures you can see that you should worry about," Hermia says. She doesn't tell me what I should be worried about, but she doesn't need to. I have a permanent set of goosebumps on my neck; the shadows move just enough I can't get rid of them because someone or something is watching us, following us, or more likely, hunting us.

Trey glances behind us, then steps closer to me. Whatever he sees, makes him push me on faster. I don't look back.

"Not far."

We pull into a narrow street, and descend another flight of stairs and what little light there is, disappears. Hermia pulls out the same brass tube she used earlier and presses another button. Light bursts from the end illuminating the street. I wish it hadn't. We're in a dead end, with a single black door. On it, embossed in red, are the five State symbols. As well as a sixth, which has a Mermaid on it, that I assume is Aurora's lost symbol. And in the middle of the alley are three human-shaped carcasses.

"Can't enter," Hermia says, "plausible deniability. I'll stay here."

"Right," I say, sounding more confident than I am.

We step over the abandoned bodies; their ribs are cracked open, their entrails missing and yet, their eyes continue to follow us.

The street is a tacky patch work of blood and remains and smells like a musty abattoir.

The door swings open as we reach it, welcoming us into a cool dark room. My heart throbs in my ears, racing almost as fast as my breathing.

A loud click from behind makes me flinch. The door's vanished, there's no way out.

The room's walls are made of a reflective surface, like glass, but I can't see out. Someone can see in though because my skin crawls the way it only does when you're being watched.

In the middle of the room is a solitary throne. I blink, and a body appears in it, or maybe it was always there. The figure is smiling at me with a set of silver spikes for teeth and clawed hands that clutch half-eaten organs. Her Imbalanced red wine-colored eyes bore into me. I've seen her twice before, once in my final sim, and once on Trey's train as we crossed the barrier.

"Eden East, Trey Luchelli," the Last Fallon says, standing up and crossing the space between us with the same floating grace as her sister. "At last."

THIRTY

'Where there is Balance, there must be Imbalance.'
Last Law - The Book of Imbalance

"WELCOME TO OBEX, land of the banished, broken and recently deceased," the Last Fallon says, smiling to herself. Her voice rasps like sandpaper on granite as she towers over both Trey and I.

The stone floor and damp chill in the air makes the room feel like a medieval prison. In the low light, she stands out like a porcelain blemish wearing the same style of white flowing dress as her sister. But the Last Fallon is corseted in the middle and covered in splatters and smears of dark red spots, which I assume is from her raw meat dinner. Like her sister, her skin is pale, but that's where the similarity ends.

Her hair, like her eyes, is blood red and pulled into a tight bun. But it's her mouth full of pointed teeth that makes my scalp prickle.

"I didn't used to look like this," she says as if she's reading my mind.

"What happened?" I ask, slow, tentative, unsure of how to approach her.

"Oh, come now, you know that story. My sister banished me. And now you and your Keepers send all the Imbalance from Earth and Trutinor here."

Trey and I look at each other, but it's Trey that answers.

"We don't send it here. Our Keepers are trained to destroy it."

The Last Fallon snorts, and narrows her eyes to examine Trey, "Imbalance, like Balance, is energy. You can't destroy energy, any more than you can Imbalance. Only manipulate it, change it, or send it somewhere else. Cecilia chose here, and now my world is deteriorating...dying, consuming itself in bad energy. A beautifully destructive but achingly slow death that my dear sister gets to watch from her Trutinor-shaped prison."

"But that's what we're meant to do," I say, my brow wrinkling, "whether it's destroyed or moved, we're meant to get rid of it. It's the first law of the Book of Balance."

Her eyes snap to my face, her lips curling into a thin smile and my confidence abandons me. She moves across the room, drifting almost, her steps imperceptible as she walks. She's a strange mix of grace and the kind of terror you find in nightmares. She waves her hand down one of the glass walls behind her. It's a hollow wall and a light illuminates the space behind it, displaying a leather book that looks like the Book of Balance. It has our State symbols on the front, but instead of white leather, it's red.

"This is the Book of Imbalance," she says, and waves her hand switching off the light.

"There's a Book of Imbalance?" Trey asks.

"I like to think of it as the book of choices," she says, a soft smile on her face as she strokes the glass. Her head twitches up, her red eyes hard and devoid of warmth.

"You've been misled. Because of my sister, Trutinor wrongly believes the first law means that where there is Balance, Imbalance must be removed. You believe *that* is the only way to ensure fate is carried out. You're wrong. The last law in this book..." she prods the leather, "says where there is Balance, there must be Imbalance. The last law is the law that rules all others, and it is also my name-sake. Balance is not all light or all dark. And fate is not finite. Yes, there is a path, a destiny written for all of us. But it is not fate that determines whether we are great, or a leader, or a criminal, it is our choices and our actions which define that. It is from chaos that we find Balance."

My head swims trying to make sense of what she's saying, and then Hermia's voice pops into my head, *'We're all meant to make choices and sacrifices, Eden. This is mine. And one day, you will make yours.'*

My mouth falls open. Rita and Tyron were Potentials forced to Bind to others because of fate, or was it always the First Fallon? Could they have chosen differently? Chosen each other? And Maddison? She's spent twenty years fighting against fate to keep Cassian, to let him live, even if that meant never seeing him. I should've known; even my final sim exam taught me that sometimes we shouldn't inter-fere and yet somehow, every Keeper's brainwashed to ignore it.

My heart stops. My parents knew, and made the

greatest choice of all: to die, and all so I could be free to fulfill my ancient prophesied fate.

I fall to my knees, my chest tight, aching with frustration and clarity that's as sharp as winter's bite. The oppression, the fighting, the secrets; this whole time we thought we were working for good, for Balance, for fate, and all along we were part of the problem. My whole life has centered on this premise, my duty to the Balance.

I look up at her, horror peeling across my face. "Who are we, if we are not meant to keep fate?"

"That, my dear, is up to you. But there's a difference between bending and influencing, and removing someone's ability to choose."

I stand, staring at Trey. I knew I loved him the moment before he took my memories on the night of my sixteenth birthday, and I know it now too, but I still can't tell him, because like then, he still isn't mine. Yet my parents died because there's a prophecy saying I should be Bound to him. Do I really have a choice? Or has it been made for me?

"Trey's life..." I start.

"I know about the Jugo," she says, cutting me off.

"If I kill Victor, Trey dies too."

The Last Fallon smiles, the candle light glinting in her eyes as she reveals her teeth. "Yes, Victor Dark has given us quite the predicament. So much potential wasted."

"Potential?" I say, frowning.

"He's a fate anomaly. Should never have been born. Maddison swore an oath to Aurora, a blood oath, to bear a female heir for her in exchange for the magic that protected Cassian from Cecilia for years. But Maddison loved Israel and didn't want to fulfill her oath and birth the child of another."

"Then how is Bo alive?"

"Well, she avoided the oath at first by making a grave choice. One that even the book of Imbalance didn't predict. She got pregnant with Victor. Which is why he is an anomaly. When Aurora found out, she's was furious. While hiding Cassian on Earth might have saved him from my sister, Aurora was only banished from Trutinor. Not from Earth."

"Aurora was going to kill Cassian if Maddison didn't bear her an heir?" I say.

She nods, and waves her hand dismissing the conversation. "Victor has to die, you understand. You must have noticed your Binding is killing him anyway."

His face materializes in my mind, his pointy features and sweaty pallor, the erratic behavior, the desperation. He knows he's dying too.

"How?" Trey says, pacing the stone floor, "how do we kill him without killing me? If I die, you lose the war."

She glides across the floor, picks up an oval shaped piece of meat and takes a bite, fresh blood dripping onto her white corset. She looks from me to Trey, and when she finishes chewing, she says, "Like I said, quite the predicament."

"But there is a way?" I say, inching closer to Trey.

"There is..."

My shoulders sag, relief pouring over me.

"...In theory."

"In theory?" Trey says.

"Victor is an anomaly. They are rare, unique, highly unpredictable."

"What do we have to do?" I say, slipping my hand into his and squeezing like it will give him some reassurance I'm not going to kill him.

She moves to a darkened corner of the room; there's a

rustle, and then she appears holding a silver dagger with the State symbols carved into the blade.

"The thing about the universe," she says, "is it has a funny way of coming around again. Cyclical, almost. This is the dagger of Obex; the dagger of choice."

"I have to use it to kill him?"

"It's not as simple as that. The knife needs to be dipped in the blood of the one that should have been born."

"Bo?" I say, my eyes as wide as orbs, "but she's his sister."

"And she has a choice," the Last Fallon says.

Reaching for the knife, I say, "What if it doesn't work?"

"You've read the prophecy," she says, stepping back into the shadows and disappearing from sight. "I guess some things will always be up to fate."

THIRTY-ONE

'Should a female heir be born, Aurora will return.'

Excerpt - *The Book of Imbalance*

THE DAGGER LIES in the middle of the booth table. It wobbles and taps again the wooden top in time to the rocking of the train. Cassian stares at it for some time before saying, "So one of us *is* going to die then?"

My arms are folded on the table, my head resting on them while I watch the knife like it might attack me.

"I think we both knew one of us was always going to die."

Cassian has the decency not to ask who and I guess, given I have a knife and he's still alive, it's obvious.

Trey is asleep in the other booth, his chest rising and falling quietly with his breath.

My eyes are red raw, but I force them to stay open.

I sit up. If one of us dies, there's something I still want to know.

"Why did you come with us? Back in the Camden, I mean."

He shrugs, "I knew I'd have to come back to Trutinor eventually. I guess you were my best option."

"No," I say narrowing my eyes at him, "that's not it."

He smiles, his dark eyes sparkling, "Not just a pretty face, are you?"

I press my lips shut, ignoring his comment.

"There are two women in my life. My mother wanted to protect you because of the prophecy. The other wanted to protect him." He points at Trey's figure.

Interesting.

"You should get some rest," I say, "in a few hours, one way or another, either we're dead, or Victor is. Let's make sure it's him."

My CogTracker buzzes in my pocket, and I flip it open. I sent Bo a message as soon as we got back on the train.

Where are you? I need to see you. Now.

Finally, she's replied:

At home. Did you go to the Binding Chamber?

I start typing a response, explaining that I had seen my mother's memories and that I wasn't sure what I felt, but that I didn't blame her and then deleted it. Because for one,

I wasn't sure if that was true and two, that's not the kind of conversation I should have over a CogTracker.

I'm on my way.

I type out another message, one that makes my fingers shake even as I press the keys.

We should talk. I'll meet you at yours at 9am.

Victor's response is instant.

Can't wait.

I fire off a few more messages, asking people to meet me in Eris Castle in the morning, hoping they get them with enough time to travel to the North. If they don't, we'll be on our own.

I rap a soft knock on the engine cab door. Magnus opens it. His face crinkles with irritation, then he sighs, and allows me in, gesturing for me to sit on a black leather seat on the opposite side of the cab. Maybe Trey's right, Magnus is softening.

"Where is it to be then, Fallon East?"

"The North. Eris Castle."

It ends where it began, I think, *with blood and promises, fate and choices.* Through the windows in the cabin, dawn streaks the sky, wiping away the darkness and replacing it with daisy yellows and deep oranges. I hope it won't be the last sunrise I see. Magnus is silent, but he doesn't ask me to leave either so I stay and watch; the greenery gets more sporadic as we pass from the northern part of the West into the Eris mountains and the North State.

After some time, Magnus finally says, "You'll keep him alive, won't you?"

"I hope so, Magnus. I really do."

I lean my head against the cab wall and let my eyes rest, but it's too rickety and I can't nod off. Magnus takes off his navy jacket, folds it up and hands it to me.

"Thank you," I say, and place it between my head and the wall so I can sleep.

———

HE GRUMBLES something under his breath that sounds like an insult, and I smile as I lose myself to sleep.

I've stood outside Eris Castle a thousand times before. But never with a dagger pressing against my spine, and never with the intention to use it. Trepidation makes my chest so tight it's hard to speak. The last time I saw Maddison, I promised her I wouldn't hurt Victor. Now there's only an inch of my Binding left and if I stare at it hard enough, I can see it disintegrating. It tingles on and off constantly. I suspect I have an hour, two at most, before I have to break that promise and end Victor's life.

Their home is carved out of a mountainside and sits in the left-over cove like a fairy tale castle. A dozen thin turrets nudge the clouds; the largest and widest sits in the center of them all, a penthouse of sorts, that the Darks live in. Two tall, black haired Shifters exit the castle, the first, Reginald Atticus, Bo's cousin, holds the door open. He smiles and nods at me. I give him the quickest smile I can and skirt past him, as if he can somehow tell I'm harboring a weapon. Trey and Cassian follow behind closing the door.

We're in a narrow corridor made of black numbered doors, chandeliers and red carpet inlaid with black filigree patterns. There are six main castles in the North, one for each of The Six houses and all of them designed the same way, divided into floors of flats for the Shifters belonging to that house's pack.

At the end of the corridor is a lift and we ascend to the top in silence. The lift tings as it opens, signaling our arrival. It's a few short steps to Bo's front door, but by the time my hand is hovering over the gold wolf-shaped door knocker, my palms are sweaty and nausea clings to my insides.

Trey takes my hand and squeezes as if to say this will all be okay, but I'm not sure it will.

It's Kato that opens the door, not Bo. He glances from Trey to our joined hands and grins at his brother. "Ladies," he says, letting the three of us through. "We'll give you some space. You must be Cassian." Kato leads him and Trey to the kitchen.

Bo is standing at the back window-wall staring out at the mountains; her hair is in a neat ballerina bun.

"Bo?" I say, taking a steadying breath and walking down into their white living room. Images of my parents' last moments in this room flash through my mind, and I try to force them away.

When she turns around, there's a moment of hesitation between us, then she runs at me, clings to my neck, and sobs into my neck.

"I'm so sorry," she says, "I'm so, so sorry."

"I know," I say, "It's okay, I forgive you." And as say I it, I realize it really is okay. It might've been her blood they used, but she didn't kill them, no one did. They made that choice by themselves, and I can't blame her for it. I need her. More than anything right now. I hold on tight, tears of relief bubbling up. Then I remember why we're here and I go rigid.

She pulls away frowning, "What is it?" she says, biting her lip.

"Bo," I start, and stop because I don't know what to say. I rub my hand over my cheek and when I look back at her, her mouth is wide.

She takes my wrist, "Your scar. It's nearly gone. Tell me you've found a way to fix it?"

I blink once, swallow hard, and say, "I have."

It must be the tone of my voice, or maybe the strain on my face, because she lets go of my wrist and stumbles back dropping into the sofa.

"Oh God," she says, shaking her head, "tell me it's something other than what the First Fallon's said."

"I..." I say, unsure of how to verbalize what I'm here to do, "I need to ask you for something."

She looks up at me from the sofa, her dark eyes pained, like she already knows what I want.

"Not you too."

"Why didn't you tell me about your blood?" I blurt before I can stop myself.

"I only found out recently; I haven't even talked to Dad, I mean Israel, about it."

The boys return, interrupting our conversation and put breakfast on the coffee table between the sofas.

Cassian glances from Bo to me and says, "Have you told her?"

"Told me what?" Bo says, looking up at us both.

I take a deep breath; I have to get it out before I can't, "Victor used a Jugo to tether his life to Trey's. If Victor dies, Trey dies."

Kato drops his jam-covered knife, and it clatters to the

plate. "He did what?" Kato says, his neck blotching with red. I don't think I've ever seen him angry.

"Insurance," Cassian says. "Pretty clever when you think about it. If his life is linked to the one person Eden can't kill, he's safe, and I," he says, licking jam off his fingers, "will have to die instead."

I glare at him, at his arrogance, at his tactlessness, and I've a mind to end him myself. But then I remember the prophecy, the fact Victor is an anomaly, the damage he's already caused, and the damage he will cause if he's left to live.

Bo stands up, her arms folded across her chest, "Taking your side in school fights and petty squabbles is one thing, but you're asking for my blood so you can murder my brother. Are you all out of your minds? How can you ask me to do that?"

I stay silent because I can't ask. I don't want to even though I know I have to. Trey is standing with his back to the window. He catches my eye, and I wish I knew what was going through his head. He's waiting for her answer; her sentence on his life. Her sentence on our friendship because if she says no, I've already decided I'll take it from her anyway.

The silence is thick as she paces across the floor, shaking her head, "I can't, Eden, I can't. Please don't ask me to."

I gasp, fracturing the tension, and fall to my knees clutching my wrist. Another section of the Binding fizzes away into the air.

Kato moves across the room, and steps in front of her. "If you don't, then my brother dies," he says, reaching for Bo's hand.

"And if I do, mine dies."

They stare at each other, identical pained expressions

etching into their foreheads. The realization that they are perfect soulmates on opposite sides of war. One of their brothers will die today, and it will be the other's fault. Blood versus love. An unforgivable betrayal that their relationship might not survive, and I can't help but think this is all my fault.

I'm sorry.

"I'm sorry..." Kato says, echoing my words as he cups her neck, and kisses her with such intensity I have to look away. When he pulls back, his hand remains around her neck and her cheeks are sticky with tears, "...But I can't let my brother die to save yours."

She stiffens as Kato's eyes burn that fiery blue of Siren magic. "Kato, please," Bo mumbles, "don't do this."

But it's too late, he's made his choice, and as her eyes roll back into her head, she slumps forward into his arms. He places her on the sofa, kissing her forehead and whispering, "Forgive me."

He turns to us, tears in his eyes. "Take it," he says, holding up her palm. "But, Eden, you'd better save my brother, because no matter how much she loves me, I just killed her brother. She won't forgive me for this."

THIRTY-TWO

The wisest fate is the one we choose –
Balance Proverb

AS I SLICE Bo's palm and smear the blood over the dagger, Cassian stands up, walks to the window, and gazes at the courtyard below.

"We don't have a plan," he says, "you need a plan before a fight."

"Is that cage fighting wisdom?" Kato growls.

Cassian glances at him; if he notices the irritation in his voice, he doesn't seem bothered by it.

"It's logic," he says, turning to me. "You were lucky Maddison and Arden were there when he attacked last time. This time we're on our own."

"Maybe," I say, hoping Arden and Hermia got my messages. "But you're right - we do need a plan."

Kato finishes bandaging Bo's hand then slumps into the seat next to her and strokes her head.

"Well, Victor was wounded by Arden. So, he won't come on his own, which means he'll bring wolves, and wolves always hunt in packs," I say.

"And they always isolate their prey," Trey adds.

"Right," I nod. "So, we need bait. I guess that's me."

"No. We need you to use the knife on Victor. If one of the wolves gets you before you get to Victor we're all screwed," Trey says. "I should be the bait."

"Well, that's stupid, he's not going to kill you, is he?" Cassian says. "I'm the logical option. If he kills me, your Binding's fixed. I'm the one he wants. I'm the textbook bait, so I'll go. Besides, I can shift and hold my own in a fight."

"Fine. You're the courtyard bait," I say, walking to join him by the window. "But don't underestimate what a pack of wolves can do, Cassian. You might be able to fight in a cage, but these guys are trained to fight *as* wolves or whatever their essence is."

The courtyard is huge, walled and completely cut off to the outside. One side has a wall at least ten feet high. The other three are inner castle walls potted with flat windows. The central square is made of stone slabs carved with the name of every resident that's lived in the castle. Around the edge of the courtyard itself are stone pillar archways and under them, ground floor flat doors.

"Kato, do you know any of the ground floor residents?"

"One. Reginald, Bo's cousin."

"No good. He left this morning,"

"His parents might be in."

"Okay, try them. If they are, you and Trey wait behind the back door to the courtyard."

"Where are you going to be?"

A slow grin peels across my face as I point to the turret on the opposite side of the square.

"There. Victor will be too busy with Cassian to notice me... I hope, anyway. When he's in the center of the courtyard, I'll attack."

"Then we have a plan," Trey says.

There's a pause. Brief, heavy and silent. Full of the recognition that even though we've all made it this far, some of us might not make it to the end. Then the moment's gone and Cassian says, "He's here."

I peer out of the window; goosebumps track down my back. Victor's standing in the courtyard, smiling as he stares up at the window as if he can see me.

Kato rests Bo's head on the sofa; she's stirring, she'll be awake soon. Cassian hovers by the steel staircase leading from their window to the ground.

"Kato," I call, as he reaches the penthouse door. "Thank you." I raise the dagger a few inches, and he nods.

"Save Trey. I mean it, Eden."

My turn to nod. "Oh, and Kato?" I move to the middle of the living room to stand next to Trey.

"Yeah?"

"Don't get killed."

He snorts, "I think we both know that pleasure is going to be reserved for Bo when she wakes up." Then he walks out the door.

Trey and I stare at each other, a million unsaid things passing between us. There are so many things I could say, so many things I want to say. But only one I should. Three little words teetering on the edge of my lips.

"I..." I start.

Love you, Trey. But I can't say the rest aloud. If I do, and he dies, then I'll have lost the three people that matter most to me.

He takes my hand. "It's fine," he says, "you don't have to."

All of a sudden, my cheeks are hot and my eyes stinging. This could be the last time I see him. He takes my face in his hands and pulls me to his lips. "But *I* do. Remember the forest, no matter what happens. I'll find you." He places his hand on my chest, over my heart, "You make me feel, Eden East. I love you, for all the lifetimes."

He kisses me on the lips. Just once. Warm, soft and lingering; it's goodbye.

Then his back is to me, and he's walking towards the door. In my head I'm shouting, screaming at myself to just say it. Tell him I love him before it's too late. But the lump in my throat is too big, and I can't form the words. The door clicks shut and he's gone. Once again, it's too late.

"It's time," Cassian says, and pushes open the window stepping onto the metal stairs.

I run into the hall, out the stairway exit and up to the rooftop.

I step outside; the air is crisp and fresh with the nip of mountain breeze.

Standing on the far side of the square is Victor, his shoulders back, arms folded. He's wearing black leathers and a white t-shirt that matches his skin tone. He might be standing like an animal about to mark its territory, but even from up here I can see the dark rings under his eyes and the sheen of sick sweat on his brow that gives away his weakness.

I sneak along the roof, keeping as low as I can to avoid him seeing me.

When Cassian comes to a stop, Victor laughs. "After all

that, she's just given you up?" he says, looking down his nose at Cassian.

"Something like that," Cassian says, keeping his eyes locked on him.

I pass parallel to Victor and reach the other side of the courtyard roof. I clamber up the turret, but my hand slips. My heart misses a beat as I fall a couple of feet down. I swing my free hand up, and manage to regain my footing to haul myself up and over the parapet into the turret. I peek down at Cassian; he's still looking at Victor but shifts on the spot like he saw me out of the corner of his eye.

From my position, I can see the front and back of the castle, although Bo's huge penthouse turret blocks part of my view. Circular turrets with points for roofs shoot into the sky like spears. This is the same view of the Eris Mountains my parents had right before they died. But the beauty of the endless, undulating white peaks doesn't dispel the knot in my chest.

I scan the rear and freeze.

On a mountain ridge, close to the castle, the skirt of a silky dress swishes in the wind. Then a puff of navy smoke fills the space where the First Fallon was. Close by, ten, maybe twenty, wolf Shifters sprint towards the castle. She must be helping Victor. I wish I could signal to the others, but there's no time. I see movement to my right: Arden and a handful of Sorcerers pepper potting towards the castle. We're outnumbered at least two to one, but three of the Sorcerers are high ranking Guild members, and most of us are Fallons. Even outnumbered we stand a good chance.

"Shall we finish this?" Victor says to Cassian.

The dagger in my fatigues presses cold and hard against my thigh.

Victor whistles and the wolves that ran across the mountain appear from behind the doors on his side of the court-yard. They run, bounding across the stone slabs, shifting into wolf form and circling Cassian.

I slip my hand in my pocket and touch the dagger, checking it's still there for the millionth time. I'll only have one chance at this. A cold wind whips around the square, and the first splatters of rain speckle the stone beneath me.

The wolves draw nearer to Cassian; he grins, disappearing as his body crumples to the ground and reappears in his wolf form with that black streak down his back.

Growls emanate from the pack; one of them howls and then they charge.

I move fast. Yanking the dagger out, I don't even think before I leap from the turret. I shoot a jet of air from my free hand to slow my fall and hold the dagger point out aiming at a spot on his back that, I hope, with enough force will puncture his heart. As I plummet towards the ground, Victor hears me and spins around causing the dagger to pierce the upper part of his chest instead of his heart. I rip it out ready to strike again, but he rolls away and a wolf steps in front of him.

Somewhere in front of me, Trey gasps; the impact of the knife must be affecting him too.

My wrist burns up and Cassian howls, hopping from paw to paw while Victor screeches on the floor. Wisps of our Binding scar drift away in the breeze, and my eyes widen at the sight of what's left. Barely a millimeter or two. I have to end this. Now.

The wolf in front of me jumps while I'm gripping my wrist and sinks its teeth into my shoulder. I scream as I punch it clean in the jaw. It falls to the ground, and I ignite my fist with electricity and fire a bolt as fast as I can into its head. It yelps, twitches and then limps backwards.

I stand up, woozy as blood trickles down my shoulder.

Trey and Kato are at the other end of the courtyard, back to back, both of them with their hands out, circling the wolves as the wolves circle them. One attacks, then recoils as one of the Luchellis takes control of their mind and fills them with pain. Trey's moving slowly. Tight tremors grip my chest as I spot the growing red patch on his shoulder in the same place I stabbed Victor.

A door opens behind me and a Sorceress in a green slip with golden hair walks out. Eve.

Trey spots her and halts. "Eve," he mouths. It's caught him off guard, and it's enough for the wolves to break rank and attack him.

A shadow swoops across the courtyard as Evelyn fires a thread of magic straight at Kato.

I'm running, but it's too late; it hits him clean in the face. He falls to the ground and doesn't move.

The shadow drops to the square, shifting from falcon to Fallon and shrieking Kato's name.

Bo rounds on Evelyn, fury burning hate into her face.

Cassian bumps into my side as he catches a wolf mid-air, preventing it from sinking its claws into me. In one sweep, he tears out its throat and flings it to the ground.

Two wolves jump me from the other side knocking me into the floor and biting down on my ribs. I yelp, kick one in the jaw and grip the other's head with both hands, flooding its skull with as much electricity as I can. It doesn't even howl. It stills so I discard its limp body to the floor and scramble up.

The snap of magic exploding against one of the flat doors sounds behind me. Arden's in the courtyard. But as they've arrived, so too have a dozen more wolves. Wooden spikes from the shattered door fly across the square and clatter to the stone slabs narrowly missing my head.

On the other side of the courtyard, Bo is guarding Kato. I think his leg twitches; I just hope he holds on. Evelyn swipes her wand at Bo. She dodges several threads of green magic until she dives to protect one from hitting Kato. The crack of bone echoes through the courtyard as Bo crashes to the ground. Evelyn's eyes narrow; her lips thin and peel over her teeth. She swishes her wand. There's a crunch and a squelching sound, then with one flick of Evelyn's wrist, Bo's calf is ripped clean off. Her scream curls my stomach, and I have stop myself throwing up as a stream of red squirts over the grass. I swallow down the vomit and drag myself upright.

Victor is lying on the slabs a few feet away, his breathing shallow, rapid. I nicked his lung at least. But as he struggles, so does Trey. He's stumbling around, throwing wild, inaccurate pulses of torture at the wolves. He sees Bo and his expression strains with concentration as he raises his arm in her direction. Her face relaxes; he must have removed her pain. Then her whole body hardens; her eyes blaze and she crumples into her wolf form. I lose sight of her as she leaps at Evelyn. I blink and Evelyn's body is lying still on the ground, blood pumping in jets from her open throat. I shake my head. There isn't time. I have to get to Victor.

Cassian's circling me, fending off the wolves that are trying to stop me reaching Victor.

I hobble to Victor's side, holding my ribs and wincing with each step and each breath.

As I reach him, I collapse and a blistering pain shoots from my wrist to my heart. I grab at my Binding scar, trying to hold it on, but the fragments are disintegrating before my eyes and as they do, my heart is slowing. It's hard to breathe;

it feels like my lungs are shrinking, withering and dying. Cassian, in his wolf form, falters and two wolves jump him.

Bodies, limbs and fur mark the courtyard like battle wounds. Arden and the three other Sorcerers are surrounding me, but they part to let Trey hobble through. He drops to his knees, the color fading from his face. He's covered in blood, smeared with dirt and fur, and his clothes are torn. Blood oozes from the spot on his chest where I stabbed Victor, and it makes me shake. What if I kill Victor and Bo's blood doesn't work?

"I can't," I say, the panic rasping into my voice.

"There's no time. Just do it. Don't make me compel you."

"But you'll die."

Victor sits up, startling me enough he grabs my throat, squeezing so hard dots speckle my vision. I pull at his arms, slapping and pawing at his face. But he continues to strangle me. I hit his temple with the butt of the dagger. Trey reaches for his own temple and Victor laughs in my face, "We could've changed everything."

I gasp one final breath, and the last fragment of my Binding crumbles away. All three of our hearts pump their last beat. Stars spot my vision. Victor's grip loosens, his face slackens and hollows with death. Over his shoulder, Trey's bright blue eyes hold my gaze and as the last of my oxygen leaves my body, finally I say, "I love you, Trey."

As my body drops like stone to the floor, I reach out and plunge the knife deep into Victor's heart.

THIRTY-THREE

'The fate of all our worlds, realms and lands rest in the choices and sacrifices of the First Couple.'

Excerpt – The Book of Imbalance

I ALWAYS THOUGHT DYING WOULD HURT ESPECIALLY after seeing Obex. I was expecting an expanse of dark, vacuous space, an infinite nothing and intense, ceaseless pain. But as the last of my air evaporates from my body, there is no pain and instead of darkness, there is bright white light.

As the blade extinguishes Victor's life, I collapse on the ground. The light becomes a thick white mist that glistens like the sun kissing the ocean on a cool morning. It descends over the square and everything inside it. My body lightens, and I'm sure it's my soul leaving for Obex. I'm tired, exhausted from fighting and ready to be reunited with my parents again.

I float up, weightless, into the white haze, a sense of serenity swaddling me like a blanket of tranquility.

Then I'm tugged. Gently at first, like the soft nudge, nudge of a hungry dog. But then it's harder, more insistent. A jumble of sounds and whispered words in my ears. I can't make sense of them. But the voices are urgent, restless, desperate. They shout, call and scream a name at me. I don't understand. I want to tell them to go away, to leave me alone, but I can't. My voice is noiseless. The prodding becomes a yank, downwards, back towards the ground. A demand to go back. But I fight the voices, struggle upwards. I'm ready to join my parents.

And then I hear the name.

"Trey."

Over and over it repeats in shrieks and whispers and shouts. Each time it hits me, like a blast of icy ocean water.

I'm scrambling now, reaching for the ground, desperate to go back. I hit the stone slabs. They're hard. Cold. Real. I sit up. Gasping. Clawing at my throat, unable to breathe.

My body jerks. The tugging isn't over. I'm dragged across the square like a rag doll until I crash into a body. The mist is too thick to see their face, but arms envelop me. Familiar. Strong. Warm. The air fills with the comforting scent of summer and frankincense. Our bodies entwine and through the mist, maroon and violet tendrils appear, looping and lacing around our forearms. Binding us.

This time, being Bound doesn't hurt. Tingles pour over us, like a cocktail of midsummer sun, static and love. A love so deep, it was etched into my soul the day I was born. I smile and think of Mother, and how she'd say I've finally found my missing puzzle piece. Only, he was never really missing. I lean into the body pressing against mine. I don't need the mist to clear. I know in my heart, I'm Bound to Trey.

THIRTY-FOUR

'Never trust a Fallon that can't keep the Balance.'

Lionel East – R.I.P.

"I'M NOT SUPPOSED to see you today," Trey says, rolling over in bed and kissing me on the lips. "It's bad luck."

"That's your wedding day, silly, and you're not human," I say, grinning and pushing hair behind his ears.

"Coronation, wedding, same thing."

"If you say so," I plant another kiss on his lips before pushing him out of bed. "Guess you'd better leave then."

There's a thud and a muffled laugh as he hits the floor, "Did you forget where we are? This is my house."

"Oops," I say, smiling and climb out of bed to help him up.

He picks me up, and I wrap my legs around his waist as he swings me around showering tiny kisses over my neck and lips.

A photo catches my eye, and I stiffen.

"Wait, stop. Put me down," I say, untangling myself and walking to his chest of drawers. Above it hangs a series of photos. Trey and Kato as children, a tall man with Trey's jawline and then a woman, with brown hair and the same crystal blue eyes Trey and Kato have.

"No," I breathe. "It can't be."

"What's wrong?" he says, coming to stand behind me and wrapping his arms around my neck.

"Who is that?" I say, pointing at the woman.

"That's my mom, Lani," he says.

Ice runs through my veins. I'd forgotten all about the woman on Earth. But now I know why I recognized her. I know what Cassian meant on the train, who the other woman in life is. Those chestnut locks, those blue eyes only Trey's family have. I reach for my hand, and the echo of where she pricked me stings with the memory.

My chest pounds as I stare into Trey's face.

Worry lines crease his brow.

"What wrong," he says, gripping my shoulders.

"Trey..." I start and falter. How do I tell him when he's spent half his life thinking she was dead?

"Your mom... She... I think Lani is alive. I have no idea how you Inherited your powers. But I am positive she's alive. I saw her twice in Camden. Lani is the one that cut my hand. She's alive; she was on Earth protecting Cassian this whole time."

A smile flickers, then disappears as tears well in his eyes. Then they're gone too. He's controlling his emotions.

"You're certain?" he says, his face cold, hard, angry almost.

I nod. I am. But now I waver, unsure of what he's thinking or feeling.

"Good for her," he says.

"Pardon?" I say, my mouth falling open. "Trey, this is your mom. I just told you she's alive after you thought she was dead for most of your life. How can you dismiss this?"

"Because if she's alive, then she left, Eden. She left me alone as a child, to look after my baby brother and an entire State. And for what? To look after someone else's kid? What kind of mother does that? Even if she is alive, I don't want to know. I don't care."

His face is rigid, stiff, but I see the wobble flash across his eyes. He does care. Deep down. Even if he needs time to process, I'll find her and I'll bring her back to him. We don't know the full story, and we can't make assumptions until we do. He taught me that.

"Knock, knock," Nyx says, breaking the tension. She and Titus walk into Trey's room and lay my dress on the bed.

Titus is suited in his finest navy uniform, polished gold symbols and buttons down the front of his blazer, his beige trousers and navy boots just as neat. His blond dreadlocks are quaffed up under his hat. Nyx is wearing a slim fitting navy dress to match Titus, and she's even tamed her hair into a slicked-back look.

"Hurry up, the pair of you; Titus and Magnus need to set off."

"Sorry," I say, glancing at Trey, "I'll be quick. Trey, help me into the dress."

Nyx's cheeks flicker pink, and she hustles Titus out so we can get ready.

Trey's hands slide down my skin, in ways he shouldn't considering how little time there is before the coronation.

"You can't avoid talking about this forever," I say, as he kisses down my shoulder.

"Then just for today."

He zips up the back of my dress and whispers, "While I love putting you in this..."

Bo appears in the door, "Hey," she says, smiling.

Trey leans into my ear and whispers, "...I'm looking forward to taking you out of it even more."

I cough, and shake him off me trying not to blush.

"You two are gross, just so you know," Bo says rolling her eyes.

"Speak for yourself," I say, and then regret it. Bo still hasn't forgiven Kato for what he did. Which makes the knot of guilt in my chest even worse. I'm the one that killed her brother and yet, she attributes it to Kato because she blames herself for my parents' death, despite what I keep telling her. She says she understands I didn't have a choice.

"I'll leave you to it and meet you at the station, Eden," Trey says. He kisses me on the forehead and then leaves.

"How's Israel and Maddison?" I ask, picking up my shoes to slip them on.

"Okay. Sort of. I mean, they lost one son and gained another. It's going to take some time."

"Have they found out who Cassian is Bound to yet?"

She shakes her head, "No. Still searching."

"What about you?" I say, glancing at her leg. From the knee down, shiny brass tubing and cogs whirl and pump as she leans from one foot to the other and flexes her mechanical toes.

"Sore," she says. "I still feel like my toes are there, but at least I had the Dryads to heal it fast. Charlie did give me the choice to try and save my leg, but he said the chances were slim because it had taken hours to get me to the hospital and by then the dark magic had soaked into my calf and the skin was necrotic. Lance and Titus made me this." She raises her knee and her foot twitches. "I'm still getting used to it. But it has its benefits."

"Oh?"

"After I finished up in Ignis, I went back to check on Angus and Obert and make sure everything was signed off and completed. The Guild administered the antidote. I filled in all the paperwork, so The Six didn't have to; I even bought them all a celebratory meal, but they still didn't see me as their general. But with this," she waggles her foot, "whole different ball game. They say I finally earned my general stripes because I'm a wounded war hero. It's like I needed to get my leg cut off so they'd respect me." She grins at me shaking her head and even though it's an awful thing to have gone through I can tell she's trying to take the positives out of it, so I smile back.

"And Cassian?"

Her face falls, she closes her eyes and takes a deep breath, "Yes, well. You can't win everything. He's as annoying and arrogant as Victor, but at least he knows he has a lot to catch up on here and he's Balanced enough according to the readings now he's Bound, so the Council are letting him stay."

"Why did you help? In the end, I mean. I stole your blood, and you knew it was to kill your brother, so why did you fight?"

She bites her lip, "I wasn't going to. I circled above the fight for a bit, watching. But when Evelyn attacked Kato, I had to do something. She was going to kill him. No matter how pissed I am at him, he's still Kato."

"How is he?"

"Good. Better. He has a scar that cuts through his eyebrow and across his forehead. I don't think he's too impressed, some rubbish about Sirens needing perfect, serene complexions. I secretly like it. Not that I've told him. Bastard."

I laugh, because I know no matter how betrayed she feels, they will find their way back to each other eventually.

"Eden?" she says, after a pause.

"Hmm," I say, buckling the last heel.

"He's my half-brother."

I stop fiddling with my shoes and look up. The Last Fallon had told me about Maddison and Aurora, but Bo hadn't, and I wanted my friend to tell me in her words.

"A few years ago, I was rifling through mom's stuff in the loft and found a diary from when she was pregnant with Cassian. It was awful. She had to cover everything up. She took forever to tell Dad. Anyway, she wanted to protect Cassian, because she wasn't Bound and wouldn't be when she gave birth. She traveled to Aurora, made a deal with her. Aurora asked Mom to bear a female to her son. She needed a female granddaughter."

She looks at me. "Mom made a blood oath, Eden. Can you imagine being desperate enough to do that? What was she thinking?"

I shake my head because I don't know what else to say. I can't imagine being that desperate. The only thing more powerful than a blood oath is a Binding.

"Well, she loved Dad. She didn't want to have someone else's child, and she was young, stupid and desperate. So, she got pregnant with Victor. She didn't know it would poison her blood oath with Aurora."

"Does Israel know?"

"I haven't... I mean, I don't know how to talk to him about it."

I nod, understanding how difficult it must be to ask her father if he knows he isn't actually her father at all.

"Do you know who your biological father is?" I say standing up, and gesturing for the door.

"Yes and no. It's Aurora's son. But I've never met him. I think I want to though."

"You should go find him."

Bo nods, "I think I will."

We exit Trey's castle and the air is hot and thick with summer heat. There's a procession of Sirens hooting and cheering as we make our way to the station, ready to travel to the East for my coronation.

As the train chugs towards home, I wonder whether Mom and Dad can see me, if they're watching from Obex, or whether they've passed on to their next life.

I stroke my dress, pushing out the soft rumples and fiddling with the jewels. Nyx fixed Mother's dress after it got destroyed in the ceremony, and stitched even more sparkling gems into it, only this time she added swathes of maroon to represent my union with Trey and the South. I smile, Mom would love it.

Nyx opens the carriage door and brandishes two objects. In one hand is the coin I keep in my fatigues; the one Father gave me. In her other hand is a glass orb, and a tiny speck of Dust. "I brought it from the tower, so they're with you today," she says, tears welling in her eyes. I smile, unable to thank her without crying and pop them in my handbag.

AS TREY and I enter Element Square, a strange bitter-sweet nostalgia washes over me. It's been more than two weeks since then and so much has changed. The same stage and drapes are at the back, but the plinth that carried my parents is gone. In its place are two thrones, one made of electricity, the other a high-backed Chesterfield chair with sculpted figures inlaid around the edges.

The last time I was here, was the Dusting. Back then it was Victor who was destined to be by my side today. Instead it's someone else.

As I round the stage Nyx, Bo and Arden are waiting for me, beaming and clapping as I appear.

My lips part as I catch sight of Trey who snuck off the train before me so he could be here when I arrived. He's wearing a suit, of sorts, skinny dark maroon trousers, with violet trims and a blazer that hugs his figure. His hair is knotted up, showing his eyes and the jaw that makes my insides melt. I still can't believe he's mine.

He laces his fingers through my hand. The vault lurking inside both of us hasn't gone, it never will. But together we're stronger, and we can use it to fight with Arden and the Libra Legion.

"Are you ready?" Arden asks.

"I am," I say, and then correct myself, "we are."

Arden guides us on stage, and I peek through the drapes. The square is just as packed as last time. Arden pushes us through, and cheers erupt from the crowd.

Trey pulls me by the hand and leads me to the center of the stage. "Are you really ready?" he whispers.

"To be a Fallon in charge of an entire State?" I breathe.

"To spend your life with me?"

I grin, and look up at him, my eyes twinkling in the bright sunshine, "I've always been ready for that."

Arden picks up the CogMic and silences the crowd, "Ladies and gentleman, it is my great pleasure to welcome you to the coronation of..."

A giant shadow sweeps over the square. I frown, look up but see nothing.

Arden starts again, "It is my great pleasure to present to you, your Fal..."

This time the shadow sweeps in front of the sun, blocking it out and throwing shade over the square.

Huge scaly wings beat the air, sending gusts of wind through the crowd. I narrow my eyes scanning the sky. The only person who might want to sabotage my coronation is Maddison. She's avoided me since I killed Victor.

But it isn't Maddison. I squint at the face attached to the wings as it shifts and emerges in front of me. It shoots enormous balls of fire and wisps of green magic- across the square. *Impossible.* Only the Fallon sisters can control all the State's magic. The creature dips and as I catch sight of its greasy blond hair and dark eyes, my legs go weak, and I stumble back, the blood draining from my face.

Father always said never trust a Fallon who can't keep the Balance...

This creature, this Fallon, can't be flying across the square because I killed him with my own hands. Father was right. But he should have added, '...Even the dead ones.'

The creature slows, beats his dark wings and hovers at my eye line.

"Victor."

THANK YOU

Thank you for reading Keepers. I hope you love Eden's story as much as I do. If you did, and you can spare a few minutes, I'd be really grateful if you left a short review on the site you purchased your copy.

Want to know what happens next?

You can be the first to hear about the sequel and rest of the Eden East series in **CogMail** by clicking the **eepurl** link below.

www.sachablackbooks.com

eepurl.com/cqA2B5
sachablack@sachablack.co.uk

ACKNOWLEDGMENTS

I'd like to thank coffee, chocolate and all the bad shit your mom tells you not to eat. If it wasn't for those terrible body-wrecking delights, I'd have crashed and burned in a pile of half-formed sentences and keyboard imprints.

I'd also like to thank night-time. I worked full-time while writing this book, so whether she wanted it or not, midnight became my best friend. Together we cried, and celebrated, as night after night I made my way through three entire re-writes (and two-hundred and thirty-seven thousand drafted words) of this book. I owe you, my friend.

There are, of course, some real squidgy, hug-in-your-arms type humans I'd like to thank as well.

My wife first, thank you for being so patient, for letting me follow my dream, and for listening to me stress over metaphors and character arcs. My son, is a constant inspiration to me. I want him to grow up knowing you have to follow your dreams no matter what.

To Mum and Dad, I've said this before, but thanks for, you know, doing it, and making an awesome kid.

Gross.

To my accountability partner, Allie Potts, thank you for peppering my life with equal doses of back rubbing encouragement and threats of eternal shame and remorse for failing to meet goals.

To Helen, thank you for being that beacon of constant positivity. For making me feel better about my writing when I was full of doubt, and for being an amazing beta reader... repeatedly! And to my other beta readers, Ali, Allie, Sarah, and Geoff. Thank you for reading the many awful versions of this book.

To Geoff and Hugh, my old skool bash buddies, thank you for coping with my democratic dictatorship; I've no idea how you put up with me.

Suzie and Lucy, for listening to me on a daily basis and coaxing me off various cliff edges.

To Esther, I'm indebted. Thank you for taking a rough diamond and polishing it to perfection.

There are too many blogging friends to mention, but thank you from the bottom of my heart for the continuous support, listening to my rambles, grumbles and excessive swearing!

Last, and most importantly, thank you to you, the readers, for taking the time to buy and read this book. I hope you've enjoyed this first part in Eden's story and want to continue on her journey with me.

ABOUT THE AUTHOR

Sacha Black has five obsessions; words, expensive shoes, conspiracy theories, self-improvement, and breaking the rules. She also has the mind of a perpetual sixteen-year-old, only with slightly less drama and slightly more bills.

Sacha writes books about people with magical powers and other books about the art of writing. She lives in Hertfordshire, England, with her wife and genius, giant of a son.

When she's not writing, she can be found laughing inappropriately loud, blogging, sniffing musty old books, fangirling film and TV soundtracks, or thinking up new ways to break the rules.

**13 Steps To Evil - How To Craft A Superbad Villain
(and Workbook) For Writers**

Your hero is not the most important character in your book. Your
villain is.

If you're fed up of drowning in two-dimensional villains and
frustrated with creating clichés, this book is for you.

In 13 Steps to Evil, you'll discover:

- How to develop a villain's mindset
- A step-by-step guide to creating your villain
  from the ground up

- Why getting to the core of a villain's personality is essential to make them credible
- What pitfalls and clichés to avoid as well as the tropes your story needs

Finally, there is a comprehensive writing guide to help you create superbad villains. Whether you're just starting out or are a seasoned writer, this book will help power up your bad guy and give them that extra edge.

If you like dark humour, learning through examples and want to create the best villains you can, then you'll love Sacha Black's guide to crafting superbad villains. Read 13 Steps to Evil and the companion workbook today and start creating kick-ass villains.

Lightning Source UK Ltd.
Milton Keynes UK
UKOW04f1912291117
313593UK00002B/472/P